D1530813

Never Trust
a Zombie

Paul Brodie

ISBN: 1492174920
ISBN-13: 978-1492174929

Published in the United States of America.

This work is fiction. All people, places, and things contained in this story are either fictitious creations of the author's imagination or are used fictitiously.

DEDICATION

For Ned's Blog
NedHickson.wordpress.com

It all started with a comment meant as a joke, on a blog post book review
for a book that doesn't exist.

Also for Jesse Gray

Jesse recommended I write a book about the psychology behind zombie
interest. I told him I wasn't qualified, so I wrote this book instead. But if
you are thinking, 'I'd rather read about the psychology behind
zombie interest,' *then head to iTunes or Amazon and check out Dr.*
Michael Britt's Zombie Fascination.

And for Laura, Alison and Lesley for pre-reading the story and giving
me feedback.

Most of all, for my wife, Kathy, for reading the story, helping me structure
it, editing it, and supporting me through all of the time it took to put it
together.

Contents

1. Small Town Trap

I can't believe I'm transferring schools again. My dad just can't seem to keep a job in the same place for very long. Thankfully mom works from home; she completes surveys online. She is the stable part of my life. Dad is a contract CEO; he's always gone and we are always moving. Companies hire him to stabilize their business and then after a year or so he moves on to another job, and I move on to another school. He just doesn't understand what this does to me, he never understands things. There's nothing I can do about it.

And here we are moving to Cranston, TX, population 2,346. We've always been in larger cities, but my parents got tired of that, so they found a nice outlying village to hide away in this time. I'm leaving a high school with close to 5,000 students to live in a town with a smaller population. This is how I will finish my public school career. A fitting swan song I suppose.

"Mom, why did you guys choose Cranston?"

"Oh, I don't know, dear, it just seemed like a nice change of pace after the last few years of urban living."

The only downside to Mom's survey job is that she doesn't pay much attention to me when she's working.

"But you love the city! What are you talking about 'change of pace'?" Mom loves the city, she doesn't want a change of pace.

"Well, sometimes it's nice to do something different. Dad likes to change his job often, he likes to change our house often, I suppose he likes to change our living style often as well."

"I'm a teenager! My lifestyle changes all the time without changing my environment or affecting anyone else! Why can't Dad change like that?"

"I don't think I'd like that...and by the way, your constant changes don't affect anyone else?"

"Oh, Mom! Forget it!" I don't like being shown up like that.

"You'll be fine Eric, you never have trouble making new friends, and you've never lived in a simple town before, I think you'll enjoy the slower pace."

I guess we'll see. I'm going to my room. In parting I say, "Sure, Mom, I'll make new friends, and I probably won't even have to try to keep up academically with these bumpkins, but still, I'd rather not be here."

***

Up in my room I check out my new textbooks. We arrived in town on Thursday; on Friday Mom took me to the school to register for classes and get my books, I'll start classes on Monday. Starting a new school is always somewhat difficult for me, but it's made worse when it happens in January, like this time. Three times we've moved over the summer so I was able to start the school year fresh with everyone else. I was still new and didn't have friends from previous years, but at least I wasn't dropped into the middle of social conversations lasting since September.

Not that it's much of an issue for me, I don't date much, but dropping in half way through the year is usually a hassle for that kind of thing. Everyone is paired off by January. And in a school with such a small population, and an even smaller senior class - I think the lady at the school said thirty-eight students - the chance of me finding any girl to interest me is slim to none. I'm just going to do my time, graduate, go to college far away and finally be able to settle down somewhere I choose. No more of this nomadic living like a criminal or storybook monster.

Dad is already fully involved with work, meaning he's not around on Saturdays either, so it's just me and Mom for dinner again. We decided to try out one of the local BBQ spots; apparently there are two things Cranston is known for, very little rain and a whole lotta BBQ. We have a small - "quaint" is the word my mother used - three-bedroom ranch house. No ranch, just the house, but down the road a way, after it forks, the ranch land begins. Our house isn't far from the center of town, a few city blocks is all. We live on Earp Street, it's a left onto First Street and that crosses over and continues on past Route 33, which is called Main Street for the quarter mile it runs through town.

It's primarily residential between home and town; the only commercial buildings in town are all on Main Street. The school, which houses kindergarten through twelfth grade, is on the other side of Main Street heading away from our side of town. Not more than a mile straight line from our house, roughly, but given the roads to follow it probably comes out a little longer. I plan on riding my bike to school, at least until the heat picks up again, I hear it spends most of the year in the 80's and for the thick of the summer it tops 100 quite regularly. Once it gets to that I can use the car, if Mom doesn't need it or as she keeps suggesting, I'll be able to ride to school with my new friends. I think she already thinks I have a solid group of friends here. I haven't even seen anyone my own age aside from our short visit to the school for me to get my class schedule and books.

"I just love all of these local businesses; no sign of franchise stores anywhere!" Mom seems to be genuinely happy in this desert wasteland. I guess that helps me feel like being here isn't a complete waste. I thought she always catered to what Dad wanted, but maybe she had some influence in this decision after all.

"Yeah, looks like stereotypical small-town America, for sure." As much as I want to be under protest with this move, I guess I am kind of interested in the dramatically different location, and I do like BBQ. I really don't need to make a lot of friends to feel comfortable here, I can get by without all that social stuff, but it would be nice to find one person I can relate to and goof off with. I'll know better come Monday.

We pull up to Josie's BBQ and Breakfast to find what seems like half the population of Cranston parked outside. Okay, that's a total exaggeration, but the place looks packed.

"I told you we should have just walked over." Mom thinks it is stupid to drive the few blocks when it is such a nice day, and in January to boot. We were in the frozen north before our move to Texas, living just outside Chicago where Dad was working. I don't mind the snow very much, but I'll admit I'm pretty excited to have winter over with already.

"Yeah, yeah, you told me so," I say.

"I guess I'll turn around and park on the other side of the street. We'll be halfway home already." Mom knows how to make her point.

"If you guys hadn't wimped out and just bought a ranch, thereby completing the Cranston experience we could be having our own BBQ outback, right after we slaughter our own steer."

"Right, like you would slaughter anything. I'd like to see that…and laugh at it!"

Mom is right; I don't exactly have the constitution of a slaughterhouse technician. I tried pulling a conscientious objector role for biology class when we did the frog dissection unit. It didn't work, and neither did my body when I had to pull the guts out of that little guy. I passed out. That was the one time I actually looked forward to an upcoming move. I was the only one to faint, and the teacher made sure to let us know that that was the first time he'd ever had a student faint during a frog dissection. Luckily for me he waited until I came to before making the announcement to the class. The jerk.

"Well then you could do the slaughtering and I could do the grilling." Just thinking about the frog incident again makes me feel a little uncomfortable in the upper digestive system area.

"Look over there!" Mom exclaims with an over the top extension of her index finger.

"What?" I follow the finger to the eight car parking area in front of the restaurant.

"They look like they are probably your age. You should go say hi and introduce yourself. I won't even be offended if you ditch me and sit with them."

"Mom, you know I'm not aggressive enough to do that, but if you really don't want me around I can wait in the car for you. Just leave me a bottle of water and crack the windows a bit." There are two boys and two girls hanging around outside the front door. They are all wearing blue jeans and button up shirts. One of the boys has a black cowboy hat. I wonder if they call them cowboy hats down here. They all look like what I'd expect from the youth of a town like this. My clothes aren't too different, I mean, I wear jeans too, but mine aren't quite so snug, and my shirts aren't quite so tucked in and I don't think I own any shirts with buttons, I leave that style to my dad.

Both of the girls look good. I don't talk to them much, or ask them on dates, girls that is, but I certainly notice them, girls in general, I mean. I bet this is some sort of double date anyway; so even if I was socially capable of introducing myself to complete strangers, I don't think it would be proper in this situation.

"The place looks pretty full, I hope we can get in, otherwise we are both sitting in the car drinking water."

"That doesn't make any sense, Mom."

"I know."

As we walk around the last car in the row alongside the sidewalk leading to the front door the kids all look at us. They are smiling, a mix between "howdy, partner" and *Children of the Corn*.

"Hello! How's the food here tonight?" Mom excitedly asks the kids.

"Perfect, as always, Ma'am." Cowboy hat responds first, and does one of those nods while simultaneously pinching the front rim of his hat and pulling it down and up, very slightly. I almost laugh. I never expected to see anyone do that in real life.

"Yes, Josie makes the best BBQ in central Texas, maybe even further. Is this your first time having authentic Texas BBQ?" This comes from the shorter of the two girls, both blonde and bearing a striking resemblance to one another, I think they must be sisters, this one being the younger of the two.

"We've had BBQ before, but this is our first time having it in Texas, right, Eric?" Mom makes meeting new people look so easy, Dad, too, but I usually struggle with it for some reason. Maybe when I'm older and I'm meeting kids it'll be easy like this for me, something to do with peer group intimidation factors. Whatever that means.

She continues, "This is my son Eric, Eric Sterling. We just moved into town this week, he'll be starting school on Monday, he's a senior this year. Are you all in high school, too?" Mom is thorough, I'll give her that, and she knows how to carry out an agenda. She knows I'd never introduce myself to these guys, and probably won't be very forward in the introduction department after I get to school, so she's taking the lead.

"Hi, Eric." The other boy and girl joins the younger sister in this standard greeting.

"Eric, Mrs. Sterling, nice to meet you." Cowboy Hat one up's them all. He must be the leader of the pack.

"You girls are beautiful! Eric told me he saw some nice looking girls when we were at the school yesterday…"

"Mom!" The shock causes me to interrupt before I realize what I'm doing, and not just interrupt, but do so in the style of a tantrum-throwing young girl. Embarrassing? Only mostly.

"Well, don't you think they are beautiful?" I can't believe it! Why is she doing this? She can't just comment on how polite Cowboy Hat is and get back to the real purpose here, dinner?!

My eyes drop to the ground as the blush in my cheek hits core meltdown temperature. My physiological response to embarrassment can stand with the best of them. I look up and notice that even with their perfectly tanned faces I can almost detect a hint of blush on the sisters as well.

"Yes," I answer, "you are both very beautiful." I smile and quickly look away again.

The hatless boy speaks up now, "And what about me?" It was the kind of well-timed comment that I'd like to be known for making, but often I miss the opportunity, thinking of the punch line just a little too late for the conversation.

"Of course, you two are equally handsome young men." Mom is happy to have struck up a reciprocal friendly tone in the conversation. She adds, "Which is probably why these young ladies are with you this evening."

"Nah," says Cowboy Hat, "Krissy and Jessie are my sisters; they're stuck with me no matter what I look like. Saturday dinners take place at Josie's; it's kind of like a Cranston rule."

"Well I'm glad we are in compliance then!" Mom seems ecstatic to hear about the "Cranston rule."

"I'm Trent, by the way, and this here is Michael, and of course, Krissy and Jessie. The three of us," singling out Krissy as the fourth, "are all seniors, she's a sophomore." Once again identifying Krissy.

"It's a pleasure to meet you all. I hope to see you around sometime, you can all come over to the house to see Eric," Mom says.

"Sure thing, we're usually around. There ain't much to do in Cranston besides work, which we do a lot of." I suppose I should start calling Cowboy Hat Trent now, but perhaps the window of opportunity for a name change is already passed. I think Cowboy Hat is going to stick. At least until I figure out how this embarrassing introduction moment with my mom is going to play out at school on Monday.

"I guess we'll go have ourselves some of central Texas' best BBQ then. Ready, Eric?"

"Yeah." I'm still keeping my eyes anywhere but in contact with the four townies.

"See ya at school, man," says Michael.

"Nice to meet you Eric, see you on Monday." Jessie says.

I look back and smile as we enter Josie's, "See ya."

***

Josie's is rather deceptive. From the outside it looks like an old stucco dive, but on the inside it's built like a large log cabin style lodge. The ceiling is high, so much so that I contemplate running back outside to catch a glimpse of the roof again. I guess I just wasn't paying attention to that on the way in. I better not mention this to mom or she'll say something like 'of course you weren't paying attention to the building, how could you with Krissy and Jessie in the way!'

The whole interior is raw lumber, well, I guess it was processed somehow, but it looks like logs is what I mean. The walls are covered with paintings and other framed items. Some look like legal documents; some are old photos, black and white at one point probably, but now more of a faded yellow. As one would expect, there are various animal heads mounted around, and a few sun bleached bull skulls.

"Welcome to Josie's! Two newcomers for dinner tonight?" We are greeted by a woman, roughly the same age as my mom, if I had to guess, but deeper lines in her face, most likely from the sun and lots of smiling. She wasn't holding back on the smiling here in the least.

"Yes, two newcomers for dinner," replies Mom, "both excited for what we've heard is the best BBQ in central Texas."

The waitress leans her head back and to the side, and then shouts, "Who's got the best BBQ?"

To which the whole crowd inside erupts in a loud, unsynchronized wave of "Josie's!"

I bet this waitress used to be a cheerleader, probably at Cranston High.

Mom and I are both slightly startled and Becca, according to her name tag, laughs and explains the pride

Cranstonites take in Josie's reputation as being the best BBQ around.

"Private table or would you like to join the masses?" Becca has the stereotypical appearance and drawl you would expect from a waitress in a small BBQ joint in central Texas. Exactly that stereotype.

"I'd be happy to sit with the locals, but I think my son still needs some time to adjust, may we have a table of our own?" Mom nudges me in the arm with her elbow and rolls her eyes. Becca laughs and invites us to follow her. As we came in the door there were some diner style tables and booths around the right side of the room while on the left were four long banquet tables. The "masses" as Becca had called them, filled out nearly every chair at the four long tables. It really does seem like the whole town is here for dinner. This either means the food is worth it, or the town is just that boring. I suppose I'll find the answers to both of these questions in short order.

2. *You Won't Know*

It's raining. They said "it never rains in Cranston." Liars. Although the comparatively dry and desert-like terrain would indicate they are correct. Rain doesn't bother me, I usually enjoy a good overcast day, and with today being my first day of school here, I really couldn't care less what the weather is. Besides, Mom said I could take the car today.

I like having Mom at home. It's nice to have someone always around, and she usually makes great breakfast. Today seems to be on par with that, as I can smell the aroma of frying pig flesh emanating from the kitchen. I have a creative writing class, so I'm trying to get in the spirit. I'm actually pretty excited about bacon for breakfast; Mom always makes corn pancakes with it, a combination that can't be beat.

With backpack in hand I head to the kitchen, by way of the living room where I turn on the TV news and ratchet up the volume so I'll be able to hear it in the kitchen.

"You know, if you want to watch TV maybe you should stay in the room with the TV?" Mom doesn't particularly care for my media consumption habits, specifically how I consume it rather than what I consume.

"I was going to stay in there but the smell of a down-home breakfast is impossible to resist," I say as I slide into a chair at the kitchen table. We aren't much for formalities when eating at our house. Dad is always at work, so meals are usually just me and Mom, and she doesn't care where I eat, or when. A lot of the time she has already eaten by the time I make it home, or into the kitchen, for a meal. Neither one of us is concerned about sitting down together, so neither of us makes an effort. When Dad is home we make the effort to be all together for a meal, but I think that's just some kind of compensatory desire my dad has for not being around more. Incidentally, he's already gone this morning, I heard him leaving as I was just waking up.

"Are you super excited for your first day at the new school?!" Mom is clearly more excited than I am. "Maybe you'll see your friends from Josie's."

"Mom, there are about fourteen and a half students at the school, I'm pretty sure I'll see all of the kids that were at Josie's the other night. And no, I'm not 'super excited' about school today. The only thing I'm excited about is being all done with high school in another five months."

"Well with that attitude you'll be prom king in no time!" she says.

"Right, prom king, that's exactly what I'm going for, you saw right through my tough-guy façade and spotted the very innermost wishes of my heart!" I counter.

"Well with that sarcasm you'll be the idol of the disaffected crowd in no time!" Checkmate.

"Thanks, Mom! I knew I'd be able to make you proud!" An outside observer might detect some venom in exchange like this, but we know it's all in good fun.

Mom has already eaten and is off to the virtual world of filling out surveys and trolling the Internet. I hope she is happy. I don't see why she would be, but hopefully she is. She's the grown up, I'm still just a kid, at least for two more months until I turn eighteen and magically become an adult. I'll let Mom worry about her life and I'll worry about mine, which right now is about to take me to some out of the way, insignificant K-12 school in Cranston, TX. I guess I'll find out if their school's reputation is anything like that of their BBQ joint.

***

Everyone stares at me as I pull into the parking lot of the school. 'Everyone' in this case amounts to about two dozen people. The rain is merely a drizzle and there are kids standing around as though it were a sunny day, just chatting. No different than any other school; the kids waiting as long as they can before entering the building for seven hours of captivity. I guess there is at least one difference from any other school, the ones I've been to anyway, there are way more cowboy hats here. And as a testament to the amazing power of the human brain to find familiar sights, there is my friend from Saturday night, Cowboy Hat, among all the other hats.

He sees me and his face lights up in recognition. Maybe the kids here are all just as bored as I am and anything new is exciting enough to cause a stir. He waves and yells; probably 'Hey, new kid!' or something of that nature, but I can't hear it with the windows up and music playing. I cued up one of my favorite rainy day songs, "You Won't Know," by Brand New, for the drive over. It's a short drive, made it in one song.

I wave and pull into a spot under a tree along the edge of the lot. As I get out of the car I notice that Cowboy Hat is stopped and looking in my direction still. Is he waiting for me? I wave again and consider yelling 'hello,' but I realize I don't remember his name. I don't think it would be very friendly, and certainly not effective, to yell

13

'hello, Cowboy Hat!' I'd have half the parking lot turn to look at me. I start out in his direction.

"Hi, Eric. You made it." I really need to remember his name now if he's going to remember mine.

"Hey, yeah, I made it. I actually went to the other high school first before I realized I was at the wrong one." I say, and give a self-deprecating laugh.

Cowboy Hat looks puzzled; apparently my dig at his hometown doesn't register as a joke.

"What other school?" he asks.

There's nothing worse than having to explain a joke of this nature, not only does it erase any hope of getting a laugh out of someone, but it also makes a person who is already feeling behind the eight ball feel like they have just been hit in the eye with the eight ball. As I gear up to explain I hear my name.

"Eric! Welcome to school!" It is Jessie. Not surprisingly, I remember her name, though I wouldn't tell Mom that. And Jessie is Cowboy Hat's sister, along with the other girl; it sounds like Jessie…Krissy. Michael is the other boy, I remember he said what I would have said and that reminded me of my friend Mike from a few years ago, so I remember his name. However, still nothing on Cowboy Hat.

"Hi, Jessie, nice to see you again." I may be shy with girls, but I can usually conduct myself with appropriate social politeness.

"Where's your class schedule, let's see where you need to go and who you have classes with." Jessie reaches out her hand and waits.

I pull my schedule from my front pocket and unfold it twice before handing it over.

"I figured we'd all be in the same classes, I mean, with a school this size I figured there wouldn't be options

beyond grade level, we'd just all switch classes together."
I say.

"For the most part you're right, but we do have thirty-eight in our senior class, sorry, thirty-*nine*," Cowboy Hat nods to me, "so they break us up into two classes for each subject. It's pretty much the slower class and the faster class."

"I guess that makes sense, forty kids would be a lot for one class," I say.

Jessie finishes reviewing my schedule and says, "You're in the faster classes."

"Well I guess *I'll* see you in gym, new guy," Cowboy Hat says in a mocking tone."

"You can follow me to class, we have the first few together," Jessie says as she hands my schedule back to me. "But then the last two classes are swapped. I'm not as good in math. And with the limited options if I don't make it to the faster math class then something else needs to get switched as well, it happens to be social science, which isn't really any different between the two levels. We have gym in the middle, but all seniors have that at the same time."

" 'Not as good in math!' Listen to her, it's not enough she's a junior age-wise but goes to all the senior classes, thereby skipping a full grade, she has to put in that the best she can do is the lower senior math class." Cowboy Hat wraps his younger sister up in a bear hug from behind and lifts her up off the ground slightly. Jessie squeals. I start to wonder if having a sibling would have made much of a difference for me with all of the moving my family has done. I've had close friends before, but I've always had to leave them. Cowboy Hat and Jessie are close friends in addition to being siblings. That would be nice, I think.

"I'm not a fan of math; I'm surprised I'm in the faster class for that. It'll be good to know someone in class already for the first three anyway." I'm surprised how sincere I am in making that statement. It's as if I'm trying to be friends with these kids. I suppose I am. They are friendly enough, and aren't holding back on making an effort to extend a welcome to me, I guess I'm captivated by their rural charms. Then again, maybe it's time to revisit my initial *Children of the Corn* theory.

Jessie says, "Don't worry about the other two classes. Do you remember Michael from the other night? He's in all of the fast classes, too. He's inside with Krissy, they have a thing going, don't know if you picked up on that the other night or not."

"I didn't notice it," I say.

I didn't notice it; not that I was really paying attention. I felt a little relief that Jessie isn't the one having a thing with Michael, but I'm not going to dwell on that right now. "How about we go inside? Maybe the rain doesn't bother folks in Texas, but where I'm from, which is essentially everywhere else, people don't usually stand around talking in the rain in the middle of January."

My new friends agree and we all head indoors. Jessie asks how many places I've lived in and what I liked most about them. I give the usual answers, fully expecting that I'll be answering similar, if not the same, questions in each class for the satisfaction of each teacher. Cowboy Hat asks what my last school was like and what I did for sports. I feel somewhat like I let him down when I say I didn't play sports. He picks back up when I tell him my last school was very impersonal and I just stuck with a small group of friends, and that I already feel oddly at home in Cranston; probably because of the significantly smaller population. It is clear he takes as much pride in his town's hospitality as he does in Josie's BBQ.

"Here's us, Eric." Jessie grabs my elbow and motions to the classroom on the left. "See you in gym, Trent."

Bingo! "Yeah, see you in gym, Trent." Cowboy Hat's name is Trent; I'll need to do a better job of remembering it. This time for real. It really won't do for me to ask Jessie something about "Cowboy Hat" at this point, it'll be best to use his real name. I better try it out to reinforce the memory.

"What's the age difference between you and Trent?"

"He's eighteen next month, and I'll be seventeen in June. Sixteen months between us. Krissy is a full two years younger than me, almost to the day, my birthday is the ninth and hers is the thirteenth."

Jessie is able to coax a classmate to move desks so that I can sit to her left. She introduces me to a few other students. Michael comes in just before the teacher, who seems to be already teaching a lecture as she enters, so he just nods and waves to me while taking his seat on the other side of the room. Mrs. Davis has already asked a question regarding the reading assignment from over the weekend when she sees me and changes direction. She welcomes me and goes through the expected rigmarole of introductions. I comply by answering her questions, trying to remember what I say so I can either parrot it back for each of the next classes or dress it up on subsequent deliveries, depending on how I am feeling.

The class is small; the kids all seem friendly and the teacher seems anxious to help me get caught up. Overall this transition is going rather well, better than I expected, but then I always have been somewhat of a pessimist. Hopefully the rest of the day will be the same. Hopefully I didn't just jinx it.

***

Creative writing was the first class. How that constitutes a senior level English requirement I'll never know, but we have a lot of reading on the syllabus, and Mrs. Davis does comes across as a stickler for grammar. What's in a name anyway? That was followed by chemistry, which was much the same as creative writing, except more chemistry and less creative writing. Now it is time for gym, and things look like they are picking up. The game of the week is floor hockey. Although not much of a sports enthusiast, I really do enjoy floor hockey, at least the kind with the plastic hockey sticks and rubber ball. At one of my previous schools they used brooms. My friends and I would joke that it was because the custodians were lazy. Pretty lame joke in retrospect. The game is better with the plastic sticks.

Michael leads me to the locker room where we meet up with Trent, you know, Cowboy Hat. The teacher designates a locker for me and lets me borrow a lock for the day. Apparently it's BYOL, and nobody told me. I did expect the need for changing clothes, so I have those at least. My previous school issued athletic clothing with the school name and mascot printed on it, but I didn't expect Cranston would have the same provision. I change and follow Michael and Trent out into the gym.

The gym is a full-size high school basketball court, but that's pretty much it. On one side are pull-out bleachers attached to the wall and on the other is about ten feet between the court boundary line and the wall. Likely most of the gym class activities are conducted outside as the weather allows it year round, but floor hockey is best played on a floor, and those are usually only inside.

The gym teachers explain the bracket system for our games and post a schedule. Then we are arranged into teams. I am on team three, without any of my three friends by the way, so I'm on deck for the second match. Each match has a five minute timer, most points in five minutes wins. Here I am just sitting and watching the current game when behind the cluster of teenagers and plastic sticks battling over a bright orange rubber ball I notice a girl enter the gym from the corner door that leads in from the hallway. She is wearing jeans and a long sleeve T. Her brown hair is down, not in any particular fashion, just down. She is pale, unusually pale for the population of this town. My first thought is that she must have transferred in from somewhere up north, like me, somewhere hidden from the sun during the winter. My excitement over the possibility drowns out any logic that might have challenged the likelihood of Cranston receiving two transfer students in the same month, let alone the same day. In fact, I think someone mentioned to me that I was the first transfer student in more than a year.

My distracted train of thinking melts away as I continue to notice this girl. She walks directly to one of the female gym teachers and hands her a note. The girl's expression remains blank through her brief exchange with the teacher (consisting of the teacher saying something and the girl nodding) and then as she takes a seat a few rows up on the bleachers, all the way to one side, away from anyone else. I guess she isn't a transfer student, just late to school, or perhaps not feeling well, the note may have come from the school nurse. If they have a nurse here, I wonder if they do.

Michael is on team four, so he is sitting next to me. Trent is on team two and in the current game. "You guys have a school nurse here?"

Michael looks at me.

"Are you feeling ill? Trying to get out of the hurt my team is about to dish out to your team?" he laughs.

"Nah, I'm fine, ready to play, for some reason the question just came to mind." I know the reason, but I'm not about to say it out loud.

"Well, there's a nurse station in the main office. Janice, she's probably the one who set up your classes, she fills in as the nurse, but I don't think she has any medical training, just experience as a mother of five kids. Most of the faculty, and even more of the students, have farm or ranch experience. You don't work with animals and not know how to handle the types of injuries that would be common among a school setting. We all pretty much take care of ourselves and each other as needed. So when you get in my way and I check you to the ground, I'll splint up your fractured wrist for you, free of charge." He laughs again. Michael has a genuine laugh, even for his own jokes, usually something that comes across as arrogant, or an indication of a poor sense of humor, but it works for him.

I laugh but don't offer a response to his threat, or discourse on the school's health care situation. I'm back to trying to steal a glimpse of the pale girl without being too obvious, which is difficult while sitting on the second row of the bleachers at half court. I have to turn my head further than just ninety-degrees to the left. I pull off a few successful glimpses by faking like I'm stretching my back and shoulders before the whistle is blown, indicating time to switch teams. Trent comes off the floor soliciting high-fives; apparently he did well in the game. I almost don't recognize him without his hat. I give him five and he says some encouraging sportsmanship phrase, but I'm not paying attention. I quickly get across the gym to the opposite side so I can face the pale girl. She is still sitting in the same position, leaning against the railing, head down, away from everyone else.

A whistle signals the start of our game and I'm able to snap back to paying attention and run after the ball. After all, this is one of the few games I enjoy playing, and the girl will still be there after it is over. This is school, where's she going to go? I let all of that out of my head and play floor hockey like I was born to do it. Maybe I was. I've never showed physical prowess like this in any other activity. But here I'm running and maneuvering a hockey stick, without tripping myself or others; although Michael almost falls victim. He, of course, thinks I did it on purpose, causing him to laugh and say "You're on, new guy!"

Whatever that means.

Our game ends with a tie, 2-2. I didn't score a goal, but I took a few shots. Team four apparently has the best goalie in the school. If that is the case then I say we did very well as a team. More importantly I now have the rest of the class to sit down and watch other games. Once every team has played their first game there will be two-minute lightening matches for tie-breakers. The teachers don't think there will be time to get to that today. I'm glad for that.

I return to my same spot next to Michael, with Trent joining us now that he isn't playing. I make one more glance up at the pale girl before taking my seat. She hasn't moved. I start to worry about my fascination with her. Is she that attractive? I can't see her face now and I begin to wonder if I remember correctly all the way back to the seven or so minutes when I first saw her from across the gym. Oh well, something still has my interest, so I best find out what it is.

I decide to go for a drink; the water fountain is just a few feet away from where she is sitting. I should be able to talk to her from the water fountain; at least I'll be out of sight from everyone else so no one will know I'm talking to her. I'm already way out of my comfort zone with meeting new people, although I don't feel so out of it. Still, I'd rather not inspire discussions of 'Looks like the new guy's got a crush on pale girl!' I think I have a real problem with making up names for people.

My plan is to go get a drink from the water fountain and then stand there to watch the game for a little bit before returning to my seat. I'll leave the rest up to spontaneous courage that I hope to develop in the next twenty-five seconds. Otherwise I'll just be standing watching the game from a terrible vantage point. My plan is garbage. Too late to turn back now.

"I'm going to get a drink, be back in a minute," I say out loud, but not specifically to anyone.

"Yep." Trent verbally acknowledges me, but he and Michael are laughing at a friend of theirs who just fell down on the court.

I watch the girl as I walk; she still hasn't moved. I guess I'm hoping she'll happen to look up and I might make eye contact with her. As it is I'm trying to watch her and walk in a straight line at the same time.

"Watch out!"

Wham! I'm knocked into the bleachers, hard. That warning came way too late. Two guys I haven't met yet help me up, one of them was the force that caused the collision and the other was the projectile.

"Sorry man! Are you alright?" The bigger kid, I think he must have been the force, is apologizing and looking me over. Maybe he has x-ray vision. I should ask him.

"Are you okay Mr. Sterling?" One of the gym teachers is standing next to us.

"Yeah, I'm fine, just caught me off guard. You guys okay?" I sit on the lower bench of the bleachers for a minute while my brain reviews the pain signals to make sure I really am okay.

"Okay, if everyone is alright, get back in the game, be careful with your momentum, Josh."

"You got it, Coach. Sorry everyone." Josh, the force, picks up his stick and gets back into the game, with the projectile right behind him. Sure, he's fine, I broke his fall.

My left elbow is a bit sore, but the pain is barely noticeable over my complete and utter embarrassment. I don't even want to look back at Michael and Trent. Jessie is in the current game; I didn't notice her after the collision though, she must be on the far side of the game or something. Pale girl! I quickly stand up and look in her direction, but she still hasn't moved! Impossible! She must have looked up to see the commotion and then just returned to her position of arms folded across knees and head down on forearms. No way she just sat through that, no one is that focused in their obliviousness. She must be asleep or something. Maybe it was a note from a doctor excusing her from class because she's sick, but if she's that sick maybe she should be at home.

Safe behind the bleachers I drink from the fountain. As I stand up again I look right at the pale girl. I can't see her face from this angle either; her hair is in the way. Now or never, or more accurately, now or later, but I choose now.

"Hey, not a fan of floor hockey?"

What did I just ask? I could blame the collision, but the truth is I never actually planned for this part of the mission. She doesn't respond or even react, so I guess I could just walk away and regroup. No, I'm here and the campaign is underway. I walk a little closer; she is sitting high enough so that her shoes are at eye level for me. "Hi, my name is Eric Sterling, I just moved in last week, this is my first day of school here."

Still no response, but at least I did a better job with my dialog. I turn to grab another quick sip of water, and when I turn back she is gone. I think my mouth actually opens as my jaw drops a little. I don't think I've ever noticed that happen before. I shrug and turn towards the court to head back to my seat and there she is, standing a few feet in front of me.

"Hi Eric, sorry about that, I'm not feeling well at all. My name is Rachel, welcome to Cranston." She is smiling, but it seems as though it pains her to do so, she must be really ill. Her hands are behind her back. Thankfully she doesn't extend one for an introduction handshake because if she's that ill I don't think I want it.

"Thanks, Cranston's turning out to be a decent place. It's nice to meet you, Rachel. I thought you were sleeping or something. I figured you were sick and that's why you weren't playing today." I explain.

"Yeah, I've been kind of sick lately, some kind of virus. My whole family has it, actually. But we are mostly on the mend now," she says.

Rachel is beautiful. She's a little soft spoken and has only shown a half smile so far. I guess there is a legitimate reason for my attention being directed at her after all. She goes on, "I was out of school all last week."

"Wow, sounds pretty bad. You aren't contagious now are you?" I do one of those weird things where you put your hands up in front of you and kind of duck down behind an invisible shield. I've been watching a lot of sitcoms lately. Rachel either ignores my ridiculous posturing or thinks it charming.

"No, I don't think I'm contagious. We haven't been to the doctor or anything, but we are all getting better, so it seems the virus is on its way out. Anyway, my parents thought I was well enough to come back to school, although I can't really seem to focus on anything and I'd rather be anywhere but here."

I don't know why but I feel really comfortable with Rachel, and it seems she is comfortable with me. I take the role of investigator for a change and asked about siblings and parents and how long she's lived in Cranston. She's an only child, mother stays home, father runs a cattle ranch a mile outside of Cranston in Franklin. Her family moved here a few years ago, after her freshman year, from Georgia.

Our conversation only lasts a few minutes before it is time to head back to the locker room. It is announced that the tie-breaker games will take place first thing tomorrow. We have to wrap up our conversation.

"I was told I'm on the fast track for classes, will I see you in the next class then?" I ask hopefully.

"Yeah, I'm in the 'fast track,' as you called it, too. Are you headed to the cafeteria now?"

"Yeah, we all have lunch together, right, I mean the senior class?"

"Yes. I just didn't know if you were leaving for lunch or not."

"We can leave for lunch?" More information, like the gym lock, that may have been nice to know ahead of time.

"Sure, seniors are free for the lunch period. You can go home or go to Josie's or whatever. Most people just take their lunch outside and eat in the courtyard. But since its rainy today they'll probably be in the cafeteria."

"Right on. I didn't bring a lunch today, just money. If I had known I could leave I might have planned to do that, I have my mom's car today. But I think I'll just stick around here. I'm still pretty new in town, I wouldn't want to get lost and not make it back in time for class." This time my poking fun at the small town gets the response I want, Rachel laughs and agrees with a good sarcastic tone.

"New guy! Come on, we gotta get changed!" Michael and Trent are headed into the locker room and waving me along. Trent winks at me when he sees me talking to Rachel, at least, I hope that's what he is winking for.

I say to her, "I guess I better get going. I'll see you in the cafeteria then?"

"Sure, I'll be there." She smiles, turns, and then walks away.

3. Praise Chorus

"So, you made a new friend, eh, Eric?" Michael starts right in on it.

"Yeah, looks like it. I can't be hanging onto you guys for the rest of my life," I reply.

"Our little guy is all grown up!" Trent grabs Michael in a headlock and gives him a noogie. I wouldn't believe it if I didn't see it myself.

"Rachel's an alright girl. She's usually really quiet. She moved here summer before sophomore year, but none of us really know her at all. Quite a feat in a town this size; somehow her family pulls it off, obscurity, I mean."

This intrigues me greatly. "Wow. Yeah, I wouldn't expect anyone in Cranston to be able to remain anonymous for very long, I haven't even been here a week and look at me."

"Well," Trent begins, "They've done it. When she introduced herself we recognized her family name, it's on the slaughterhouse just outside of town, apparently her great-grandfather started the slaughterhouse, but it has been in different ownership since him. The name was never changed. Her dad is from Texas originally."

"For not really knowing her you seem to know a lot about her," I say.

"Well, Trent probably knows her better than anyone else; he kind of almost dated her the first year she was here," Michael offers.

"I see. Almost? So one of you decided not to get into it?" I ask Trent.

"Something like that." Trent doesn't seem to want to get into this discussion. He is changed and ready to head out now. I put my gym clothes back in my bag and remove the borrowed lock from the door.

I have one more question for now, "Slaughter house? Rachel said her dad runs a cattle ranch."

Trent answers, "Yeah, Rachel's dad bought the ranch and slaughterhouse his grandfather started some years ago. So both, she wasn't lying. She told me once she was 'unsettled' by her family's business."

Michael chips in, "Well, Eric, are you officially interested in Miss Sutton?"

"Is that Rachel's last name, Sutton?" Just to clarify.

"Yeah, Rachel Sutton, of the Strange Suttons of Harrison County."

We are headed out of the gym now.

"The 'Strange Suttons of Harrison County'?"

"Don't worry about it, man, her family just has a reputation," Michael says.

Trent adds, "Rachel is an attractive girl, but also a strange girl. However she's nothing much, as far as strangeness is concerned, when it comes to her folks."

"What's that supposed to mean?" I won't say I'm feeling defensive, but I suppose I am.

"There are some rumors about the family, something that isn't uncommon for outsiders. I'm not saying Cranston is a bunch of gossiping bumpkins, but some of the older folks in town are very traditional and not really enthusiastic about new or different lifestyles, so rumors get started. Rachel is a cool girl; she just wasn't interested in me."

I can tell Trent is being sincere with me. He did like Rachel, but apparently she didn't like him. I'll have to ask about those rumors later. For now I decide to be extra diplomatic, "So, Trent, I'm not saying I'm going to go ask Rachel out right now, but if it gets to that point someday…"

"Go for it, man, but good luck to you. She's had a few guys ask her out now, but she never goes on a date with any of them. She'll hang out, but as soon as a guy asks 'Will you go out with me?' she either makes excuses or avoids the guy like the plague."

"Well alright then. I guess we'll see how it goes. What are you guys doing for lunch? I didn't know we were allowed to leave school. I told Rachel I'd meet her in the cafeteria today, but I'm all for getting out of the building for a bit some other day." I decide to get off the topic of Rachel for a moment, although I guess I didn't actually do that, fully.

"We go to Josie's on Mondays. They have a good lunch deal to get rid of any excesses from the weekend. They go all out for Saturday nights, and a lot of food is eaten, but there's usually an excess, which becomes Monday's lunch." Michael's response seems a little Pavlovian.

"Okay, well, I'm not big on brown-bag lunches, so if you guys are going out somewhere tomorrow count me in," I say.

"Will do, Eric, I guess we'll see each other after school." Trent says.

"I'll see you next period in math." Says Michael.

"Hey guys! Eric, you coming to Josie's with us?" Jessie pounces on us from behind, throwing one arm around her brother's neck and the other around mine, pulling me off balance a bit, but thankfully I don't fall.

"I didn't get the memo soon enough, I already made lunch plans for today," I say.

I nearly forgot about Jessie since I saw Rachel. I'll admit I was thinking about becoming interested in Jessie earlier in the day, but I guess I got distracted. Teenagers, so fickle.

"You made plans?" Jessie questions.

"Yeah, I'm going to the cafeteria," I answer.

"How is that better than Josie's? Advanced warning or not." That's a fair question from her.

"A fair question, Jessie, and I guess I don't have a fair answer as I have never eaten at the cafeteria here before and…"

Michael interrupts, "Eric met Rachel Sutton in gym class."

"Oh, I see! I didn't know Rachel was even at school today?" She looks to her brother and he shrugs as he takes a Smartphone from his pocket and starts tapping on the screen.

"She came in late. I ran into her by the water fountain and we started talking. Maybe we were drawn together because we are both foreigners around here," I muse.

"Perhaps. Well I'm glad you are making friends; don't be a stranger though, huh?" Jessie says.

"Of course not, I'll tag along with you all for lunch tomorrow, I promise." I offer up a Boy Scout salute, or what I assume would be a salute for a Boy Scout. I never was one myself, I don't actually know what they do, something about holding a few fingers up on the right hand. "I thought you were a junior, anyway, they let you out of the school for lunch, too?"

Jessie says, "I'm a senior, I technically skipped junior year. I'm a senior with all the privileges."

"Yeah, all the privileges: leaving the school for lunch. Let's head out guys." Trent fulfills his group leader role and kicks off the lunch plans. "Eric, catch you later."

"See ya'll later," I say.

Jessie turns and smiles at me, Michael nods, and Trent, who has just put on his hat and pulled it tight, does his signature pinch and pull on the front brim. I like these guys. I guess I'm not as a-social as I usually tell myself I am. Maybe it just takes the right kind of people to help me out of my reclusiveness. And now on to the next level.

***

The cafeteria has double doors which are both held open by small hooks affixed to the wall. I enter and begin scanning for Rachel. Straight ahead is the food line, with a small kitchen in the back. There is a cooler filled with bottled juice and water next to the cash register at the end of the line, and next to that a small rack chips. The room is rectangular and has ten round tables spread about, each with six chairs; none being occupied by Rachel Sutton, the pale girl. To the right is a door that leads outside. The door is closed, but I see that some kids are outside at the concrete picnic tables in the courtyard. The period start bell has already sounded, so it *is* lunch time, and I'm a few minutes late after talking with my new clique, so I expected she'd be here already. But I don't see her.

My resolve falters and I wonder if it is too late to run and catch the clique. I'll check outside before I give up. I am hungry, and this is a cafeteria, so there's also the option of just getting food and eating lunch. On my way to the side door I hear my name.

"Eric, aren't you going to get some food first? Before going outside, I mean."

I turn around and there she is; she must have walked in right behind me, or I'm blind, either way, there she is.

"Hey, yeah, I was just looking for you. I thought maybe you were outside so I was going to check first." Again I surprise myself with how naturally I'm talking with her.

"Sorry I'm late. Here I am!" she says cheerfully.

"Do you want to grab some food and then find a seat?" I motion toward the lunch counter with my head.

"No, you go ahead, I'll grab a seat over here. I'm still not feeling well. I have some water, I'm just going to drink that," Rachel says.

"Oh. Do you need anything? Tylenol or something? Maybe they have some saltines or bread. I can ask," I offer.

"No, thank you, I'm alright. I'm just still recovering, but I'm okay. Go get your lunch and I'll be right over here." Rachel points towards an empty table in the corner. Most of the tables are empty. There is one full table with some loud boys, another table with a couple of girls and then two other tables with one person each.

I say okay and then go to the line. The lady behind the counter introduces herself and asks if I'm the "fella" from up north. I answer that I am and she smiles warmly, welcoming me to Cranston. The people certainly are nice around here. The lunch provision is spaghetti with meat sauce, always a winner in school lunch form. Not. I can only imagine how hard the garlic bread will be. I add a bottle of apple juice and a bag of chips to the tray at the register. The same lunch lady meets me there. I pay and turn towards the table where Rachel is sitting. She's looking at me.

I expect her to quickly look away, thinking she doesn't want me to know she has been watching me, but she doesn't. I smile at her. She just keeps looking at me, not really smiling, but not frowning either. Just relaxed and paying attention with her eyes. I head over.

"How's the food here? Judging by the crowd I'd say it doesn't hold a candle to Josie's, huh?" I ask.

"It's all the same to me. Cafeteria or Josie's I mean. I'm not as impressed by the local cuisine as everyone else seems to be. I guess I've just had enough cow to last my lifetime," she says.

"Right, your dad's a rancher, I guess you get your fill of cows after a while? Are they right near your house or is the house separated from the livestock area pretty well?" All I know about ranchers is what I learned from movies and reruns of *Bonanza*.

"We do have some cattle in a barn closer to the house, a few milkers, but most of our stock is significantly removed from our home area. They smell too bad to have them any closer. I just get sick of the smell, the lowing, the regularity with which they appear on our meal calendar and also the smell." She laughs at herself and I smile again.

"The only animals I've ever lived with are a couple of cats, but that was years ago, we didn't take them with us when we moved that time. I was never really attached to them anyway, so I didn't miss them," I say.

Rachel says, "I like cats well enough. So you've moved around a lot? We only moved the one time. We used to live in Atlanta. This is quite different for me, Cranston that is."

"I've never been to Atlanta, but I've lived pretty much everywhere else. Not really, but it seems like it. My dad is a hotshot in the business world, he moves around to different companies, takes over for a year or two and then finds another group to get in with, and we move. I haven't gone to the same school for two years in a row since third and fourth grade. It almost happened at my last school, I was there for my whole junior year and then the first half of this year."

It feels good to open up about my frustration over moving, so I continue. "You know, I've really hated moving around so much. I've had a few good friends and I've missed them when we moved. I've gotten used to areas and then had to leave them. My parents try to be the constant foundation in my life, but they don't do much more than give lip service to that reality, my dad mostly. Mom makes an honest effort, but even she doesn't seem to fully appreciate what I'm experiencing. Interestingly, I've always wanted to just stay in one place for a long time, but recently I've been thinking about how fast I'll be out of here as soon as I graduate, even though my parents have implied they'd like to stay here long term. I don't know why but they seem to really like this place."

"So you are going to leave as soon as you graduate? Going to college, or going back to one of your previous homes?" Rachel asks.

Still hanging onto the feelings of resentment towards moving and the relief of venting I keep my gaze fixed on the bottle of juice in my hand, which is where it rested after my monologue.

"Well I guess I'm not going to leave directly after school is finished. College will be my destination. I don't actually have a school picked out yet, but I'm in the process of all of that. I'll likely be here for the summer and then leave for school in the fall." I wonder if she is asking me when I'd be leaving for a specific reason, or just to keep up the conversation.

"Well, the summer here is hot and uncomfortable," Rachel says.

Nothing else follows. That's kind of awkward, maybe she was just keeping up the conversation.

"I've experienced some hot summers. San Diego was hot. Phoenix was hot. I guess this will be more of the same," I say.

Rachel just nods and takes another sip from her water bottle.

I ask her, "So what are your plans for after graduation? You hinted at not being a super-fan of Cranston, are you headed back to A-T-L, that's what the kids are calling it these days, right?" I resume filling my mouth with some of the worst spaghetti I've ever had. Cranston should stick with grilled cow.

"Yes, A-T-L, that's the way the natives say it, in certain circles. I always just call it home. But I don't know if I'll be going back there or not. I'm still trying to decide on college, and my parents are here, so I'm not sure what I'm going to do yet. I always wanted to get out of the country and see some of the historic places we read about in text books, but I don't know if I'll get to do that or not." She seems to wince as she says the last part, not as much in pain as in fear, or guilt, as though she is saying something she shouldn't.

"Are you okay?" I ask.

"Yes, what?" She looks honestly confused.

"You seemed to wince; I thought maybe you were in pain, something to do with your convalescence, perhaps?" Sometimes I talk like a professor, I attribute it to my preference for reading old fiction.

"Oh, yeah, just a little pain." She hesitates, and then says, "I'm surprised you noticed that, you are very perceptive, Eric Sterling."

"I...don't remember...telling you...my last name." I do the best horror-movie-dramatic-pausing I possibly can, letting all emotion drain from my face. I guess I'm a better actor than I realize because my pale friend Rachel seems to become even paler and she looks as though I caught her in a terrible lie or cover-up job.

"I thought you did, you must have, I wouldn't have known it..." She stumbles along until I interrupt.

"I'm just messing with you. Yeah, I introduced myself with my last name before. Sorry, I was just having a little fun," I laugh.

"Oh, ha ha, I guess I'm a little gullible sometimes. It's not that I've been asking about you or accidently overhearing things in the office this morning. I promise I'm not a stalker-type," she says.

I didn't think she was a stalker-type until she said it. Funny how that works. I'm pretty sure I gave her my last name, but she certainly looked like I caught her in something. Like she observed, I'm pretty perceptive.

"So what didn't you hear about me in the office this morning?" I raise one eyebrow and test the tensile strength of the garlic bread by ripping it in half. Not as bad as I thought, actually.

"Well, I didn't hear that you just moved in, just you and your parents, dad's a big corporate guy, mom stays home. I also didn't hear that you are somewhat of a genius academically, as far as school is concerned, but not very much of a people person." She reports back to me as though she had been rehearsing it.

"Wow. You didn't hear much at all. I guess Trent was right," I say.

"What did Trent say?" she asks.

"Well, he was just telling me that Cranston has a bit of a reputation for gossip and rumors. That's all."

But that wasn't all, he told me she is kind of strange, and her parents are, too. I hope my face isn't as telling as hers was, or that she isn't as perceptive as I am.

"Oh," she says.

No expansion or agreement. Maybe she agrees, maybe she doesn't. Maybe she doesn't want to discuss Trent. Maybe I don't either.

"So Trent said you two almost dated once." What!? Well if I didn't reveal anything in my facial expression before I'm sure I will now.

Beginning with a sigh, she says, "Yeah, sophomore year, my first year here. Trent and I were becoming pretty good friends. He asked me out and I didn't really want to pursue that avenue, so I kind of stopped talking to him. I guess I didn't really handle it well and it came across as though I had been leading him on or something and then just stopped talking to him, but it wasn't like that."

Rachel seems to be trying to clear up any rumors she might think I've heard. I really don't know what to say next.

"I'm sorry, I didn't mean to bring that up. I mean, I hadn't planned on mentioning it to you, but I guess I just did anyway. He saw me talking with you earlier and so we were talking about you and he mentioned that."

Shoot. I shouldn't have said we were talking about her. This is falling apart quickly. This is a more familiar method of conversing with a girl at school. I guess I'm settling into my own again.

"I see. Yeah, that was two years ago and he can't seem to get over it. He never talks to me. I didn't think it was that big of a deal. It's funny that he's the one who said something to you about gossip. No one talks to me anymore. I know people talk about me but I don't get talked to, you know what I mean? I wasn't much for dating my first year here, and after turning down a couple of guys, which is pretty much everyone in a school this small, no one else ever asked me, and then rumors began and pretty soon even the girls wouldn't talk to me."

Rachel drops her eyes to the bottle in her hands. She rolls it over and over, the horizon line on the label graphic looks like an animated heart monitor line, rising and falling as the bottle turns.

"I am sorry for bringing it up. I understand something of the culture shock you might have experienced. My last school had more people than this whole town. And as far as dating, well, I'm not exactly busy on the weekends if you know what I mean." I smile sheepishly, trying not to come across as arrogant, or condescending, or anything but sincere and friendly.

She begins, "It's alright. I guess I'm just really bothered by the culture of this school, the whole town, it's exclusive. If you aren't born and raised in Cranston then you are excluded. They make a good show, but it doesn't last. I think it has developed for the occasional tourist that comes through. They put on a good show of being friendly, just long enough for the traveler to spend their money on some local food or products and then it's back to hating the outsiders. Tourists that don't stay here very long never see it, but those of us who are permanent outsiders catch the full force of it when the appearance of friendship wears off."

She looks me in the eyes and sighs again. "I suppose that's why when I was in the office earlier and heard your name I listened. I didn't notice you in gym until you started talking to me, but once we were talking it seemed like I had just been rescued from being stranded on a deserted island or something. I hoped you'd be from somewhere else and we could be friends, without all this small-town baggage."

I'll never forget the earnestness in her voice or the smile on her face right now. She's almost pleading with me, but not necessarily me, just another person to be her friend. I thought I felt lonely coming to this town, but I haven't felt anything compared to what she seems to be communicating to me right now. Perhaps I will understand better after being here a little longer, but hopefully I'm not here long enough for it to come to that. For the time being, I feel compelled to be friends with this pale girl, and I don't mind that one bit.

"Rachel, I promise not to turn into a townie on you. I don't know about what you've charged this town with, but I'll tell you I would have been eating it up with a spoon the day we rolled into these here parts - sorry, just poking fun at the local jargon – but everyone I've met so far has been really nice." I ponder what she said about the tourist for a second and chew some garlic bread, thus creating a minor tension-building pause. She waits patiently. "Now that I think about it, I could see how the reception I've received could play right into the scenario you've described."

"Eric, I'm not trying to turn you against your new friends or anything like that. I'm just saying I haven't had a great time here, and I'm sure it has a lot to do with me as well, but, well, I don't know, I'm not trying to give you a warning, just saying I had a glimmer of hope when I heard there was someone my age new in town." Now it is her turn to take a pause, only she doesn't have any heavy grit garlic bread to gnaw on, so she just looks longingly out the window. "I hate how formal it sounds, but can we be friends, Eric? I miss having someone my own age to talk to."

"Don't you keep in touch with friends from Atlanta at all?" I ask.

"Yeah, I do that, I mean I miss having someone my own age to talk to in person, I guess."

I nod and finish off the garlic bread. I pop open the bag of chips and offer them to Rachel, but she shakes her head no with a smile. We sit in relative silence while I crunch on the sour cream and onion flavored potato chips. I think about where to take the conversation next.

"How are the teachers for our next two classes? Tough?" I ask.

"Nah, nothing in this school is tough. I felt like I stepped a few years backward in school when I came here. I imagine you feel something similar to that yourself?" she responds.

Spot on. "It's only been a few classes so far, but yes."

I haven't wanted to say anything yet since it is only my first day, and I don't want to offend anyone, but what they consider the fast track is closer to my sophomore experience than my first half senior year experience. I wonder if I could test out of school altogether at this point.

Rachel asks, "So do you think I'm strange? I mean, our conversation hasn't been very typical for our peer group, I don't think. I hope I'm not coming across as needy or clingy or something, although I suppose that's exactly how I sound from what I've said."

There's something about this girl that makes everything she says seem normal. She uses facial expressions, but there isn't anything hanging on the words, or in the way she says them. Her tone isn't flat, but it is somewhat dead. There's no implication behind it. I guess in a way that is strange, but I find it more appealing than strange. Not even appealing, but hypnotic. Like the contrast between her pale skin and dark hair.

"Strange? Let me tell you something about strange. Four days ago I thought I was going to get through the next few months of school without talking to anyone. Then I went to a restaurant with my mom and she dragged me into a conversation with some kids standing in the parking lot. Next thing I know I'm talking to them, however briefly, but then two days later I'm at school and it's like I'm best friends with these guys. Then I meet a beautiful girl and actually start a conversation with her, and find easiness about it that I've never experienced before. You want strange? I give you myself over the past few days. I'm living strange right now," I say.

"But you didn't answer my question." She doesn't break her expression from when she asked her question. I know she heard everything I said, but she's waiting for my answer before she reacts.

"I don't think anything you've said so far makes you strange," I answer.

"So far. Meaning you expect me to do or say something strange in the not too distant future?" She still hasn't broken that same blank expression that accompanied her question. I'm starting to get nervous. I seem to be moving back and forth between my old awkward self and my new smooth self.

"Give me a second." I motion for a pause. "Okay. Rachel Sutton...what's your middle name?"

She almost betrays a smile by a twitch of her mouth and her right eye. "Esther, it's my grandmother's name. I come from a long line of Bible readers."

"Rachel Esther Sutton, I don't think you are strange, not with any negative connotation, however you are not altogether contextually normal, if you will allow me to explain. You see, there is something that is, at least, superficially different about you in comparison to the other students here, thereby making you strange, or rather, out of place with the status quo. I don't fully know what this is yet, but I am drawn to it. Additionally, as we are teenagers, I think it would be shortsighted of me to declare that I don't think you are likely to do anything strange in the near future, as it is simply part of our age-graded nature to do so. My final verdict is that I do not find you unappealingly strange but do expect that you have the potential to be strange."

"Well…" she begins, but I interrupt her straight away.

"My middle name is Stay. My mom likes names that sound like sentences."

With that Rachel brakes into a good laugh. At first I just smile, trying to contain a laugh, but then it breaks free. We both laugh for a bit and then she says, "Thank you, Eric. Thanks for talking with me. I hope we can talk again."

"So do I. I think we should be able to pull it off," I say.

"Lunch is just about over, do you know where the next class is?" she asks, returning her water bottle to her backpack and zipping the bag closed.

"Yeah, I think it is in the same room as my last class. I noticed there aren't many classrooms."

"Right. Not a difficult place to learn," she says.

We both stand up. I take my tray to the garbage and then drop it off at the return counter. When I turn around Rachel is already out the door. That's odd. I thought she would have waited for me. Should I walk briskly to catch up, or is this some kind of message that I shouldn't be following too closely yet? I guess I'll just walk normally and see if she turns to look for me or slow up a bit. Either way, we're headed to the same room.

***

At the end of the last class Rachel is up and out of the room before anyone else. She sat at the desk closest to the door so it isn't difficult for her to accomplish the task. Michael seems to be on a mission himself, getting out of the classroom with haste, probably to meet up with Krissy. I decide to set out after Rachel. As soon as I step into the hallway Trent grabs my arm and gives me a squeeze on the bicep, not like he is checking out my muscle tone, but like he is holding me back. At least, that's how I interpret it, and given the two options, I think I prefer the second.

"Hey, man, how'd your lunch date go?" He is smiling and sounds sincere, but the grip on the arm and the lingering thoughts of what Rachel had said make me a little suspicious, more than I would have expected. As though he picks up on my thoughts, Trent releases his hold on my arm.

"Ah, it was nothing like a date, we just chatted about moving and the social challenges it presents. Rachel is a really nice girl; I'm looking forward to talking to her again. How was your lunch?" I ask, trying to change the subject.

"Did you make plans to drive her home or anything?" Now my suspicion is increasing, why didn't he answer my question?

"We didn't make any plans. I don't know anything about her plans for getting home from school. We never discussed that. What are you all up to this afternoon?" I try again to change the subject. Perhaps I'll need to do some investigation work before I get wrapped up too tightly in Trent's clique.

"Michael and I have basketball practice. Then the girls and I have chores to do at home, and homework. Weeknights aren't very free for us, but our parents are good about letting us have the weekends off. At least after morning chores, there's a lot to do on a ranch." Trent seems to be off the topic of Rachel, at least for the moment.

Jessie joins us. "Hey Eric, how was the rest of your day?"

"Not bad. Got some homework, didn't feel too far in the dark on the topics in class, I think I'm gonna make it after all," I declare.

"That's great! So what do you have planned for tonight?" she asks, obviously fishing for details about my conversation with Rachel. Or I'm just paranoid now.

"Homework, I guess. My dad said he'd be home for dinner tonight, so we'll have a family dinner, that's a rare occasion, especially this soon after starting a new job. He usually works long hours for the first few weeks and I rarely see him. So I guess dinner with the parents, homework, and probably television, my constant companion."

"You're a Suburban alright. That's what we call you guys that don't have farm or animal chores every day," Jessie says.

"Charming," I say.

"So nothing planned with Rachel tonight then?" Jessie smiles and waits for the answer, as though her question was perfectly normal and not prying in any way. This time her facial expression tries to cover up just how prying she knows her question is.

"Nah, the wedding isn't until next week." I try to make it sound humorously sarcastic, but I think it comes out as bitingly sarcastic.

"Ouch, have you met our friend Michael? I think the two of you would get along great." She calls me on it, but she doesn't seem offended, just laughs it off.

Trent, seemingly amused by his sister, says, "Well, I gotta get to practice. See ya tomorrow Eric, unless you wanna play some ball?"

"No thanks, I'm not one for basketball," I say.

"Maybe baseball in March then, eh?" Trent suggests.

"Yeah, we'll see," I laugh.

Trent turns to his sister, "Jessie, find Krissy and get on your way home, tell Michael to stop drooling over my baby sis and get to practice."

"Aye, aye, captain." Jessie gives a mock salute and turns away, waving to me as she leaves.

"Bye." I'm left standing alone outside the door of the classroom. I turn to my right to find my locker in order to deposit a few books I won't need at home. A locker door a few feet away from me closes to reveal Rachel standing behind it. She looks at me.

"Hey, I thought you left, you seemed to get out of the class pretty quickly," I say. Wondering how much, if any, of the recent conversation she had heard.

"Class was over, so I left. I thought you responded quite well to Jessie. She did that on purpose you know. She saw me standing here when she walked over. But, I don't think you responded the way she wanted you to." Rachel says, answering my unspoken question. Apparently she heard it all.

"I'll have to apologize to her tomorrow. Both she and Trent seemed pretty interested in my interaction with you. Are you sure you and Trent never actually dated?" I almost don't ask it, but then I decide to keep up with my new practice of being extra forthright in conversation.

"How much time do you have? I could explain my theories on the Janson siblings, but it might take a while. Which direction are you heading in for home?" She asks.

"You didn't overhear my address in the office this morning?" I tease.

Rachel proves she can dish it out herself, without skipping a beat she says, "No, only your phone number, social security number and favorite color."

"What is it then?" I ask.

"Which one?" She raises an eyebrow and leans her head forward a bit.

"Color," I say, as I take a step closer to her, though not encroaching upon her personal space by any means.

"Brisk magenta." She loudly whispers, hanging on the final syllable for an extra beat.

I burst out laughing.

"I guess you weren't kidding! Now the only question is how did the school people know that one?"

Rachel, smiling, says, "It's a mystery!"

I return to her question, "I live over on the other side of Main. The guys told me your dad's ranch is a little bit outside of Cranston? Which direction?"

"The opposite direction from your house, I'm back further up this road a way. I didn't expect you were in my direction, no one is, but I thought I'd ask."

"I have my mom's car; do you need a ride home?" I offer.

"I actually have a car myself today, what with the rain, and still recovering and all," Rachel says.

"Oh. Good then. At least you aren't walking, I don't know how far it is, but like you said, you are convalescing, so driving is better." I wish she didn't have a car. Or I didn't. "Do you have a bunch of ranch chores to do every day? I mean, when you aren't feeling ill?"

"No, my dad has a full staff of workers. I don't have to do anything farm related unless I want to. I'll be honest, I don't usually want to. Dad spends a good deal of time working, but Mom and I stay in the house or the yard and leave the farming and wrangling to the men-folk."

Awkward silence. We have no reason to stay at the school any longer, and we both have our own method of transportation. Neither of us knows where the other lives. This girl doesn't seem to mind talking to me, but she might have a habit of walking away hastily as soon as a conversation ends. I can't let this conversation end without a plan to meet again, more than just class tomorrow.

She breaks the silence, "I guess I'll see you in class tomorrow?"

"Yeah! No. Yes. I'll be in class. I'll see you in class tomorrow. There's nothing to do around town tonight?" See those straws? See me grasping at them? I think she does.

"No, not much happens around here that isn't planned. Are you a good planner?" she asks, hopefully.

"Not usually, but I wish I were." The hope in her eyes diminishes as I say this.

With resolve she says, "Good luck on that. I'll see you tomorrow, Eric Stay Sterling. Enjoy your homework."

I've failed. "Thank you Rachel Esther Sutton. The same to you. See you in the morning."

And she is around the corner.

4. Teenage Politics

"Hey, Eric! How was your first day of school?" Dad is sitting on the couch with his feet up when I walk in through the kitchen door.

"Hi, Dad, school was alright. You're home earlier than I thought you'd be," I say.

"Yeah, I decided I'd had enough for the day. This new place needs a lot of work. I'm going to ease my way into it," he says, turning the TV off. "So, tell me about school. Get the place figured out yet?"

"Seeing as how there are all of about 15 people in the entire school, and the building is the size of a football field, I've got it figured out pretty well," I answer.

"I hope the small town simpletons can keep up with you, wise guy," he says and throws a pillow at me.

I catch the pillow and toss it back. "Only time will tell."

Mom enters the conversation, and then the room, "Eric! Did you see your new friends?"

"Yes, I saw them, and spent pretty much the whole day with them. The school has two tracks, one for smart kids and one for dumb kids; I'm considered a smart kid," I explain.

"Of course you are, dear," Mom seems to say reflexively "Did you meet any other nice people?" From

48

the lilt of her voice and how she smiles I know what she means.

"You mean did I meet any other nice girls?" I ask.

Dad laughs at first, but then seconds Mom's question.

Having had an unusually social day, I decide to answer their question rather than skirt the topic. "Yes, I did actually. I met a really nice girl name Rachel. Rachel Sutton. We had lunch together."

My parents' faces freeze. I don't know if it's because I had lunch with a girl on my first day at the new school, or because I actually told them about it.

Mom's excitement can't be contained for long. "Yay! Tell me about her? What grade is she in? What does she look like? Do you have classes together? Did you ask her out?"

Dad and I ignore the onslaught of questions with a knowing look at each other, but he has a question of his own, business related, of course.

"Sutton, you say? Any relation to the Sutton Slaughterhouse in Jefferson, just over the Cranston town line?"

"Yeah, that's her family. Her dad runs the ranch and slaughterhouse. Apparently it was her great-grandfather who founded them, and then her family has been out of state for while, but now they are back. Her family moved here two years ago from Atlanta. How do you know about the slaughterhouse?"

"It's the primary employer for non-ranchers in this town. I did plenty of research on the local economy before we moved here. Interesting fact, the ranch house, likely the one your friend lives in now, was a funeral home since the early 90's until, I suppose, her family moved back and reclaimed the family business. I read about that, but didn't understand the connection between a slaughterhouse and a funeral home, well, I guess there's some kind of abstract, unpleasant connection, but it makes sense that if the family left, perhaps the slaughterhouse and the ranch house were sold separately. Small towns have such interesting histories." That sounds like dad, business and trivia.

"That makes sense," I say.

I'll have to ask Trent about that funeral home business. Maybe that's where some of the rumors about Rachel's family come from.

"Come on, Eric, so what about Rachel?" Mom has remained quiet for as long as she can, but she won't wait any longer.

"She has brown hair," I say.

Following a substantial pause, to let Mom's anticipation grow, I continue, "She's a senior, too. We are in all the same classes. I haven't asked her out yet, I thought maybe I'd wait until at least 24 hours after she and I met before doing that."

"Fine, fine. You take your time, wise guy. Just keep me posted." Mom gets up from the sofa, "What should we have for dinner tonight?"

"Not spaghetti," I suggest. "Do they have any pizza places in town? I don't think I noticed any."

"No pizza in town," Dad says, and then asks, "What are our viable options?" He follows Mom into the kitchen. I sit down in his place on the sofa and pick up the remote.

***

Dinner went well, we ended up having meatloaf. Mom and Dad had more questions for me about my day at school, and I was forthright with the answers. Then the conversation moved on to Dad's experiences thus far. I'm not embarrassed to admit I didn't pay attention very well. I did think about Rachel a little bit, but not exclusively.

Now it's time to do some homework, but first I think I'll do a little personal research on Facebook. I login to find a friend request from Jessie waiting for me. This makes things a little easier. I was going to add her, Trent and Michael anyway, but now I don't have to search. Based on the reaction of Rachel towards Trent and Jessie, I doubt she has them as friends, but I'll check their lists. I was right. How about Michael? Nope. Now for the name search…no Rachel Suttons that match the pale girl. How about Sutton Slaughterhouse…a few hits as a place of employment, but overall there's no business page or anything like that. No one with the last name Sutton associated with it either. Rachel isn't on Facebook? How does she keep up with her friends from Atlanta? Maybe she does one of those codename things for her profile, to prevent people from creeping on her like I'm trying to do now.

Thwarted in my recon mission I decide to resort to homework. I don't mind schoolwork so much; I actually enjoy learning. Sometimes I don't care to learn what the syllabus demands at a certain time and in a certain way, but overall I enjoy learning, so school isn't so bad. Still, I won't miss high school at all; I hope college is a bit more enjoyable. I'm sure it will be. It can't be any worse, right?

After two hours of reading what I needed to read and writing what I needed to write I decide to go to sleep. Lying in bed I rehearse scenarios in my head for the next day, planning for what to say to Rachel and wondering about when I'll first see her, either before school or in class, and whether or not she'll talk to me right away or wait until no one is around like last time. I think I'll go in a little bit early, just in case she's there early, too. And then there is lunch time to consider. I prefer to spend it with Rachel again, but I did promise the Jansons I'd do lunch with them. I can try to organize a situation where we all have lunch together, but until I find out a little bit more about this rift between Rachel and the townies I think I'll keep these two friendship groups separated. You gotta keep 'em separated! And like that I guess I'll fall asleep on a distraction from classic rock music. *The Offspring* is considered classic by now, right?

***

Tuesday morning brings bright sunshine. Not a cloud to be seen anywhere in the expansive Texas sky. With Cranston qualifying as a desert, and the clouds all rolling out over night, the temperature is a bit brisk when I walk out the front door. But with the way the sun is rising fast and filling the sky I don't expect it will be long before things warm up.

I enacted my early arrival plan with some skillful verbal maneuvering. Mom asked if I wanted the car again but I turned her down, stating that I'd prefer to get to know the process of walking to school, just to see how long it takes. In reality, I want to walk to school for two reasons, first, so that I won't have a car in case Rachel wants to offer me a ride home, and secondly, I can leave a lot earlier under the guise of not knowing how long it will take me to walk in. My perfect plan fooled Mom; she didn't seem suspicious of my wanting to walk at all. I kind of thought she would. This indicates I even fooled myself with my plan, not bad for a Tuesday morning.

I'm still not sure what to do about lunch. I suppose there is always the possibility that Rachel won't mention it to me, and then I'll wimp out and not say anything to her. I want to ask the clique what their lunch plans are before I see Rachel.

I hope my no-car plan pays off. Walking to school is fine, for some people, but if I have access to a car I'd rather drive. Then there is always riding my bike, which is what I expected I would be doing most days anyway, not counting on having the car. Of course, I can't very well give Rachel a ride home on my bike, so that option is out. The things we do for cute girls we barely know, with reputations of being strange. But not as strange as her parents, that's what Trent said. I wonder what is so strange about her parents. Something to do with funeral homes and slaughterhouses no doubt, people are pretty predictable sometimes. I'm sure it will come out eventually, and when it does I'll know if my prediction is right. Trent doesn't seem to be too tight-lipped, and if it's true what Rachel said about the rumor and gossip habits of Cranston then I'll know all the misinformation I want to know in short order.

***

I have a pleasant walk to school. It's a pretty direct route, just a few streets to navigate, so it isn't difficult to become familiar with, but walking does help me to recognize the buildings and shops on Main Street. There is one diner in addition to Josie's, seems to be geared more towards breakfast, but it is a 24 hour operation, its right next to the gas station, *Mobil* pumps and a small two-bay auto repair garage. There is a small market, or convenience store, along with basic groceries and whatever else, called The Cranston General Store. It has probably been there since the town was founded. It looks like they've modernized it pretty well, at least on the inside, from what I could tell walking by the window.

There's a hardware store that doubles as a farm equipment retailer. I suppose they have auto parts there as well; I didn't see any signs anywhere else for that type of product. A combination barber shop and salon sits on the corner of Main Street and School Street and was the last business I passed on my way in.

Between Main Street and the school are just houses, nothing fancy, small yards and one story single family homes. Most don't even have a garage. Pretty different from the areas where we've lived before. We've been in large two story suburban houses and multi-floor apartment buildings. I like the small house we have now; it's a good size for us. My parents actually bought this one as opposed to renting, like they usually do. I guess they actually plan on staying in Cranston for a while. Only time will tell for me.

Just like yesterday I spot Trent in the parking lot, but this time the rest of the crew is with him as well. They are leaning against Trent's truck and all but Krissy are facing away from me. She doesn't pay any attention to me as I walk up, probably because we've only seen each other the one time outside Josie's. I'm at the back of the truck before I say hello. Jessie jumps a bit, she has a good startle reflex apparently. A chorus of hellos issues forth.

"Didn't see you drive in," Trent says in a half-questioning statement.

"I walked today," I say.

"You should have called; we could have picked you up," Jessie offers.

"Thanks, but it's not a problem, I could have driven in but I chose to walk today, for the experience. I was curious how long it would take to make the walk. Looks like I allowed way more time than was necessary." Checking my watch I note that it is twenty-minutes since I left home. "And also, I don't have anyone's phone number."

"Ah! That's right, give me your phone," Jessie commands. I hand over my phone and she enters a couple of numbers. I listen in as Michael and Trent continue their conversation from before I walked up. Jessie hands my phone back to me. "There, now you have our numbers, and I have yours; I texted myself from your phone."

54

"Solid," I say.

"Now where did you say you live?" Jessie asks.

"On Earp Street. Headed away from here it's the first right on First Street."

"Oh yeah, my friend Chris lives over there. I know where it is." She smiles, content with her sense of awareness, I suppose.

"Yeah. So, I didn't drive today, but what is the plan for lunch? Do you all want to head out somewhere? I didn't bring any food, just money." I don't have any other small talk to make, so I stick with the script I've been rehearsing.

"Josie's or the diner, or the General, but they don't really have any lunch options. Sometimes we just get snack foods instead of lunch type food," Michael says.

"We could just do the cafeteria," says Trent. "I don't have any real cravings for anything today. Cafeteria food will suffice."

Well, that would simplify things I guess, if we eat lunch here then it shouldn't be much work to get Rachel to join us, unless *she's* planning to leave for lunch.

"If we stay I vote for eating outside, it's way too nice out to sit in the cafeteria." Jessie doesn't offer a preference for what to eat, or where to get the food from, just where to eat it.

"I don't care what y'all do, I'll be eating alone in the cafeteria like usual." Krissy joins the conversation, only to be met with some cries of fake sympathy from Michael and Jessie.

"Let's eat here today." Trent gives the final word on the subject. I decide to bail out of the conversation, now that this part of my reconnaissance is completed.

"Cool, cafeteria it is. I mean, for food, then eating outside." I give a slight bow towards Jessie. "I'm going to head inside now, gonna hit the bathroom before class starts."

"Good luck," Michael says with a wave.

"Thanks, see y'all later," I say, unaware of using the jargon.

"You're getting the language fast!" Jessie says as I smile and turn, waving behind me as I walk towards the school.

Under my breath I say, "*Yeehaw.*"

5. Come Out and Play

I scope the halls looking for Rachel, both of them, the halls I mean; there is only one Rachel. She isn't in the hall or by her locker, so I decide to pop into the classroom and see if she is there. She isn't, but the teacher is and she engages me in conversation. I want to get out and watch the parking lot for Rachel, until I realize how creepy that sounds and resign to submit to conversation with Mrs. Davis. I have to give a report on everything I have done in my old school for the first half of the year. She seems impressed by the speed of our curriculum. Another student comes into the class and has a question for Mrs. Davis, which frees me up. After putting my backpack on the chair where I sat yesterday, I return to the hallway. Class doesn't start for ten more minutes.

Still no sign of Rachel, but the Jansons and Michael are making their way down the hall.

Trent says, "Where you headed, Eric?"

"Just wandering a bit, still a lot of time before class starts," I reply. It's true, I am wandering; I have a purpose, but technically I am wandering as well.

"Don't be late for class," he says.

"Of course not. Wouldn't miss it for anything." Okay, now that is a lie, I would totally miss it, and regardless of the inflection in my voice and Trent's inability to understand dry wit, no teenager alive would mistake the sarcasm behind such an answer to that question. More specifically, however, I would miss class if the alternative was talking with Rachel some more. But first I have to find her.

I return to the parking lot to look for Rachel. A shiny *VW Jetta* pulls into the parking lot right as I finish my scan of the perimeter. This car is unlike most of the other vehicles in the lot, which population consists primarily of pickup trucks; I know that's the stereotype for this area of the country, but stereotypes are often based on reality, and this one certainly rings true. Other than the trucks there are a lot of older cars. By which I mean the cars were built before their drivers were born, and that's including the teachers. The *Jetta* is recent and sparkly. Not a cheap car, I imagine. I don't know what the laws in Texas are regarding window tint, but in some of the places I've lived this car would be illegal. Something inside me says it is Rachel's. Probably just wishful thinking.

I take to leaning against the wall of the school, a few feet from the front doors. The blue metal-flecked car pulls into an empty spot. I wait for the driver to emerge from behind the seemingly mirrored windows. I try not to be conspicuous, but suddenly realize that I'm the only person outside the school at the moment. Starting to feel slightly embarrassed, I consider going back inside. Luckily, the driver's door open and there is Rachel, or it could be in a few more years. I was wrong a moment ago, there are two Rachels! This woman has the same hair and pale skin, roughly the same height, but slightly older looking. The passenger door opens and there is Rachel. *This* time I'm sure of it. The doppelganger must be her mom. She got a ride to school from her mom.

Oh, Henry! My plan has backfired! Rachel got a ride to school and I walked, it's "The Gift of the Maji," more or less. Probably less. But here we stand: each of us with a car yesterday, neither of us with a car today and…and her mom is with her. At least I don't have my mom with me, although I'm sure she'd love it. They're both walking towards me. I wave to Rachel and her mom looks at her. She waves back, her mom just smiles at me.

"You must be Eric," says Mrs. Sutton.

"Yes, I am. I guess you are Mrs. Sutton? Hi, Rachel." I use my best formal voice.

"Hi, Eric. This is my mom, Dr. Arlene Sutton."

Before I can correct myself and apologize for missing the title, Dr. Sutton says, "Eric, I understand you were speaking with Rachel yesterday. Well I came here today to tell you to stay away from her!"

The look on my face must have interrupted her fun, because the doctor's stern countenance shifts into a contorted smile. Some sort of giggle, almost a chortle, is let loose before she says, "I'm sorry, I was just trying to have some fun with you. I'm not very good at keeping a straight face."

Rachel rolls her eyes. "I told her not to do it, but she insisted. She always likes to embarrass me. Or at least try to, I'm used to it now, and I expect it whenever she meets my friends…meets someone new, so I don't really let myself be bothered by it."

"She ruins all of my fun," Dr. Sutton says.

I'm surprised by the doctor, not because of her failure at keeping up her tease on me, but just in general. She doesn't seem as reserved as Rachel did yesterday. I suppose her behavior could be identified as strange, like Trent said, but it isn't the kind of strange that turns you off of someone. Of course it is way too early to make that sort of judgment. People often do have a side of themselves that they keep hidden, I learned that one from Billy Joel.

Here I stand, facing Rachel and her mother, who she looks exactly like, with nothing coming to my mind to say.

"You had me going, Dr. Sutton," I say in hopes of initiating conversation, but neither of them pick it up or make a movement towards the door. I ask, "So, what brings you to school today?"

"Rachel didn't tell you?" Dr. Sutton looks at Rachel with mock disbelief. "The 6th grade is having a science fair and as a scientist I've been invited to be a judge and speaker for the event."

"Oh, that sounds cool, what kind of science do you do?" I ask and then wonder about my phrasing. Is that an appropriate way to ask that question? Maybe it should be, what kind of practice are you in? I don't know. I'll think about that later.

"Before we left Atlanta I was working with the CDC, specifically I was in virus research." Something changes in her voice. I'm not a psychological expert, but if I were on TV I'd probably be drawing some conclusions about the change. As it is, I notice that her voice seems to waver a bit, but I just don't know what that means. I recall Rachel acting similarly yesterday when she said something, but I don't remember what it was now. Best keep the conversation going.

"Wow, are you working here in Cranston or do you commute?" I ask.

"I'm not officially working anymore. I still keep contact with the CDC and consult on some things, but for the most part I'm sort of retired from that world." Again, a little uneasiness, but this time I think there's enough to actually draw a conclusion: regret. That makes sense, a scientist working with the CDC in Atlanta who

has to quit her job to move to Cranston-population-insignificant, TX would likely be a little resentful. I wonder if that's how it went down or if I'm just making things up.

"Oh, I hope you don't mind that I asked, I was just curious," I say apologetically.

"I'm not offended. When it came time to leave, I was ready to do so. Right, Rachel?"

"Right, Mom," Rachel says, and seems to take on some of the regret seeping into the tone of the conversation.

Looking to change the subject, I ask, "How does the science fair work? Is there a school-wide display of projects or something?"

Rachel responds first, "They'll be taking over the gym after we have our class, when we go to lunch. They'll have an assembly for the elementary grades with my mom as the speaker. After that the 6th graders will present their projects to everyone. It's not one of those events where each kid has a table and a poster board set up."

"That sounds good. But we don't get to miss any class time to see it, huh?" I ask.

Dr. Sutton laughs, "Spoken like a true high school student. Anything to get out of class!"

I smile and think, 'Duh.' But my polite upbringing has been too influential for me to say something like that, at least not to the mother of the girl I've got an irrational infatuation with. I only call it irrational because I don't know much about her yet, we just met, and I've been practically stalking her this morning. As I focus my attention on the matter I wonder if I should ignore Rachel for a bit. Nah.

"You two better get to class, school is about to start, right?" Dr. Sutton says.

"Spoken like a true *parent* of a high school student," Rachel says.

We all laugh and start towards the door. Inside, Dr. Sutton says goodbye and heads to the right, Rachel and I head left.

"Nice car," I say.

"You were watching for me?" Rachel says. "I mean, were you watching for me?"

"I like what you did there with the rewording. That's subtle, but remember, I have a keen sense of perception," I say.

"And I have a keen sense of you not answering my question," she says as she walks a bit faster away from me. Once again, the school is small, so it is only a few more steps to her locker, where she stops.

"Okay, I'll admit it, I was watching for you." The easiness I feel in talking with Rachel is back, just like yesterday. I don't think I've ever experienced this before. "I didn't expect you to get out of that sorority sister car. I figured you'd drive something more befitting a rancher's daughter." I don't know where I'm going with this.

"You mean like a pickup truck, or like a horse?" She has the locker open, but pauses while reaching for a book to look at me and wait for my answer.

I say in all seriousness, "I mean like a private helicopter."

This time it is a chortle, which means with her mom earlier it was definitely a giggle. Sometimes you just need to hear a chortle to appropriately calibrate your ability to define it.

Rachel says, "You should teach the straight-faced delivery method to my mom. As you saw she hasn't gotten it down yet. As for the helicopter, I don't know how ranchers in Chicago do it, but down here we stick to cars for travel around town. Besides, one of the horses has the helicopter today."

It is a cheesy joke, but I like it. It's pretty much on par for anything I'll come up with. I'm quickly running out of time to discuss lunch plans. We aren't alone, the hallway is full of students, as full as this school can be, but no one else is involved in conversation with us, so now is my time.

"I walked to school today, so I'm eating lunch at the cafeteria again. I told Trent and the gang that I'd eat with them, so if you aren't leaving for lunch, will you want to sit with us?"

Rachel looks at me, smirks, and then says, "I'd like to eat lunch with you."

It seems like one of those moments where a sentence is left hanging in build up for a 'but,' so I intervene. "But not with them?"

"You said it, not me," she replies. "I can handle sitting with them occasionally, but" she leans in and lowers her voice a bit, "they all just strike me as insincere and immature and I tire of their antics really quickly." She straightens up and flashes a quick smile.

"I hear you. Some of us are just more mature, old beyond our years, right? Sit with us today and then tomorrow we'll do something else, how's that sound?" I ask.

"What will we do tomorrow?" Rachel asks.

She caught me. "I don't know. Something else? I just mean you and I can have lunch and I won't make plans to go or sit with the others."

"I don't want to interfere with your friends, Eric. You met them before you met me, and seem to get along fine with them; I don't want to impose my personality clashes with them onto you."

"I met them merely hours before I met you. Besides, you and I are outsiders, we need to stick together. I don't want to turn into one of them; if they are like you said they're all part of some small town cult-like community. Maybe not cult-like, but zombies or something, drones that don't think for themselves." From the look on Rachel's face when I say this I think for sure that Trent, Michael, Jessie and Krissy are all standing right behind me. But she isn't looking past me; she is still keeping eye contact. I casually turn and look around to see if it seems like anyone heard me. There is no indication of it.

"Yeah, you're right," she says, relaxing from the shock of a moment before. "You and I *are* outsiders; we don't want to become part of the drone population." If it were possible I'd say the color drained from her face after I said that last part, but she's so pale already.

"In any case, you smell better than Trent." I decide that my communication skills are going through some sort of changes, like when my voice cracked a few years ago. Sometimes the awkward things slip out or don't sound how I intended them to in my mind after I say them. I hope this is just a phase I'm passing through.

"You can smell me?" Rachel's brow wrinkles a bit.

"That's not what I meant, and no, actually, but I can smell Trent."

"Can you smell him now?" Rachel is getting playful again.

I laugh a little, "Well, no, not right now, but I smelled him yesterday."

Rachel interrupts me, "You did?"

I hold up a hand, indicating I need a moment. I think I did that yesterday, too. Maybe I need to slow down.

I compose my thoughts and deliver as eloquent an explanation as I can, "Given the socially appropriate physical proximity for holding a conversation, I was within smelling distance of Trent after gym class yesterday and noticed a slightly unpleasant odor emanating from his person."

"Only slightly unpleasant?"

I laugh and give up. "Gimme a break!"

"Alright, alright. Well played, sir," she says and closes the locker door.

In a moment of great synchronicity, the class bell rings, so we scurry inside the classroom to take our seats.

***

They have two bells before first period: one for a thirty second warning and another to signify the start of class. They don't have homeroom here. Any announcements come through in the first five minutes of class. I guess it really is a homeroom, technically, because first period is five minutes longer than the other ones. But announcements and the Pledge of Allegiance don't take five minutes, so I guess first period classes are just longer than the others over the long run.

Anyway, Rachel and I weren't the last ones through the door after the warning bell, but it was after the bell that we walked in, so people were looking towards the door, a conditioned response I suppose, and Jessie seemed to take notice of how we walked in together. As she had secured the seat for me the day before, and I didn't want to break from that new pattern, I reserved the seat next to Jessie with my backpack earlier. Rachel took an empty chair in the front of the class right by the door, similar to the location she occupied in the two classes I had with her yesterday. I suppose that's her regular seating preference. When I sat down on Jessie's left she turned fully towards me and made a cooing sound and face to accompany it. I played dumb and just shrugged. From my peripheral field of vision I could see that Jessie raised an eyebrow and pursed her lips then shifted in her seat to look forward again. First period continued on like any other day of class.

We have three minutes in between classes. Rachel took a similar front-of-the-room seat in this class, and I'm once again sitting where I sat yesterday. Today we are watching a video about glaciers, but rather than pay attention I'm replaying my conversation with Rachel from before first period for about the tenth time since it happened. We didn't chat at all during the room change. I suppose it will be lunch before we talk again, depending on what she does in gym. She seems fine to me, I guess she's more fully recovered, but I don't know if she'll play hockey or not. I'll be in the first game for sure to run the tie-breaker. Maybe I'll be able to figure out a way to sit with her while I'm not playing. A way that won't bring obnoxious comments or looks from Jessie, but I'm starting to think that might not be possible. Of course, I may be letting Rachel's bias influence me. That would be unfair, but at the same time, I don't owe Jessie anything, and I'm not being rude to her, even if I'm starting to think she is somewhat obnoxious.

There's just a lot of guesswork right now because I don't know anyone very well. I jumped right into these two separate friendship dynamics and both are unfamiliar to me. I should be able to fill in more of the gaps at lunch today with all of them together. At the least it will be awkward for everyone and should lead to each side telling me more of the back-story later on. It might even get interesting. But before I get there I have to endure the glacial melt and a few games of floor hockey, which isn't all that bad. I'm also interested to see if the cafeteria can redeem itself after yesterday's offering. I can't see how they could do any worse.

***

My team won the tie-breaker, but then lost the next game, stalling us in the bracket, at least for the day. More important to mention is that Rachel didn't go to gym today. I caught her at her locker after second period and she said since she was still excused from gym class she was going to help her mom with some stuff in preparation for the science fair assembly, something about a laptop, projector and PowerPoint slideshow, but she'd catch up with me in the cafeteria for lunch.

It now being lunch, I'm sitting at a table in the cafeteria waiting for her. Everyone else is up in the food line, but I decided to wait for Rachel before getting my lunch. I'm actually pretty hungry; I hope she gets here soon. There she is.

My face involuntarily lights up. Kind of like the moment in the movies when the nerd girl walks into the room after her magical transformation, which usually consists of taking off the glasses and putting her hair up. Big transformation. Anyway, Rachel's entrance catches my attention and I wave and shout her name. Too loudly, I suppose, as everyone looks over at me. She doesn't seem to mind.

"Hi, Eric," she says as she makes her way to the table. She sits down next to me, placing her backpack on the table in front of herself.

"Did you get things set up with your mom alright?" I think I worded that poorly.

"Yes, she's all ready to go. They'll be setting up right now and then the kids will be brought in after a few minutes," she says.

"Sweet. Too bad we can't go see it," I say.

Rachel says, "I actually was able to participate last year, it wasn't that great. But if you just want to miss class then I guess it's worth it."

"Hmm. Oh well. It's only my second day of classes here; I guess I don't need to be trying to get out of them already. Do you want to grab something to eat?"

"I'm not actually very hungry. I had a good breakfast," Rachel says.

"Are you sure? You don't want anything at all? I can get you something," I offer.

"Thank you, but no, I'm all set." She takes her water bottle from her back pack.

"Okay. They all want to eat outside; I was just sitting here waiting for you. Do you want to head out and meet up with them or wait for me?"

Rachel smiles and takes a drink of water. "I'll give you two chances to guess it."

"There are only two options to choose between, so that doesn't sound like much of a challenge," I say.

"Well?" she asks.

"My guess is you'll be waiting here for me."

Rachel winks at me and recaps her water bottle.

"I'll be right back."

I pass Trent on my way to the lunch line as he heads towards the outside door.

"We'll be out in a minute, Trent," I say.

He looks at Rachel sitting alone at the table, and then back to me and smiles. "Cool."

My wait has allowed the crazy lunch rush to work its way through before me. All of a dozen or so people have come through. I don't know how they keep up with the volume!

Chicken nuggets and mashed potatoes for lunch today; this is one school lunch that I've never been disappointed by. When I turn around after paying for lunch I look at Rachel. Our eyes meet and we maintain the gaze. I start walking towards her and become aware of a sensation of anxiety at the possibility of tripping over something, so my stride shortens and my pace relaxes. I don't want to look away, so I try to prevent falling by adapting my locomotion. It isn't a far walk, so I'm at the table pretty quickly. Rachel stands up, shoulders her backpack and then reaches for mine, which is resting on the floor.

"Let me carry this for you," she says.

"Thank you."

We exit the lunchroom. It certainly is a nice day out, Jessie made a good call for eating outside. At the picnic table the group secured Michael is recounting some jokes he heard on TV last night.

Rachel and I sit down next to each other on the side with Michael. Trent and Jessie are sitting opposite us. I start in on my lunch. Michael finishes his monologue and everyone is quiet for a minute while we eat. Jessie asks Rachel about the science fair, and Rachel answers her questions. Trent and Michael start discussing basketball practice and Jessie drifts into their conversation. Rachel and I start our own conversation. I wish we were alone.

"How did your team do in gym?" Rachel asks.

Of course I'm absolutely pleased that she is asking about this, something that has nothing to do with her. It shows she is concerned with me. Either that or she takes her gym class floor hockey spectatorship very seriously.

"We won the tie breaker, but lost the next game. I enjoyed it. I even scored a goal."

"Well good for you!" Rachel says.

"Yeah, he carried his whole team, scored the only goal." Michael joins the conversation, to our surprise, and my dismay.

"I'm a covert hockey star," I say.

"Too bad we're in Texas and not Canada, maybe you'd have found your calling in life," says Trent. I guess everyone is in on the conversation now.

"Right, my calling in life is indoor gym class floor hockey." I decide not to hide my disdain for the praise of sports achievement.

I think Trent understands me this time. He says "Just remember you said you'll come out for baseball."

"I did say that. I will try it, but no promises of making the cut," I confess.

Rachel asks, "You play baseball?"

"Not exactly. I enjoy it more than some other sports, but I don't really play."

"Do you have a favorite pro team? I've always been a Braves fan, supporting my home town," she says.

Trent and Michael go back to their own discussion. Jessie has flagged down one of her other friends and they are talking.

"My dad took me to some games when we were living in San Diego. Other than that I haven't really ever followed any pro sports. So maybe I would vote for the Padres," I say.

"I recommend the Braves. You should think about changing your preference."

"I'll take it into consideration. So what time is your mom done with the science fair? Does it last after school is out?" I ask.

"It's done when school is done, nothing extra. Why?" Rachel asks.

Not willing to give my real reason, I only say, "I was just wondering if you were going to have to wait around for her after school. That's all."

But that's not all; I want to know if I'll be able to spend some time with her after school. Of course I didn't drive today so I can't offer her a ride home. And she's with her mom so she probably won't offer me a ride home, or if she does it won't quite be the same.

"Do you have afterschool plans?" she asks.

"Me? No, I just… I just have homework I guess."

"Oh," she says.

It's on me now, time to ask the question, make a plan.

"Do you have anything planned for tonight?" I ask, through restricted vocal cords, due to nervousness.

"Tonight? No; homework also, I suppose," Rachel says.

"Maybe the two of you should do homework together," Jessie suggests. I forgot the others are still here, or at least, I'm pretending to forget. Now I wish they weren't, I don't like this type of interference. Rachel doesn't look at Jessie, at least not right away, I do though.

"Maybe we should," I say. I can't tell for sure what is being expressed in Jessie's face, either jealousy or contempt. I don't know if one would really be better than the other right now, and I'm not sure who the feeling is directed towards: me or Rachel?

"Speaking of homework," Rachel begins, "I need to see Mr. Owen about an assignment I missed last week. I'll catch up with you in a bit, or see you next period." And with that she stands up to leave.

"Oh, okay." I'm not done eating yet, otherwise I would just follow her, but I don't want to seem too zealous. "I'll be here, I guess, until next period. I'll see you here or there."

"Bye, Eric." Rachel doesn't even acknowledge the others sitting around the table.

I watch her enter the cafeteria before rotating back to face the table. I deliberately look at my food so as to avoid making eye contact with the others. Silence ensues while I eat my chicken nuggets.

Soon, Trent says, "I told you she was kind of strange. Right when the talk turned towards you and her doing something outside of school, just like I said." Surprisingly he doesn't sound arrogant about it, only observational.

Jessie isn't so observational, "Rachel is nice enough to talk to, but you don't want to hang out with her, Eric, she's very weird."

Before Michael can add his two cents I better start a rebuttal.

"What's so strange? I don't see it. I think some awkwardness exists between you guys and her and that's all it is. I don't know why that awkwardness exists, but it wasn't until you said something, Jessie, that she just left, so maybe she feels the same way about you that you feel about her?"

Jessie's mouth sort of drops open, but she recovers quickly.

Trent comes to his sister's defense. "I'd say you were right Eric, except for my experience with Rachel proves otherwise, and how she acted with other people who tried to get close to her."

"Be friends with whoever you want, Eric, I don't care. I'm just trying to save you some hassle is all." Jessie gathers her things and she and her friend leave.

"I'm sorry if I offended you, but I don't think there is anything wrong with Rachel," I say as Jessie walks away.

I make eye contact with Trent and Michael alternately. Michael smiles and shrugs and finishes off his chocolate milk. Trent says, "Maybe things are different with Rachel now. Maybe she just doesn't like the local guys. Jessie's got a crush on you, but don't let it go to your head, she hasn't found any guys around here that she's too keen on so anyone new is likely to spark her interest. Don't sweat her."

Rather than damage the remaining bonds of friendship I might have with these guys I say, "Thanks. I won't worry about it. I really wasn't trying to make Jessie upset, I just felt like Rachel should be defended, seeing as how she wasn't here to do it for herself."

Trent nods and raises his bottle of juice in salute to me. Whatever differences exist between me and Trent, I like him. He's got a cool attitude, perhaps a little slow on the uptake with sarcasm, but that's not really a bad thing. So far I can see he is loyal, takes care of his family, and is outgoing in the friendship department. I think I'll pump him for information now.

"I appreciate your experience with Rachel, but the claim that she and her family are super strange seems kind of strange to me, I don't see it. I don't want to get into gossip or rumors, but is there anything specific that you can tell me about her? About why they are the 'strange Suttons'?" I ask.

"Alright, Eric, I'll explain a few things, but, I guess it really is just rumor and gossip. You know how small towns are," Trent starts in. I'm not sure if he is asking me a question or making a statement, or perhaps it's a rhetorical question. He's still looking at me and not talking, so I guess I better give an answer.

"This is the smallest town I've ever lived in, so all I know about them is likely stereotyping from TV and stuff," I answer.

"Well, that's all probably pretty accurate as to how it really is. We are tight, and when outsiders come in, they don't understand the heritage, they have a different lifestyle, and the feelings of strangeness go back and forth, you know? Well, I'll just tell you from the start. When the Suttons arrived in Cranston they came with the story that they were returning to their family heritage, but there were still some folks in town who were here when the original Suttons were around. Small town, everyone knows everyone, or everyone knows someone's grandfather. So there were some questions, but it's not easy to go up to someone and say 'you aren't who you say you are' so it just gets talked about in the background.

"And we talked about it in the background. I guess it didn't help that the previous owners of the Sutton's house had taken on the business of undertaking, so Rachel's house used to be a funeral parlor. You can guess how that factors into the rumors."

We all chuckle a bit as we contemplate how ridiculous we are, I guess that's what we chuckled at. Trent continues his story.

"The Suttons are claiming a heritage that is in question, they move into a funeral home and then no one ever seems to see Rachel's dad anywhere except at work, and her mom is some important scientist that just up and quit and moved to Cranston? Sounds funny, I guess. Rachel was great when she moved here! We were pretty excited to have a new girl around, a hot new girl."

Trent looks to Michael for affirmation. Michael shrugs.

"Rachel and I struck up a conversation quickly, not unlike your experience with her. Maybe not quite as fast. After a week or two, I don't remember now, I asked her to go to a movie with me. She said yes at first, but then the next day she was kind of off with me. Then the day after that she barely spoke with me except to say she couldn't go to the movie with me. I asked why but she never had a good reason, just that she didn't have time, or something like that. It was lame, whatever it was. But we went from starting a friendship to being barely even friendly classmates. She never comes to school activities or sporting events. We never see her around town. So I guess the rumors started to fill in the blanks about what she is doing outside of school. We didn't figure she was working for her dad. The people in town who do work for him could've confirmed that, but that'd be weird for anyone to ask about it. Not sure why I thought of it now. Anyway, I guess it was just the family heritage question and then the anti-social behavior that led to the rumors. I think Rachel is a nice girl, but she never attempts to defend her family against the rumors, so that seems to give validity to it all."

I interject, "Or she sees it as pointless to refute the rumors because they are just rumors. Also, I think you mean a-social, not anti-social. Just one of those things that kind of bother me, I learned about it in school last year. Anti-social means something specific, like being opposed to society. A-social means what people usually think anti-social means, which is to be less enthusiastic about social gatherings, kind of like introversion, I guess."

"Nah, introversion isn't about not being in groups, it's more about preferring to spend time alone to reenergize and relax. Introverts can do big groups, but they usually don't like to do it for very long." Michael says, somewhat to our astonishment, which he must be able to read on our faces. "I read a book about it. I guess I'm kind of an introvert myself."

Trent looks at Michael, strangely, then slowly turns back to face me and says, "Okay, so a-social, I'll remember that."

I smile sheepishly. I think the different terms should be used correctly, but I always feel kind of pedantic when I correct people on it. Anti-social is so widely misused that it can probably be used legitimately in both cases.

"I'm sorry," I say, "I didn't mean to turn this into a discussion of grammar and social psychology."

"It's cool, I like learning," says Michael.

"Yeah, it's a good diversion from the topic. But I just want to say that I don't mean to influence you against Rachel, I just don't want to see you have the same experience I did, but you aren't me, so who knows what might happen. Hopefully good things for you both."

"Thanks, Trent. I hope so, too," I say.

We sit in silence for the few remaining minutes of lunch period. Rachel never returns.

***

I take the bull by the horns in the next class and move seats from yesterday so that I can sit next to Rachel. She doesn't seem to mind. I ask her about the assignment she had gone off to find out about. She explains what it is and that it isn't a big deal. I am careful not to bring up lunch, the Jansons, or spending time together. Not that I don't want to further our conversation and make a plan of some kind, but I think it best to wait for a more opportune time.

That time comes after final period. I walk with Rachel to her locker. We aren't alone, but it doesn't seem like anyone is actively taking an interest in our conversation this time.

"So do you want to do homework together sometime?" I ask.

Rachel doesn't stop transferring books from bag to locker. "Yeah, I guess so."

Ask a general question, get a general answer; I clarify, "How about tonight?"

She asks back, "How about it?" She closes the locker door and looks at me, then asks, "Do you need to stop by your locker?"

Her question implies that she is willing to go with me if I have to. I like that. I don't think I need to go to the locker, but I'm going to go anyway. "Yeah, I think I do."

"Okay, where is it?" she asks.

"Just around the corner." I point. I suppose there is some system to locker assignment, as in grouping by grade, but it is hard to tell. There aren't very many of them and the lockers are assigned in 7th grade. Then the same locker is kept through graduation, so the different grade areas sort of shift each year. And then there are newcomers like Rachel and me, who get assigned an empty locker not necessarily part of our grade's area.

We walk to the locker, and as it isn't a very far walk and the hallway is still relatively congested, we don't say a word.

As I begin to spin the dial for the combination lock she asks again, "So how about it?"

"Tonight? Do you want to do homework together? You could come over to my house. You could stay for dinner if you want and then I can drive you home." I shuffle a few books to make it look like I really did need to come to the locker.

"That sounds good, tonight I mean; I don't know about dinner though. I should probably not be out too long. The assignment I need to make up is going to require a lot of writing, which means typing, which will be easier if I'm at my house."

I flash back to Trent's warnings. She isn't brushing me off completely, but she is limiting the plan. I shouldn't let that stuff get in my mind.

"Okay. Great. I don't want to interfere with your other stuff. Would you rather come over after dinner then? I could come pick you up whenever," I say.

"No. Before dinner would probably be better, then I could have the rest of the evening to work on the paper, it might keep me up late," she explains.

She does have a legitimate reason for limiting the time she spends with me tonight.

"Cool. So we could just go to my house now then?" I ask.

"Sure, I just need to tell my mom," Rachel says.

Here is where I remember I didn't drive to school today.

"Oooh, I just remembered, I walked to school today."

"Oh, okay. We could walk to your house, or my mom can drive us," Rachel suggests.

"How about we walk? It seems nice enough out there, not too hot, and it isn't a bad walk. I survived it this morning so I should be able to handle it again. Unless you'd rather catch a ride, that's cool too." I need to be more decisive.

"I don't mind walking, but if my mom will need to pick me up later then she might want to see where your house is now. She'll offer to drive us either way, really."

"I can drive you home later. I have access to a car I just wanted to walk today instead," I say.

"Okay, let's walk then. First we just need to find Mom so I can tell her," she says.

We find Dr. Sutton in the gym talking to one of the science teachers. She sees us walking over and ends the conversation. The science teacher smiles at us and walks away.

When we get close, Dr. Sutton says, "Hey kids, how was school?"

"Same as usual," Rachel reports.

"I had a good day," I say, and then ask, "How did the science fair go?"

"It went really well. We get a lot of repeat projects from year to year, the standard fare of volcanoes and what not, but it's always a good time. Thanks for asking!" Arlene Sutton is a very friendly and upbeat woman. My mom is kind of like that too, but in a more reserved way. What I mean is that you can read it on Dr. Sutton's face more easily than with my mom. Dr. Sutton is more expressive, I guess.

"So, Mom, Eric invited me over to his house to do homework, we were thinking I could go with him now and then he could drive me home in time for dinner. I have a paper I missed last week that I'll need to do later this evening. Is it alright if I go with him?" Rachel asks.

Dr. Sutton's excitement from a moment before morphs into a look of concern. She seems like she is considering a very important question. Trent's words fill my mind again and I begin wondering if maybe Rachel's parents are part of the reason why she seems to not want to spend time with anyone outside of school. I didn't think Rachel's question would be so difficult to consider.

"That sounds okay. You'll be home by six?" Dr. Sutton asks her daughter.

"Yes," Rachel promptly replies.

Then to me, Dr. Sutton asks, "Will your parents be home, Eric?"

A little surprised by the question I answer, "My parents? Yes, my mom is always home. I don't know when my dad will be home tonight, he works crazy hours most of the time."

Dr. Sutton looks back to Rachel and finishes deliberating. "Okay. If you're home by six. Let me just gather my things and I'll be ready to go."

"We decided to walk to Eric's house," Rachel says.

"I walked to school today, but I will be able to drive Rachel home later. By six," I say.

"Are you sure you wouldn't like a ride? Where do you live, Eric, is it far?" Dr. Sutton asks.

Rachel answers the first question before I can take on the second. "We are fine walking, Mom, thanks for the offer."

"We live on Earp Street, it's off of First Street on the other side of Main," I add.

"Yes, I know where that is. Okay, well you two have fun. I guess I'll just head home now. Eric, it has been great meeting you. See you at home, Rachel."

"Nice to meet you, too, Dr. Sutton," I say.

"Bye, Mom," Rachel says.

Dr. Sutton gives a sort of slight, informal bow and then walks across the gym.

I turn to Rachel , "Shall we?"

"Let's," she replies.

This time we exit the scene together.

6. Make Believe

It is beautiful outside. The air temperature is perfect and the sun is shining. We talk about entertainment likes and dislikes for nearly the entire walk. Some people don't put a lot of stock into music preferences as a way to judge someone's personality, but I can't think of many better ways to do it. Me? I'm stuck in the late 90's for music preferences, mostly. I was barely walking when most of what I listen to was written. I think the music then was more authentic than what is being written today. I wonder if every generation feels that way. I do listen to some contemporary stuff, in spite of all of that.

Rachel is into most music. She prefers country and folk. Having grown up in the South that makes sense, and now being in Texas she fits in well in this regard. After some friendly teasing about some of each other's votes for best albums ever, we agree upon No Doubt's *Tragic Kingdom* as the all time greatest album...that we can agree upon. I give her a list of bands to look into. She even records a few of the band names into her phone to look up later.

Beyond music we briefly discuss movies and find vastly different interests there. I love a good horror movie; Rachel says she never watches them at all. I think comedies are also pretty brilliant, while she prefers musicals and anything made prior to the 1960's. We finally hit television shows by the time we get to my house. The walk seems shorter when talking with Rachel.

As I reach for the door knob I remember my mom. She's going to get all kinds of excited when she sees I brought a girl home on my second day of a new school. I should have prepared Rachel for Mom's line of questioning that will likely ensue. We enter the house.

"Mom, I'm home," I call.

"How was your day?" she calls back, likely from the office.

"Not bad. I brought a friend home with me," I say.

Rather than a verbal response we hear a chair moving and then footsteps down the hall. Mom appears around the corner head first, meaning she was leaning, not diving, but clearly impatient for the extra second it would have taken to fully walk around the wall before looking for who was there. Her eyes get big when she sees Rachel and then she smiles.

"Hello, dear! Welcome to our home." She takes Rachel's hand and shakes it vigorously.

"Mom, this is Rachel Sutton. Rachel, this is my mom, Nancy Sterling," I say.

"Hello, Mrs. Sterling, pleasure to meet you." Rachel is very polite, taking the hand shaking like a pro.

"So, Rachel, tell me about yourself," Mom says.

"Mom, that's not why she's here," I say. "We have homework to do; you'll have to save your twenty questions for another day." I don't want to spend the afternoon doing homework alone while Mom talks with Rachel.

"Well, how about that?" Mom says, with an air of having taken offense. Maybe she has, but I don't think so.

"It's alright, Eric, I don't mind introducing myself." Rachel is more diplomatic than I am. "I'm originally from Atlanta, my family moved here about two years ago. My dad runs a ranch and my mom is a scientist, but she doesn't work anywhere anymore. Cranston has been a bit of a culture shock for me, but it seems like it is getting better with time. My favorite color is orange, I like baseball, I'm undecided about what I want to study in college, but I do plan on going, and I think fresh pineapple is the greatest food on the planet."

I'm impressed. Mom is, too, "Either you rehearse that in front of the mirror each night or you are a girl who really knows what she likes and wants. Did you know Eric has a hard time deciding what to eat for breakfast most of the time?" Mom is good at keeping a straight face, so she doesn't betray her joke like Rachel's mom did this morning.

"Thanks, Mom," I say. "But it isn't really a struggle for me. I just eat whatever you prepare." I don't think that really helps my case any, now that I've said it out loud.

Smiling, Rachel says, "He hadn't told me about his breakfast indecisiveness yet, obviously. I wouldn't be here if I knew that about him." Rachel apparently can keep a joke going; she must get that from her dad.

Mom laughs. "I like you, Rachel. Are you staying for dinner? Please tell me Eric invited you to stay for dinner."

"He did invite me, but I have to get home earlier rather than later in order to work on an assignment I need to make up from last week. I was sick and missed some school. But thank you for inviting me," Rachel says.

"That's too bad that you can't stay, and about you being sick last week. Are you all better now? Was it the flu?" Mom looks very concerned.

"We don't think it was the flu, but something viral, probably. We should be all better now. We being me and my parents, we were all hit with it. I won't get you sick. My mom cleared me to go back to school, so she's not worried about us being contagious." Rachel seems very comfortable talking with my mom. I hope that means she's really comfortable with me. She certainly doesn't seem as edgy as she did around Trent and Jessie.

"Well that's good. Not that I was worried. You said your mom is a scientist?" Mom asks.

"Yes, well, she has her MD, but she has also specialized in virology. That's what she was last working on with the CDC." Rachel pauses momentarily, as though she said something she wishes she hadn't. "But that's all I know about it."

She did that before, acted like she said something she shouldn't have. Maybe mentioning the CDC invites a lot of questions that she just doesn't know the answers to. Maybe she regrets mentioning it as soon as she says it.

"Wow, from the CDC to Cranston? That must have been a change. She isn't here investigating some weird viral outbreak is she?" Mom asks excitedly; she loves those movies where some form of disease spreads rapidly around the world. Kind of odd, if you ask me, but then I love those kinds of movies where an alien force invades the planet and a hand full of super people fight them off. Meanwhile, whole cities fall victim to the battle and are seemingly written off as acceptable casualties. There's definitely something incongruous between Hollywood and reality.

Rachel is more timid now, "No, nothing like that, nothing that I'm aware of."

"Too bad, that would be a great story, and liven this place up a bit," Mom says.

"Yeah, Mom, it's too bad we didn't move to a rural town with a fatal disease going around and no known way of combating it. What a gyp," I say.

Mom laughs, but Rachel doesn't. Maybe her mom *is* here to study something. That would probably explain any strangeness. If the community knew about it I think that would certainly explain the coldness towards the Suttons, the locals wouldn't want the attention or whatever would result from their secret being exposed. Rachel must know more than she is saying. Or it's just my preference for conspiracy reaching a peak once again. Mom likes disease outbreak stories and I like conspiracies that cover them up. I guess we aren't so different in preference as we are in perspective.

"So what kind of homework are you two working on? Some kind of project?" Mom asks.

"Nah, just doing homework at the same time in the same location," I say.

Rachel nods in agreement.

"Okay, well I'll be in the office if you need anything. Nice to meet you Rachel, I hope you can come over for dinner sometime. Maybe we can have your parents over too. I'd like to get to know some people around town as well," Mom says.

"Sure, that sounds fine; we'll have to plan something some time. Nice to meet you, Mrs. Sterling."

"Want to go to the kitchen table?" I ask Rachel.

"Uh, sure, that sounds fine, whatever you prefer," she answers.

Mom retreats to the office and I lead Rachel through to the kitchen. I drop my bag on the table.

"There's more room to shuffle books around and whatever. Would you like something to drink? Soda, juice, water?" I ask.

"Water would be great, thank you," she says.

"Are you hungry at all? Just a snack of some kind, popcorn, chips or anything?" I offer as I retrieve our filtered pitcher from the fridge.

"I'm fine, just water, thank you," Rachel says.

"Sure, on its way." I fill up a couple of cups for us and then empty a bag of nacho cheese flavored chips into a bowl. "Chips here if you change your mind, but be quick about it, I might eat them all myself."

"Have at it," she says, giving a wave of disinterest.

For a few minutes we behave like we are at a library, or in a controlled study hall. Neither of us speaks, we just do homework. I'll be honest; my intent on inviting Rachel over to do homework wasn't to actually do homework but to spend time with her instead, hopefully talking and getting to know her. I need something to break the ice now.

"Do you understand the assignment for Writing? Does she want us to write our own poem similar to the one on page 173 or are we supposed to analyze the one we read?" I understand the assignment, but I want to get a conversation rolling.

"I'm pretty sure we are supposed to write our own poem of a similar nature, you know, with a moral to it," Rachel says and then looks up at me from her science text.

Her green eyes pop against the pale skin. She is still unusually pale for the people in this area, but she looks more energized than she did yesterday. Even her hair seems to have more volume today than yesterday. Hair volume? Did I just notice and make an observation on hair volume? At least I didn't say something about it out loud.

I shake the hair volume thought out of my head and say, "Okay, that sounds right. I just got confused by the way I wrote it down I guess. Do you have any idea what you are going to write about?" Encouraged by the eye contact I want to keep this conversation developing.

"Actually I already wrote it. I did it during the lecture in social science. I write a lot of poetry, as a hobby, so it isn't much of a task for me to put something together for a class assignment," she says coolly.

"I'm impressed. Outside of school I don't think I've ever even *read* a poem, let alone wrote one, unless you count songs, which I don't, and you knocked it out same day during another class. Not bad at all." I hope I'm not coming across as over anxious in my praise. Just to be safe I add, "That is, unless the poem is bad. I haven't actually read it so I don't know. Maybe I should reserve judgment until I've heard it." I smile invitingly; I hope that's how it comes across anyway.

"Hmm. I'm not so concerned about what other people think about my poetry that I can be sucked into your little game, Eric. But if you'd like to see how good my poetry is, you can read it, if you want." She hands her notebook over to me and then leans back in her chair. We are sitting directly across from one another at the table in the kitchen. It is square and sits four comfortably. We have only eaten our meals here so far, since the move, perhaps if we ever have company over for dinner we'll use the dining room.

I read Rachel's poem:

What changes the body, changes the mind
From changes, results that you sometimes can't find
Looking out from within acts to distort your view

But looking in from without presents its own bind
And in either direction the changes are true
With the end result that you find yourself new

"Wow that reads like a real poem. I don't know if I understand it though. I'm not much for poetry." I try to be reassuring, but mostly I'm apologetic.

"It might not mean anything," she says reassuringly, "That's the beauty of poetry."

We both laugh a bit, but I'm not sure I know why.

I ask, "So does it mean anything?"

Rachel considers the question for a bit and then says, "Yes. It does mean something, and though I tried to mask it in generalities, it is significant to my personal experiences lately. Kind of like being a teenager in general, but also more specific."

"I see," I say.

But I don't see.

I continue, "I think I'll have to be a little more simplistic in my poem. I don't have any real deep feelings about life. I guess I do, but I don't know how to conceptualize them in a motivational way, or anything like that."

"Well," Rachel begins, "poetry doesn't have to fit any given mold. There are a lot of different styles of poetry. We've gone over the sonnet, the ballad, the elegy, the ode, the free verse…and you probably know what a limerick is?"

"I've heard of limericks before, yes. But I wouldn't know how to write one."

"That's okay; I don't think a limerick would count for the assignment anyway. You should probably try free verse. You could plan for three stanzas, four lines each. They don't have to rhyme, just tell a story. Or you could use couplets, you know those, when every two lines rhyme with each other, for example, '*I woke up this morning at 6 o'clock, and then I put on my flowery frock.*' Something like that."

"Wow, that's pretty good, you get up at 6 am?! Quite the early bird. Oh, and the poem example was good too, I know that style," I say.

"Yep, 6 am, pretty much every day. That's what I do," Rachel says. "So do you want some help with your poem?"

"You want to help me write a poem?" I ask.

"Yes, if you want me to, or we can sit here and separately work on whatever else we have to do."

"I like your plan better. Let's write a poem." Sounds like Rachel and I are on the same page for this homework session.

"Okay, what topic do you want to write about?" Rachel asks.

"Let's see…I want to write something new and trendsetting…has anyone written poetry about love before?" I wait for a reaction and get it in the form of a raised eyebrow and mock laughter. "Okay, love has been done. I like humor. Can you help me write a funny poem?"

"I guess, but humor isn't necessarily about the topic, it's how the topic is presented, so you still need to pick a topic."

"I see. Well how about moving?" I suggest. "That's something both of us know about. Can we do a poem about moving and make it funny?"

Rachel says, "Well, I don't know, I think both of us are pretty negative towards moving, so maybe we can't make it funny."

"Good point, but let's try it out anyway. And it doesn't have to be funny; it can be whatever it ends up being." I pull out a piece of paper and click my pen. "Let's get started."

***

We get lost in time as we work on writing a poem about moving. We include imagery of leaving a familiar, comfortable location and entering a vast, unknown, strange territory. It doesn't end up funny, but we do end up sitting next to each other on the same side of the table. It was never about the homework anyway, it was never about the poem, it was about developing our relationship. Pass or fail in the writing class, I'm successful in my plan for the afternoon.

With a completed revised draft, we decide to call it quits and drive Rachel home. As she assembles her books and papers to stuff them in the backpack, Rachel gets a paper cut on her ring finger.

"Your finger is bleeding," I say.

"What?!" She exclaims.

"Probably a paper cut, it's amazing how much those can bleed. You don't always even feel the cut, it just starts bleeding," I say and start to feel the effects of imagining blood. For whatever reason I don't mind the sight of my own blood, but seeing it coming out of another person gives me the shivers. "Just a heads up, I'm not good around blood. I'm not going to pass out or something, but it wigs me out a bit. A paper cut shouldn't be too bad though…does it hurt?" I decide to stop talking about it.

She puts her finger to her mouth.

"No, it doesn't hurt, I didn't even feel anything. I didn't bleed on the table or the homework did I?" she asks.

I look around and don't see anything, "No, it doesn't look like it. It's no big deal if you did."

Until I get back to my homework later and find dried blood and pass out, but luckily she won't be around to see that, if it should happen.

"Yeah, I guess not, I just don't think it is very polite to bleed on other people's furniture." She sounds more excited over a little cut than is necessary.

"Maybe where you are from, but in my family bleeding on the furniture is a sign of respect." I shake my head to show I'm just making a failed attempt at humor. She smiles, but doesn't remove her finger from her mouth.

"Do you need a sterile adhesive strip?" I ask.

"A what?"

"Band-Aid," I clarify.

"Oh, no. I think its fine. You ready to go?" She shoulders her backpack.

"Yeah, I'm ready; we can head out this door." I open the kitchen door for her and we enter the garage. I follow around to open her car door for her and she looks at me like I'm strange.

"Aren't you going to drive?" Rachel asks.

"Yeah, I intend to, just wanted to open your door for you first. You are riding in the car right?" Her joke was better.

"Aren't you the gentleman!" she says.

"Just living up to my mom's expectations."

"So that's what that looks like," Rachel says and drops into her seat.

Ouch. Does Rachel have an issue with her mom? I wonder if that comment was just off the cuff and meaningless or if there is something to it. I don't think I'll ask just yet. If she has an issue with her mom, I can find out about that in due time; however, it's not really my business.

I close her door after her and pass around to the driver's side. Once in the car I hit the button for the garage door opener and then put the key in the ignition. Rachel grabs my arm and I stop and look at her.

"Thank you for opening the door for me," she says sincerely.

I smile, "You're welcome, Rachel." She pulls her arm back and relaxes into the seat. I kick over the car and shift to reverse. As I back out I realize Rachel reached over with her right arm. Her left ring finger received the cut, and though it was no longer in her mouth, her fist was balled up and resting in her lap. Why would she reach across with her right hand and not use the hand that was closer?

There's no question as to my status as a conspiracy theorist and day dreamer. My mind is creative, I can't help it. It spins wildly out of control sometimes. I like to make connections, sometimes when no connections even exist. I start to make some connections now. Rachel was really sick and missed a week of school. Yesterday she still looked really pale and sickly, but today looks remarkably better. Trent and Michael said she is sick more than most people, or, when she gets sick she seems to be worse than other people, missing a week of school at a time. No one spends time with her outside of school. I've never seen her eat any food. Her mom is a scientist doctor, which she seems to not want to discuss. Her family moved from the city to as rural a place as you can find. And now when she gets a simple paper cut she acts like her blood is infected and deadly. She's a vampire! Okay, maybe not a vampire, but maybe she's a hemophiliac or something blood related, which makes her feel self-conscious.

If she has some kind of terminal sickness that could explain the apparent hesitancy she has in developing friendships, especially with guys. Maybe her family wanted to get her out to the rural area in the hopes of clean air picking up her health. Maybe her mom quit the CDC so she could provide specialized care, something that perhaps is a sore spot in some way, which makes Rachel hesitant to discuss it. Perhaps something in there is the reason for her comment about living up to Mom's expectations. Maybe she has something contagious and that's why she's so afraid with the blood thing right now. I hope my flippancy wasn't offensive to her. But she knows I don't know anything about it, and she seems very forgiving.

"Thanks for helping me with my poem," I say, but it's not what I want to say.

I want to find out her secret, but I know it's pretty forward and invasive for me to just ask about it. Maybe the problem Trent ran into was that he started drawing similar suspicions and asked Rachel about it before she felt she could trust him. That would make sense of the situation in my mind. I don't want to make that kind of mistake. But then, she did touch my arm. Maybe she already trusts me enough to discuss it. Of course, if that's the case then she'll bring it up when she is ready to discuss it.

"You're welcome. It was fun; I think you could be a good poet if you wanted to. You think quickly and that's important in poetry." Then, as though she is reading my mind, "But quick thinking can also get you into trouble, so it's like Voltaire says."

"Voltaire? Is that the fortune telling machine in the movie *Big*?" I ask.

"No, I don't think so, I don't know, haven't seen the movie, but Voltaire was a French philosopher. The idea is that power is coupled with responsibility," She explains.

"Oh, that's what Spiderman's uncle said, you should have cited Spiderman's uncle instead of Voltron," I say.

Rachel laughs, "Right. I'll remember that for next time."

I decide to throw caution to the wind. It seems to be working out for me these last two days. Amazing how everything seems to be working out exactly how I want it to. Time to raise the stakes.

"Rachel, do you mind if I ask you a personal question?"

"I don't think I can answer that completely until after I know the question you want to ask," she responds. Yes, she is very diplomatic.

"Good point. It's about your being sick last week."

She doesn't immediately respond so I take a quick glance at her. Her expression is blank. She is staring straight ahead out the windshield.

"What's on your mind, Eric?" Rachel asks.

"I'll tell you up front that I'm operating on rumor a little bit, so please forgive me for giving any credibility to it, but I'm curious, and I think fast, like you pointed out, so maybe I'm getting into that danger zone you and Voltron were warning me about." I'm getting off track, I need to just ask. "Anyway, Trent told me you seem to be sick more often than most people and when you get sick you are sick for a longer time. Just like last week. I probably shouldn't pry, but what you had last week wasn't just the flu or something, was it?"

We are already passing the school, so it isn't far to Rachel's house. She could probably remain silent for the rest of the ride and then get out without saying another word. This might be it; she might never talk to me again. This might be what happened with Trent. I can't take it back now though, I've asked the question.

"We can't control whether or not we hear rumors. I know that. And sometimes it is difficult to not give any attention to what we hear," she says.

At least she's still talking to me, for the moment. I wait for her to go on.

"Eric, pull over," Rachel says.

Oh great! It's way worse than not talking, she's going to get out and walk home! I offended her. I can feel my stomach knot up as I obey her command.

I pull off onto the shoulder and shift the car into park. I'm looking straight ahead, afraid to look over and see her climbing out of the car. She isn't making any movement towards leaving. I look over and she's looking at me.

"It's a long story," she says and shrugs her eyebrows. "I'd like to tell you, if you want to hear it."

Surprise and relief wash over me entirely. I shut off the engine and undo my seatbelt to rotate in my seat and face her more directly.

"I do want to hear it. I'm sorry for being nosey, but I'm a curious guy. I didn't mean to impose…"

Rachel interrupts me, "Don't worry about it. I wouldn't tell this to anyone else. I haven't told this to anyone else, but I want you to know and I want to trust you with it. I know we only met yesterday, but I feel something about you and I want you to know this about me. I'm glad you asked."

She pauses for a bit and I nod reassuringly.

"You'll probably end up with more questions than answers, but I'm just going to tell you everything. I'm not supposed to tell anyone, but I don't care anymore. I'm seventeen years old and I can't confide in anyone but my parents, which doesn't actually happen. Can you imagine how lonely that is? It's terrible. Of course, my telling you might put you into some minor trouble, but hopefully we can avoid that. This is an absolute secret. Do you still want to hear it?" Rachel asks. A new intensity and sincerity filling her voice.

"Yes. Power and responsibility, I got it," I say.

"Good, because what I've told you already is enough to get us in trouble, so I might as well tell you the rest now.

"A few years ago we were living in Atlanta and Mom was working at the CDC. Her group had a virus that was found in the heart of a jungle somewhere in South America, Brazil, I think. It was found in lizards or something. Some aspects of the virus made them think there was a way it could be modified for Alzheimer's treatment, because of the interaction with the brain. They began isolating and separating and merging parts of the virus until they reached a formula that matched their goal, at least on paper. Unfortunately, an accident in the lab exposed several of the team members to the virus before they got to the point of animal testing.

"Well, I guess they had their animal testing then. Four members of the team were exposed; my mother was one of them. Immediately they were quarantined. Being a virologist, Dad and I knew it was always a possibility that Mom would be quarantined without any explanation to us. We were able to talk to her on the phone and she explained as much as she could at the time, which was that she may have been exposed to a virus. They didn't notice any symptoms or issues for three days, so they decided that the virus hadn't taken hold, although there were traces of it in their blood. Someone made the decision that there was no danger and the quarantine was cancelled. Mom came home.

"Two days later she got sick. She woke up early in the morning with a headache and feeling nauseated. She knew what was happening and called the office, authorizing a new quarantine expanding to anywhere the team members had been over the two days since being released. A containment unit was dispatched to each team member's house. By the time the unit arrived Mom had already vomited blood, and died."

Died?! Is that what she just said? Rachel had started out keeping eye contact with me, but somewhere around the first mention of quarantine her gaze wandered out the window and is now resting on her hands in her lap. I don't know what to say, so I remain silent.

"Mom was dead; Dad was holding her in his lap on the floor in the bathroom. I had woken up from the commotion and was standing watching, horrified and scared. Dad was in shock. I checked her pulse and picked up the phone lying on the floor, still connected with an emergency dispatcher at the CDC. My mom's team doesn't use 911, they have their own emergency services. When I found the line was still connected I told the dispatcher that Mom was dead. I said she wasn't breathing and I checked her pulse and she didn't have one. I asked if I should attempt CPR or something, and he said no. He said to stay away from her and that Dad and I should get away from her body and that the decon unit was almost there.

"When they arrived we were taken into the van and were taken back to the CDC and processed through a decontamination session. It was awful, but I didn't think too much about it at the time; my mom was dead. Or so I thought. After several days in a hospital bed under constant observation I was led to a sterile room where I found my mom and dad sitting at a small, white plastic table. Mom was alive again."

Rachel looks up and meets my eyes again. Her expression doesn't change, she just looks.

I feel impelled to speak, "That's heavy."

She gives one of those laughs that sounds more like a sniffing sound, "No kidding."

"So your mom was resuscitated? That's pretty amazing. Did she have one of those near death experiences?" I ask.

"Well, not exactly resuscitated, and she doesn't remember any kind of NDE thing where she saw a light or anything. What I learned was that Mom had been taken to the same emergency location as Dad and me, along with the other team members and their family members. We were all processed through decon and then each family was admitted to their recovery/quarantine unit. The families were together. Two of the team members were single, older men, but the fourth had a few kids. Their whole family was infected, just like mine.

"Mom said they didn't try to resuscitate her because it would have been impossible at that point, given the amount of time before the team arrived and given the danger of the virus involved. They discovered that the virus had killed mom, and that she was still dead, in that her heart was no longer beating at a life sustaining beat and her lungs were pumping very shallow and minor amounts of air through them, but the virus was animating her body and her body seemed to be alive.

"My mom was a zombie. And shortly after our little reunion, the virus took its toll on me and my Dad, and we became zombies, too."

7. *Your Neck*

Rachel looks back out the front window and rotates in the seat so she is facing her body forward as well. She settles into the seat. I do the same, rotate around and face forward, trying to make sense of what I just heard. Zombies. There are no such thing as zombies, are there? This is too outlandish, it sounds like a movie. She's messing with me. The whole "stop the car" thing and then telling me she's a zombie. I don't believe it. She's playing a game! It's gotta be that, right?

"You are a zombie?" I finally say.

Rachel answers simply, "Yes."

"You're joking with me, right? You did a great job, I almost believed you."

"You should believe me, it's true. But I can see how you wouldn't believe me. Zombies don't exist in real life. That's what I have been telling myself for years, but here I am." She's still looking out the window, totally blank.

"So you are telling me that you are dead? Right now, you are dead?" I ask.

"Correct." Rachel turns her head to face me. Our eyes lock. She reaches over, again with her right arm, and grabs my hand, gripping around my index and middle fingers. She guides my finger tips to her neck. "Check for a pulse."

I laugh, but realize she is dead serious. I even *think* in puns. "Okay," I say.

She lets go of my hand and I touch my fingers to her neck, just below her jaw. I don't feel anything. I move my fingers around slightly, searching for a pulse. Her skin doesn't feel dead, not that I know what a corpse's skin would feel like, or a zombie's for that matter. Her skin is soft and warm, not at all what I'd expect from a living dead girl. She doesn't smell putrid either. TV and movies have either lied to me about what zombies are or she is lying to me now. Did I actually just have that thought?

I can't find a pulse, so I reach to the other side of her neck. She waits patiently.

"I don't feel a pulse, but that doesn't mean you're dead," I say.

"Check my wrist." She holds up her right hand.

I check her wrist and again don't feel a pulse. "Nothing."

"I told you so." Rachel relaxes a little bit. "I'm sorry. I don't like being a zombie and talking about it brings me down. I'm telling you the truth, though. I guess technically I'm not a zombie, at least not a Hollywood zombie, but the result is the same. I died. My parents died. Several other people my mom worked with, and their families, all died. The CDC calls it viral reanimation. The virus stops the heart and circulatory system. It invades cells, essentially making the body a static collection of cells, meaning they never change. Then the body starts 'living' again, but not in the same way. They still haven't figured out how the virus does it. This is why they were testing it. If they can figure it out it essentially cures everything from cancer to old age. The only downside is that it kills all living things, all the ones they've tested with at least.

"We don't lose our personalities and become mindless drones intent on killing and eating our victims, like in the movies, because who we are exists in our brains, in the millions of neural connections that exist there. The virus animates those connections and we think and feel the same way we always have. We can even learn, although it does seem more difficult sometimes. The scientists working on this, my mom's team, and now those that picked it up in the aftermath, can't figure it out. They can observe what happens after infection, but they can't figure out how it happens."

I'm starting to believe what she is telling me, as outlandish as it is. Her story makes sense in theory, but zombies?!

I say, "So you are a zombie, but you aren't going to eat my brain?"

Raising an eyebrow, Rachel says, "Empty calories."

We have a good laugh, but I turn serious again with some more questions.

"Did the CDC send you here?"

"Yes. After a few weeks of quarantine they determined the threat of contagion to be limited to blood or heavy concentrations of saliva and stuff. Really, it's only barely more contagious than HIV. They thought about classifying us all as HIV positive and then letting us go about our business as usual, but decided against it. There were six others infected in total, the two older men and then the other family. All wound up in the same reanimated situation. The father in that family was on my mom's team, his wife and two sons were infected in the same way my dad and I were. After they all reanimated and the dust cleared, when they knew they were zombies, the father killed them all by poisoning their food. Kill the virus, stop the reanimation. He couldn't handle the implications of the situation. The other two, Frank and Mark, both moved here with us."

"Why to Cranston?" I ask.

"Because it's out of the way, we had a historical tie to the area, and the slaughter house provides something we need."

"Whaaaaat?" I say in a slow, drawn out, almost comical way; comical if my imagination wasn't spinning wildly.

"I told you we aren't zombies like in movies, where we're slow moving and constantly decaying, focused on only one thing: eating human brains. We aren't like that, but we do eat brains. We need to eat brains. The virus metabolizes brain matter best. It is what the researchers initially found in the cases of the virus in nature, that the infected animals would primarily eat brains. Usually of their own species if they weren't carnivores or omnivores already, likely because those were the brains they had easier access to. They also were observed to eat the brains of animals they normally hunted. Herbivores can't sustain the virus as well because they aren't as equipped physically for killing animals and eating their brains. I never cared for the science behind it. It was hard enough just to accept that I needed to eat brains.

"The virus helps out, though; it creates some type of craving for brains. I don't understand it. I don't have any desire to kill anyone in order to eat their brain, but I do crave brain. Hence the slaughterhouse, the CDC thought it was the perfect cover for the reanimates, that's their official name for the five of us. When cattle are slaughtered for human consumption the brains are usually discarded or sold for animal feed filler. Our slaughterhouse follows the discard method, but we don't discard to incinerators or bio-landfills. It's really not that outlandish that we eat brains, only mostly." She laughs.

"We joke about being vegetarian zombies, because we don't eat human brains, only cow brains." She laughs again.

"That doesn't make any sense," I say. "You are still eating part of an animal. That's not vegetarian at all."

My comment stops her laughter. She tries to clarify, "Right, but the story is that zombies eat human brains, and we don't, so we aren't the stereotypical carnivore zombies."

"I get that, but I don't think vegetarian works. Hollywood zombies aren't just carnivores, they are cannibals. You aren't cannibals, but you are still carnivores. If you called yourselves cani-*bulls*, c-a-n-i-b-u-l-l-s, instead of canni-*bals*, then I think that would work."

Rachel screws up her face to think about it. "Hmm. Fine, I guess you're right. Maybe I'll suggest that tonight. Of course I'll have to take all credit for it if they like it, as they can't know that you know."

I raise my arms and place my hands behind my head, fingers interlocked, affecting a high level of self-satisfaction. "I'm not in it for the glory. My satisfaction comes by way of knowing that proper, functional communication is being used," I say.

"Anyway," Rachel continues, "When the old family slaughterhouse was remembered, and the idea suggested, the people in charge thought it was a great plan and everything was arranged. Cranston's population increased by five and so far our secret has remained secret. As far as I know I'm the first to break the silence."

"That's intense."

Funny that I'm not absolutely horrified by what I'm hearing. Rachel has just told me that zombies exist and that she is one of them. She is dead, and carries in her a virus that could make me dead, and yet I sit a foot or two away from her and joke about what to call a non-human-brain eating zombie.

"I can understand the secrecy, I guess, but if there is a scientific explanation for it all, why not go public? Why do you have to be hidden away somewhere and not explain it? I'm not freaking out, it makes sense and I understand it. I think people in general would as well."

Rachel says, "I've never really thought about it. They told us how it had to be, and given the nature of the circumstances either we were too caught up in the shock of it all to question, or maybe at the time it seemed like the best option. Then the routine just took over. Maybe it has to do with how our brains operate now, given that we aren't exactly 100% in that regard."

"Maybe. So are you all under arrest in some way? I mean, is it like the witness relocation program where you have CDC agents supervising you and making sure you don't tell the world who you really are? Are they trying to cover this up? It didn't seem like it was an error on their part, just an accident, albeit a very serious one."

Rachel sighs, "Well, they weren't doing anything wrong, but this whole project was pretty secretive. They weren't ready to tell the world that there was a real zombie virus. They were afraid of how the public would react, or even other scientists. What they concluded is that we'll remain for a long time in exactly the state we are now, so long as we feed the virus."

I interrupt, "And the virus only wants brains? Is that why I haven't seen you eat anything else?"

"No, well, yes and no. The virus needs brain matter to live. I don't really need to eat anything else because my cells don't degenerate, sort of. Cells can be damaged, and then they do regenerate, but slowly. In general though, cells don't die of old age. Does that make sense? Somehow the immune system still works. We can eat, and all that digestive stuff still works, but we don't really need to, and certainly not as much as you need to. So we eat other foods with the brains, but honestly I can go more than a few days without eating anything else and be fine. We do need to drink water though. The virus can become dehydrated and that could lead to death."

"Absolutely fascinating," I interject. "When you were sick last week, what was that about? Can you still get the flu or a cold or something?"

"So far the only type of sickness we've gotten is when we don't eat enough brain and the virus gets weak. Every once in a while our slaughtering frequency slows down and there are fewer brains for us to eat. We have some frozen and all of that, but occasionally the supply runs down and we get weak. It's not a big deal, really."

"That's less fascinating and more gross now," I say.

"Understandable. As you can imagine, I don't have many friends over to the house, and I'm not really excited about spending a lot of time at other people's houses. Today was an exception."

"Trent told me you were kind of private."

"That's putting it nicely. I've been outright cold to some people, just because I didn't know how to handle all of this stuff."

"I think you are doing fine handling it right now," I say.

"Yeah, but I've broken the only rule we have! The CDC doesn't have anyone living here to monitor us, getting back to your previous question, but they do keep tabs on us. It's a point of contention, but they send spies out occasionally to pose as tourists and try to find out if anyone in town knows anything about us," she explains.

"They don't want you telling the secret or they don't want you infecting other people?" I ask.

"Both probably. But there really isn't much danger of us infecting anyone. We all stay away from living people pretty well, as far as in situations where the virus could be communicated. My parents have each other; Frank and Mark are old and have a lab set up where they work on things for the CDC occasionally, along with still studying this virus and its effects on us. They are happy to be reclusive. I don't think the town even knows they exist. I'm the real concern for the CDC. Not only am I the only one with any social interests, I'm also enrolled in school and have the potential to seek intimate relationships, posing a risk for viral communication. It was a bit of a struggle to get them to permit me to attend public school."

"You *are* on a kind of probation. House arrest in a way. That's rough." I don't know what else to say. Given the circumstances, saying anything is pretty impressive.

"It hasn't been too bad, but it has been bad enough. For the first year after getting here I struggled to find the right social approach, and ended up developing a reputation as being unfriendly and strange. When you reached out to me, I saw an opportunity to start a fresh friendship, one that wasn't tainted by the rumors and reputation. Apparently I wasn't fast enough to beat the rumors, but hopefully I've at least given you reason not to believe them."

Now it's my turn to laugh. "Don't get me wrong, I'm happy that you wanted to be my friend, and I'm really happy that you trust me enough to tell me all of this, and I'll keep it a secret, but I have to say it's funny that you think you have given me a reason *not* to believe you are strange."

I watch Rachel's face as she processes what I just said, and it is apparent when she makes the connection. "Okay, that is funny. In my effort to squash the rumors of my being strange I confess to you that I am a zombie."

"Yeah, I think that's what YouTube would call an epic fail," I say.

"Indeed."

"I have another question for you."

"What's that?"

"How much danger is there of me catching this virus from you? Not that I'm going to start wearing latex gloves or a hazmat suit, unless you know of a place that sells them cheap? Just kidding. I'm not afraid of catching it, but I'm curious. You seemed to get anxious over the paper cut and still haven't moved that hand anywhere near me since. How contagious is it?"

"If my blood gets into your blood, then you will likely develop the virus. However, the transfer would have to happen within about twelve hours; otherwise the virus would die in open air or whatever. My blood is thick, so I can keep tabs on where it is pretty well. Also I avoid as many blood-letting activities as I can. There is always the risk of catastrophic accident, but the CDC relies on statistics and doesn't expect that the five of us in this small town pose that much of a threat in that regard."

"Okay, so as long as I don't go vampire on you and drink your blood, then we should be alright?" I ask.

"As far as I know."

"Not that vampires are real, *right*?" I ask with a heavy influence of snarkyness.

"As far as I know," Rachel says with a smile. She then reaches over with her right hand again and grabs mine. "Thank you for listening to me and not freaking out. I'm sorry I chose you to tell this to, but I had to tell someone. I don't mean I'm sorry I chose you, but I'm sorry that you have to be the one to learn about all of this. And I didn't just choose you because you were new in the area. Maybe I did, but I've moved past that and I'm happy with how this is turning out."

"I'm glad you told me, but I think I'm even more glad that you are glad that you chose me to be the one to tell. I'm also happy how this is turning out…except the part about you being dead, that's really a crushing bummer, but I'm glad that you are reanimated."

"Thanks." She says. "We should probably get moving again; Mom does worry about me when I'm out, especially alone with a boy. That's probably not all zombie related worry either, although it certainly does compound it. Hopefully you can just drop me off and not have to talk to anyone, it might be hard to hide the fact that you know all of this now, at least so soon after hearing about it."

"Right, that might be tough. I can loop around passed your house and then on the way by again slow to a crawl and you can jump out onto your lawn. I'll never even have to stop."

"Great idea, let's do that," she agrees.

Luckily we don't have to do any extreme maneuvers when we get to her house. No one is in the yard, so I pull into the driveway, but stop about half way up at Rachel's request. It's a good rural Texas driveway, long and dusty.

"We should do this again sometime," I say.

"Confess reality-bending secrets?" Rachel asks.

"Sure," I say, picking up on her farce. "Tomorrow I can tell you how I'm really Superman."

"Tomorrow after school, you mean? I think that would work for me," she says.

That wasn't exactly what I meant, but I'm happy about it. "Yeah, tomorrow after school, we'll talk some more."

"Okay. Thanks again for listening to me and being understanding. I'll see you in the morning. Bye!"

"You got it. Good night!" I say.

She closes the car door and jogs up the driveway to the house. I watch her go and as she opens the front door I slide the shifter to reverse, throw my right arm over the passenger head rest and back down the driveway.

8. Delirium Disorder

That was pretty peculiar. I guess I've watched enough television and seen enough movies to be desensitized to extremes. I'm shocked, but I believe what she said. I'm still not entirely sure it isn't a joke, but I feel like I should believe it. Rachel is a zombie. I've got a crush on a zombie. I suppose I should be frightened, or concerned, but strangely I'm not. It seems so normal. Rachel is a zombie. She is dead, but not dead. I wonder if she has super-human abilities. I guess not. She said the virus affects her brain capability in some ways, but if her cells don't really degenerate maybe she is stronger than normal or something. I'll have to ask.

It's funny how learning something so immense doesn't really alter my manner of thinking. I'm hungry and I want to have dinner. I know I have homework that still needs to be done. I want to date a girl that is a zombie. It's all pretty much the same, I guess. I wonder if it will be difficult to keep this secret. I suppose we'll have to do some creative truth bending when it comes to having her over for dinner with my parents. I wonder if her parents will even let her invite me over. Her mom seemed nice enough at school today, but that was without any definite invitations extended, and likely no expectations of needing to address the subject of their health. I guess we'll handle that when it comes along.

I pull into the garage and hit the button for the door to close. I sit for a moment before going inside. Mom will ask how my date was, even though it wasn't a date. She'll ask all kinds of things about Rachel. I need to make sure I don't say anything incriminating. I'm pretty good at telling Mom what she wants to hear, so I should be okay. I'm level-headed, so I don't think I'll get all choked up or flustered if she says anything about zombies, brains or death. But I won't know until it happens, I suppose. Time to face it.

Just as I expected; Mom is in the kitchen getting dinner ready. Dinner or not she would have been waiting here for me to get back.

"It was great," I say before she has a chance to ask anything.

"What was great, dear?" Mom asks as she feigns focus in a recipe book.

"Yeah right, you know what I'm talking about," I say.

"What? Your date with Rachel? That's great, I wasn't even going to ask…" She trails off as she fumbles in a drawer for some measuring spoons. "I'm glad it was great, though."

"No questions? Wonderful, I'm going to get to my homework, don't bother calling me for dinner, I'm not very hungry." I know I can hold out on this charade longer than she can.

"Okay! I want to know everything, sit down and tell me about her!" Mom breaks quickly.

"Oh, what's to tell? She's an attractive girl, I'm an attractive boy, as Avril Lavigne says, can I make it any more obvious?" Mom has a weak spot for Avril Lavigne. Initially I thought it was weird, but then I realized it's just funny to see her bopping along to that style of music.

"I know that part already. What did you two talk about? Did you meet her folks when you drove her home? Did you make plans to see her again? Maybe a proper date?" Mom queries.

"We made rough plans to hang out tomorrow after school. I didn't get to really ask her on a date yet, but I will. Mostly we just talked about school. She told me a little more about moving here, and that she hasn't really connected with anyone yet. I didn't see anyone when I dropped her off. But I met her mom at school today, and she was cool," I say.

"Right. Dr. Mom. Did Rachel say anything else about the CDC? It seems mysterious and exciting, but I bet there are a lot of scientists working there who have incredibly boring jobs. They probably enjoy them, but for normal people I bet they are boring. No offense to Rachel's mom," Mom says.

"Rachel didn't really say anything else about the CDC," I explain.

Nothing I'm at liberty to repeat, that is.

I continue, "She just said her parents wanted to get away and had a family heritage in this part of the country so they came here. The ranch and slaughterhouse used to be in her family, it was started by her family."

"I remember Dad mentioning the slaughterhouse the other night. Pretty big operation then, huh?"

"I guess. Whatever Dad and I talked about the other night is all I know. Rachel has told me she doesn't have to interact with it at all, they have employees for that stuff."

Mom says, "I'm sure a seventeen year old girl isn't very interested in beef production."

"Probably not." *Just the brain part of it* I think to myself.

"Well invite her over for dinner soon so Dad and I can get to know her. Do you want to invite her over by herself first or invite her parents, too?" Mom asks excitedly.

"How about we invite her first, and then see about her parents. But how about you let me take her out on a proper date before I invite her over here?"

"That's fair, but don't dawdle on the invitation," Mom says and turns back to her ingredients. "What's her favorite music?"

"You always judge people based on the kind of music they like." I guess that's where I get it from.

Mom looks at me over her shoulder and then sticks out her tongue and shrugs.

Smiling, I say, "The best band we could agree on is No Doubt."

"I like No Doubt and Gwen Stefani!" Mom starts singing something to herself, but it is barely intelligible, thankfully.

Sitting at the table I remember Rachel's cut finger and start looking for blood. I don't see anything, but have an urge to disinfect the table before dinner.

"I'm going to clean the table."

"Thank you, Eric," Mom says.

I move my school stuff to my room before finding a bottle of spray cleaner and grabbing a few paper towels. If there is any zombie virus I don't want it getting into a reusable dish towel or something. I guess I'm slightly nervous about contracting the virus. That's normal though, right? I shouldn't want to become dead and then reanimated. At least not until I know whether there are super powers associated with it. The living forever without really degenerating or getting older part sounds okay, but I'm sure there are some terrible side effects. If it was all good then why would the CDC hide it? It can't be just for the brain eating thing, can it? If we all turned into this type of zombie and only needed brains we would just sell cow brains in the grocery store rather than throw them away or turn them into dog food. There must be something else, maybe something Rachel doesn't know about.

I wonder if the fictional accounts of zombies are somehow based on this real life version, or if the real life version gets labeled this way because of the similarities to the fiction. I'll have to hit up Wikipedia later tonight to do some research. Maybe there are historical accounts of this virus showing up in the world; unless, of course, the CDC got to them first and removed all records from public knowledge. Research will have to wait for later, for now I need to wipe the zombie blood from our kitchen table before dinner. That would make a great status update. Rachel might see it as violating our trust agreement though.

I clean the table and almost put the spray bottle away before I decide a second wipe down might not be a bad idea.

"You are very thorough with the table cleaning tonight, aren't you?" Mom says.

"Uh, yeah, I guess so," I reply. Mom doesn't push the topic, and I am happy to let it go. "Is dinner ready?"

"Twenty more minutes," Mom casually answers.

"I'll be on the computer."

"Okay. I'll call you when dinner is ready."

"Thanks," I say as I head toward the office.

I guess I could take the next twenty minutes to do some homework, but I'm not going to. I've got some more important research to conduct. After a few minutes of scanning the top articles returned in a Google search for "true accounts of zombies" I feel like I have a good handle on the topic; that handle being that zombies simply don't exist outside of the minds of Voodoo priests and horror movie writers and fanatics. Granted, I haven't given the search much energy, but I didn't see anything about a zombie virus, well, nothing credible. I don't know what I was expecting. I guess with the secrecy Rachel has described I shouldn't expect to read anything at CDC.com about it. Maybe Rachel is pulling my leg. The only real evidence she gave me is that I couldn't feel her pulse. But I'm not a doctor, so that evidence isn't very strong.

According to a few different web pages the term zombie wasn't originally used to describe what it does today. It has evolved. It popularly referred to a person under a spell of some kind, more hypnotized than reanimated corpse. The brain eating undead is a more recent concoction of fictional fancy. Either the true accounts have never made it to print or they don't exist. Or zombies don't exist. Why am I willing to change my whole concept of reality just because a girl told me she's a zombie? She's a pretty girl. That's right.

I spend a few more minutes reading about the history of zombies on Wikipedia until Mom calls me for dinner. Zombies can't be real. Rachel is playing a big game on me and she's got me going really good. The only question now is whether she's insane or extremely clever for coming up with this whole thing. I'm tempted to call Trent, maybe ask a few pointed questions, but I decide not to in case I let something slip. I need to sleep on this for at least a night before I delve into it any deeper. In any case, I suppose I'll find out more tomorrow.

***

The morning is calm and warm. I love days like this. When I ask Mom if I can take the car to school today she asks why I would want to on such a beautiful day. Normally this would be a great day to ride my bike, like I have been planning to do, but I need to be prepared for driving Rachel somewhere if the occasion arises. I tell

Mom I am going to head off campus for lunch and want to make sure I can get somewhere and back in the allotted time. A good enough excuse, I get to take the car. I head out the door with some toaster pastries and arrive at school before I know it, meaning it doesn't take long when driving.

I look for the Jetta I saw Rachel arrive in yesterday, but don't see it. I park facing away from the school and notice Rachel sitting under the large tree between the parking lot and the road. Perfect. What I don't notice is Trent's crew hanging out by his truck. The second I step out of the car I hear him call my name.

"Eric! Hey, man, over here." I turn my head to see him waving me over.

I smile and nod, then give a little wave. I don't want to go over there; I'd rather go to Rachel. I close the car door and look towards Rachel as I turn away from the car. She isn't looking up at me. She is reading. I guess I'll go say hi to those guys before going to Rachel. I don't want to alienate the Janson crew completely, I'm simply developing a strong preference for Rachel's company.

"Hey, guys. What's up?" I say.

"Nothing."

I'm glad I walked all the way over here. We all stand looking at each other for a few more seconds. Michael and Krissy decide to go in the school. Jessie tags along with them.

"I'm not going in until the bell rings. It's too nice out today," says Trent.

"It is nice out," I agree. But consumed with the desire to talk to Rachel, I add, "Well, I'm going to say hi to Rachel. Catch you later, Trent."

"Oh, I'll go with you," Trent says and leaves his leaning perch against the bed of his truck to throw his right arm around my shoulders.

"Cool." But I only sort of mean it.

Whispering, Trent asks, "So did you ask Rachel out yet?" I'm glad he whispered. Not that I've really had any reason to not expect him to show tact. He's been a nice guy so far. I need to get my mind straight and stop making up some ridiculous divide between my new groups of friends. Maybe I have a real problem with my imagination getting away from me and jumping to wild conclusions about people. Maybe I'm really gullible as a result. That would explain my taking the bait on Rachel's zombie story. I wonder if there is any way I can talk to Trent about that without breaking my promise of secrecy.

I decide to be friendly instead of jerkly, which isn't officially a word, but I would use it more often if Webster would include it in his next edition.

I answer Trent's question, "Nah, not yet. She came over to my house yesterday for a bit and helped me with some homework, but I haven't asked her out yet."

Trent squeezes me around my shoulders and makes a congratulatory sound. If I were more of an athlete I might be able to recreate it myself, but I'm pretty sure it is positive. "Baby steps," he says.

"Yeah, baby steps, that's usually how I approach girls. She's cool though, I'm going to ask her out."

To my surprise, Trent slaps me on the back and says at regular volume, "Alright, Eric, well I'll catch you later. Hey, Rachel!" And then he turns around and goes back towards the school. He really is an alright guy.

"Hey, Trent," Rachel shouts back. When she looked up to respond she looked at me, and with Trent walking in the other direction, she stays looking at me.

"Good morning, Rachel," I say as I stop at the edge of the parking lot, a few feet from her spot on the grass. "Isn't the grass wet with dew?"

"Yeah. I'm sitting on a text book," she says.

"Good plan. Thanks again for helping me with the poem last night."

"Did you revise it at all?"

"No, I thought about going over it again, but got adequately distracted by some research I was doing," I say, hinting at the topic I am interested to get back to.

"Research, huh? For school? I don't know many people that get distracted from homework by doing homework."

"Now who's the one with the keen perception?" I playfully query.

"Give me three guesses as to what you were researching?" she counters.

"Go for it." I drop to a crouching position, unwilling to get my pants wet in the dewy grass and unwilling to break my personal rule of never sitting down in a parking lot. I once sat in a parking lot and came up with gum stuck to my pants. I never saw the wad on the ground before I sat down. It traumatized me. Discarded gum is rather vile in my opinion. I don't know why the grass doesn't have the same danger potential in my mind as the parking lot does, but if the grass wasn't wet I would sit in it. I guess I could pull up a text book, but I'm not going to.

"Okay, let's see, my first guess is that you were searching for lists of reasons why music in the 90's was better than music today."

I guess she is building up to the zombie topic. I thought she was being mostly serious when she asked about guessing. Maybe she is mostly goofing on me again.

"No, I don't need to read reasons for that, I already know them all," I say in correction.

With a smirk she says, "Okay, my bad. Guess number two: you were researching the origin of the poodle shaving method that results in the dog having bands of fur around their ankles and midsection only."

"How did you…! Next!" Two can play at this game.

"I was just messing with you; I know what you were researching," she says as she picks up a small scrap of paper from the ground beside her and places it into the book to mark her page.

That's more like it. "I figured you knew."

"Of course I know, you were researching the effect of low birth weight among giraffes."

Maybe she really isn't thinking about the zombie thing at all. Maybe she just doesn't want to bring it up here and now and this is her way of communicating that to me.

"You guessed it. I didn't realize I was so transparent that you could know me so well after such a short period of acquaintance." My words come out awkwardly as I adjust my thoughts from joking about zombies to assuming Rachel is avoiding that subject.

"Keen perception, you said it yourself." She holds her hand out to me. I stand up and grab it so she can pull herself up to standing. I then reach down and pick up her text book for her. When I stand up again we are face to face, inches apart. I hold the text book up between us and she grabs hold of it. For a moment we are connected like a circuit through the book. At this point in our relationship this is better than a kiss. But it doesn't last nearly long enough. A strange voice breaks up the moment. Rather, an unfamiliar voice, I guess; the voice sounds normal, I just don't recognize it.

"Good morning, Rachel," a low, but gentle voice says, with a clear southern drawl on it.

Rachel spins around in an instant pivot. My head snaps to the right to see a rather frail looking man, passed middle age, but not quite ready to be part of the "regular" breakfast crowd at McDonalds. He is wearing tan slacks and a blue button-up shirt, with the collar open. Bifocals rest upon his nose as he peers over the top of the frame. Apparently he could do with trifocals.

"Frank...you startled me. Sorry. Good morning," she says.

We all stand quietly until Frank looks at me. Rachel adds, "Oh, this is my friend, Eric. Eric, this is Frank, he works for my father, and lives with us."

Was Frank one of the other CDC scientists with the virus? I can't remember. I guess it must be one of those guys if he lives with them. I thought she said those guys never left the house.

"Hi Frank, nice to meet you. I'm Eric." I guess I didn't need to add my name.

"Yes, Eric, I've heard. It's a pleasure. I thought school would have started by now, you two aren't truant are you?" Frank asks in mock suspicion, laughing at his tease.

I smile and look at Rachel. She doesn't look amused, clearly startled by Frank's appearance.

"School is about to start any moment. We were just about to head inside," she says.

"Yes, I saw you standing up and expected as much. Just wanted to say 'Hi.' It's such a nice day I decided to take a stroll up and down the road," he says.

"I hope you enjoy the walk, Frank. I guess I'll see you later," Rachel says with a wave and turns toward the school.

"Nice to meet you, Frank," I add with a wave of my own and then turn to follow Rachel.

"My pleasure, Eric, my pleasure." I look back over my shoulder and the old man is just standing there, smiling. I give him a quick head-to-toe-and-back-again scan before looking forward. I could see him being a zombie. He's a little strange at least, but I'm probably just thinking that because of the way Rachel reacted to his appearance, or presence. He looks normal to me. I'm not doing so well with my words this morning, spoken or not.

Rachel doesn't seem like she is about to say anything so I don't say anything until I am sure we are out of ear-shot of Frank.

"Nice fellow, Frank," I say.

"He's alright," she says. Clearly this isn't a good topic for discussion right now. I think I'm going to have a rough day if we don't get a chance to talk about this until after school. My curiosity is going to prevent any type of real focus on schoolwork. But to be honest, that's nothing new.

I wait until we are inside the school to ask a question. "He's one of the guys that…"

"Yep," Rachel interrupts. Again, from the inflection in her voice I think that's all I'm going to get to say on the subject until we are legitimately alone.

"What are your plans for lunch?" I change the subject and begin to hash out a plan for getting us alone.

"Staying here. Maybe going to the library to read," she says shortly.

This isn't the same girl I was talking with a few minutes ago. Before Frank showed up.

"Not hungry today?" I ask.

We are standing by her locker now. Rachel looks up at me, her face void of expression.

"Not really. I'm also enjoying my book and would like to keep reading it."

I want to ask if I can join her in the library, but I decide to hold off on that impulse for a bit. Instead I ask, "What book? I didn't pay attention earlier."

"Just some young adult novel about romance and supernatural stuff. I like those books, as poorly written and pointless as they usually are. I guess being a teenager and all I can relate."

"Supernatural stuff like vampires and z…monsters and stuff?" Her right eyebrow shoots up at the sound of the z, causing me to change midsentence. Finally, some recognition of the topic I'm *un*dying to discuss.

"Yes, that kind of stuff. I think these books are ridiculous but once I start reading them I get swept away into some mind-numbingly fantastic fairytale world. It's almost like being asleep while being awake. I think, actually, if I remember correctly from the psychology class I took back in Atlanta, that the brain is more active while sleeping than it is when reading a book like this." A smile seems to be creeping back onto Rachel's face.

"So what you're saying is that you don't recommend it to me?"

"I'd love to have you read this book and then we could discuss it. This is actually the second in a series; I'll bring you the first one tomorrow if you promise to read it." The seriousness seems to have passed completely now, except I think she is serious about me reading the book.

"I'll be happy to read with you in the library during lunch," I say.

"Don't you need to eat?"

"Eating is over rated."

"Says you." She says.

We have another brief moment before the warning bell rings and we snap back to reality. School. Rachel opens her locker and I stand there. She swaps some books and then we head off to class. No one seems to care when we walk into the classroom together, no one except for me at least.

***

The third day of floor hockey brings more games in our bracket system. Today the teams who lost early are playing the more recent winning teams. The bracket is like nothing you would find in a professional sports league, except maybe bowling. I don't know how bowling works. Rachel is still excused from gym class. After changing for class I see her perched at the top of the bleachers, buried in her book. Better than being buried in a cemetery. Sometimes I feel the embarrassment that would result if I said something like that out loud, even though I don't say it out loud. It's true though, about my preference for her burial status, even while I don't really know what is going on with her I'm glad she's here and not in a cemetery in Atlanta.

And that brings up something important to ponder, later, perhaps while lost in a good video game. Is it a sign of good psychological health to have a crush on a zombie, assuming Rachel actually is one?

I decide to sit with my team until our game, after which I'll head up and interrupt Rachel's reading. Walking along the bleachers at floor level I keep looking up at Rachel. She looks down at me briefly, and smiles, then goes right back to her book. That's good enough for me right now. I sit next to Chris on the second row of bleachers at half court.

Chris is in all of my classes. He's quiet, small, not short, but just small. I haven't talked with him much, just in gym class actually, and then only briefly. Seems nice enough. Nice enough to let live. In my last class I took to deciding who I'd let live if I became a blood thirsty zombie, provided I have the cognitive faculties necessary to make that decision when the time comes. I figure it can't hurt to plan ahead. Maybe if I make the choice of whose brains I'll leave alone now I won't have to make that decision later when I'm not quite at 100% for moral judgment. It never hurts to plan ahead.

Chris and I engage in some small talk and the time quickly passes until our team is up. We are playing against Trent's team. He and I end up guarding each other. The ball quickly goes towards my team's goal, being on offense I'm away from the action, with Trent standing idly by.

"Who was that old guy that you and Rachel were talking to this morning?" Trent asks. "I've never seen him around before. Did he say what he was doing? Is he a tourist?"

If Trent doesn't know who Frank is then I don't want to be the one to tell him. If I say something to him about a guy living at Rachel's house it could open up a lot of discussion that I'm not prepared for. I could say he's her uncle visiting, but then that creates a scenario that Rachel would need to participate in or correct. Usually the truth is always the easiest route to take, it certainly would be here, but sometimes easy doesn't help keep secrets. In fact, secrets usually aren't easy.

"What? That old guy? He said he was out taking a walk since it was so nice out." I try to play it casual and keep my eyes on the action of the game.

"Did Rachel know him?" Trent asks.

"I don't know. He just said hello and then we said hello and he said he was out for a walk. We agreed that the weather was nice and then told him we needed to get to school."

If Trent had been watching the whole interaction he could probably tell that that isn't what went on in the conversation. But if he was watching it wasn't from his truck. We walked past it on the way inside and I don't remember seeing him.

"Oh." That's all he can say before the ball comes flying in our direction and we get involved in the game.

My team loses. After the game I pass off my stick to someone else and head up the bleachers to Rachel.

"What was Trent asking you about?" She says without looking up from the book.

"He asked about that old man we saw this morning." I decide it would be best to play up the story I just told Trent, just in case anyone can hear me. It wouldn't do for me to use Frank's name. Rachel seems to relax a little when I don't say Frank's name.

"Oh yeah?" I interpret this to mean *'and what did you tell him?'*

"He asked if either of us knew the old guy because he's never seen him around and implied that this isn't a big tourist time of the year so he was wondering where the guy came from. I told him how the man said hello and then we chatted about the nice weather and told him we had to get inside for school." I take up residence on the bleacher bench to Rachel's right.

"That's what happened. Should have asked Trent if he was spying on us," she says, still not looking up from the book.

"I did ask him that. He said he's absolutely captivated by you and can't stop watching you." As soon as I say this I wonder if it will be taken in jest or be offensive in some way.

"You mean you," she says and looks up at me. When she looks at me this way I do mean me.

"I'll admit it. When I look at you I don't want to look away," I say.

Although no hint of blush appears in her cheeks, Rachel's facial mannerisms betray a slight embarrassment. She really doesn't have a pulse.

Rachel explains, "I meant *you* as in when Trent looks at *you* he can't look away." She sweeps the bleachers with her eyes before looking at me again, squinting, "But I admire your honesty."

I look at her and raise a quizzical eyebrow. We communicate with our eyebrows a lot.

She clarifies, "I admire your honesty about being a gawker." Clearly I wasn't honest with Trent, her clarification confirms that we are on the same page in this conversation again.

I nod and look out at the game, covertly scanning our classmates to determine if our conversation is being monitored.

It's clear to me that we'll need some time alone today after school. I need to ask her some questions about this secret. I'd like to know if Frank's appearance was a fluke or if that kind of thing is going to happen regularly. If so, we'll need to get our story straight. Maybe Frank is getting sick of the seclusion and he wants to be incorporated into the community. If that's the case a story will likely come from Rachel's parents that she can then share with me. Hopefully it doesn't interfere with what I just told Trent. If tomorrow it turns out that Frank is Rachel's visiting uncle or something then I'll have some explaining to do for Trent when he finds out. Which he likely will. This is Cranston after all. I guess I can always spin it so that Frank and Rachel don't have a warm relationship and when I met him this morning the connection hadn't been revealed to me. That won't actually be so hard to explain away if it comes to it.

"So, Rachel, do you have some time after school today to hang out? I mean, do you want to go get a milkshake or something?" I ask.

She places her bookmark and closes the book before answering my question. "Sure. Something sounds good.

Just need to be home in time for dinner again. Six o'clock."

"Alright. Good. Did you drive to school today?"

"No, I always walk; Mom drove me yesterday because she was coming here. I would've walked anyway but I like my mom's company. She isn't a fan of walking in heels."

"I see. Well I'll drive you home afterward." I say.

"You mean you won't just drop me back here where you found me and leave me to walk home?" She fakes sweetness, dripping with sarcasm, as though I was doing her a huge favor, or more accurately, pointing out the goes-without-saying obviousness of my statement.

"I'll bring you wherever you want me to. Home, school, Houston, it's all the same to me."

"Good to know." She opens her book, removes the scrap of paper, places it on the bench beside her and continues reading. I watch her long enough for her to turn a page and she never looks up, so I watch the games until the end of class.

"So you are going to the library now?" I ask Rachel. She replaces the bookmark.

Rachel says, "That's my plan. I'm hooked on this book!"

"Okay, I have to go change; I'll see you in class after lunch. Enjoy your book."

"Thanks, Eric. Enjoy your lunch. I'll see you soon." Rachel smiles, slides the book into the outer pocket of her backpack and runs down the bleachers.

I watch her go before making my own way to the locker room. I had hoped she'd change her mind and come to the cafeteria with me, or maybe ask me to join her in the library after I eat. But she didn't. I'm in that state where I just want to be around her constantly. I guess she has more restraint on her impulses than I do.

Maybe that's a benefit of being a zombie, or she isn't feeling the same impulse that I am to spend as much time together as possible. It's probably just the zombie thing, hopefully. That is, if she actually is a zombie. I don't know what kind of evidence I'm going to need to really accept it if it's true.

In the locker room I decide to have a follow up discussion with Trent regarding the rumors about Rachel's family. He never gave me any specifics, just generalities about the Sutton's not being who they say they are, their house formerly being a funeral parlor, and overall asocial behavior. Knowing what I know now, the funeral parlor makes a little more sense in how it ties in, but I wonder if Trent knows anything about that.

"Trent, good game today," I say, figuring it best to start the conversation out light and in his sphere of interest.

"Hey, Eric, yeah, it was good. For someone who claims low athletic ability you do pretty well for yourself out there. I'm looking forward to baseball season."

"I'm telling you, floor hockey is it for me, but I'll at least try out for baseball." I don't know how I'm going to get around that one; I don't really want to play a school sport.

"Trying out is all I ask," Trent says and turns back toward his locker.

Michael chimes in, "That's because anyone who tries out makes the team. Small school, low bar for making the cut."

"Great!" I say with sarcastic enthusiasm.

"It won't be so bad, man, we'll have fun. If you don't want to play much you can still be on the team. You can fetch my Gatorade for me or something." Trent slaps me playfully on the shoulder.

"That I should be able to handle."

"Besides, maybe with you on the team Rachel will come out to a game occasionally. It's just my selfish interest, but I'm curious if that would bring her out into the public or not. No offense, I'm just saying," Trent explains.

"I understand, it's cool. Maybe she would come to a game, I don't know yet." Well, that's convenient, Trent broke the subject himself. "I'll tell you, though, if I do play on the team I'll want Rachel there watching."

"You're really taken with this girl, huh?" Michael asks.

"Yeah, I am. I find her fascinating and just want to get to know her better." I'm building up to asking more questions, but I also mean it.

"Not to pry, but did you talk with her about any of the rumor stuff that we told you about yesterday?" Trent asks.

"We did, actually. Sort of. I don't want to betray her confidence, so I guess all I can say is she understands why some of the rumors were started, but doesn't think them justified?"

"Rumors are probably never justified," Trent agrees.

"I'm probably letting curiosity get the best of me, but I'm still kind of unclear as to the specifics of the rumors. You mentioned something about the Suttons not being who they claim to be, and then some ghost story stuff about the funeral parlor, and Rachel's dad being secretive, but what about it? Do you think Rachel is a ghost or something?" I ask. I hope I'm not going too far here.

Trent and Michael both laugh at the ghost question.

Trent says, "Nah, we don't think she is a ghost. That story would be more fun. I guess specifically the story that is going around is that Rachel's dad is some kind of hit man. So it isn't so much about Rachel as it is her dad. Something about the claim on the heritage, her dad's personality as reported by the people who work for him, and the connection with the funeral home doesn't help his persona as a bringer of death. I don't know, I'm sure it's all distorted. Maybe he was a federal agent or something and is under some kind of protection now, or maybe he was a hit man and is in witness relocation. These are the speculations, the rumors just grow out from there. All we really know is that the Suttons keep to themselves...and maybe to you."

Trent's seriousness melts away with his final comment.

I smile. "Maybe to me. I guess we'll see."

9. You're Not Alone Anymore

I decide to avoid classmates and secure a few minutes alone for thinking so I leave school for lunch. Unsure of whether or not I will run into anyone at the places in town, I go home. I tell Mom I forgot my wallet, so I had to come home to get it, and once here I figure I'll just stay to eat. Mom thinks it is great having me come home for lunch. She is disappointed, however, that I don't have Rachel with me. I try to play it cool and just shrug in response.

When I get back to school it is only a few minutes before the next class so I head on in and sit down. Rachel comes in shortly after and I ask about her reading. She says it was fine, and then says nothing more. We walk to our next class together and she asks about my lunch. I give her a report and soon we are in the next class ready to begin.

When the last bell rings we stop first at her locker and then proceed to my car. She calls her mom to tell her she'll be home by 6. This is what I overhear:

"Hi, Mom. I'm going out for a bit, I'll be home by 6 though...Yeah...Eric, the one you met yesterday...Yes, again..." She looks over at me and smiles. "I don't know, we are going to get a milkshake if we can find anywhere in town to get one...Yes...Yeah, I know...Okay...I know…I'll be home at 6. Bye…Bye, Mom." And she hangs up.

I can only assume the last part of the conversation was about Frank. That is, I can only assume until I ask her. "Did she mention Frank?"

Rachel looks back at me with a serious face. "Yep. He told her that you and I were 'too close for our own good' this morning."

"They must have different standards where he's from, I didn't think we were close enough." I can't believe I just said that out loud.

"You do, do you? Well, don't go telling my mom, she wouldn't want to hear it," Rachel sighs.

"Yesterday you told me Frank and the other guy don't leave the house. What was he doing going for a walk?" I ask.

"Spying. That's my guess. He must have started walking shortly after I left. He seemed to be coming from the opposite direction when we saw him. He probably walked right by while I was reading and then stopped and watched from somewhere. Mom didn't say he had been sent out to spy, but after last night I think that's what is going on. Let's start driving and I'll tell you about it."

I was going to ask, but now I don't have to. "You indicated it might be difficult to find a milkshake around here?"

"Yeah, they have slushies at the market, but I don't think anyone does milkshakes. There are some places to get ice cream cones, but I don't think any of them do milkshakes."

"A whole town without milkshakes? That doesn't seem possible." Really, I'm having a hard time believing this. Strangely, a harder time than I'm having believing

I'm speaking with a zombie. It's funny how the teenage mind works.

"Just go to Main and turn left. We can drive for a while, if that's alright with you, I mean," she says.

"Yeah, fine by me. I've got some questions and I think we should just talk for a while anyway."

"Okay."

I start the car and the stereo blares to life. It's interesting how loud the stereo is when you first start the car compared to when you turn the car off. We both jump a little in our seats as the loud volume startles us, but I quickly recover and adjust the knob to an appropriate background level of sound.

Rachel clears her throat and then asks, "Is this the radio?"

"No, MP3 files from a thumb drive," I say.

"Oh," she says, with a tickle in her voice that makes me think she's getting ready to tease me. "I didn't have you pegged as an enthusiast of jilted teenage girl rock music."

There it is.

I reach over and press the next button to skip away from Avril Lavigne's "Everything Back but You."

Alright, to be fair to my mom, I also like to listen to Avril Lavigne.

I explain to Rachel, "I like anything with a steady beat and solid guitar."

"Mhm-hm."

We drive for a bit. The next band to come up is The Graduate, a rock group from Illinois that I picked up on at my last school. I saw them play once. Hopefully this will restore musical credibility for me in Rachel's eyes.

"This song is called 'Justified' by a band called The Graduate. What do you think?" I ask.

Rachel turns the volume back up a bit and listens. "Sounds pretty good. I don't care if you listen to Avril Lavigne, it just wasn't what I expected to be blasting from your stereo."

"There are many sides and shades to Eric Sterling."

"We can do without third person narratives," Rachel says.

"Fair enough."

We drive along, making a left onto Main, listening to the music.

Rachel seems to be looking around a lot. I wonder if she's looking for spies.

I turn the volume down again and break our conversational silence. "So, what happened last night that makes you think your mom has sent spies out after you? Was it just that you came over to my house?"

"Not just that, but partly. Mom was concerned that I was already spending time alone with you after having only met you the day before. She is always concerned that the CDC is going to come after us and focus on me as the weakest link. Also, I'm not so sure that Mom *sent* Frank out."

This just keeps getting better and better. "What do you mean, *come after you*? And if Frank wasn't sent out, then how does that factor in?" I ask.

"Okay, that's a two-parter. First of all, when they figured out what happened to us they immediately set to work on finding a cure for the virus, unsure of whether or not it would kill us or if they'd be able to resuscitate us once the virus was dead. At least, that's what they told us they were working on. Mom is under the suspicion that they were actually studying us and trying to determine if it was possible to live a regular life under the effect of the virus. Mom thinks they want to use the virus as a way to enhance life for everyone. After they studied us for a while she thinks they found that being a reanimate wasn't so bad.

"Mom started asking questions and trying to get involved with the research, but they wouldn't let her. Finally they suggested we leave Atlanta and set up life somewhere else. That's how we ended up here. They gave us a story about finding a cure for the virus and getting things back to normal. Mom didn't think it would be possible, but she hoped for it. Frank and Mark were included in the initial research when Mom wasn't. She thinks they are supportive of the plan to use the virus to infect the general population, thinking they'd be doing everyone a favor. She thinks they might have pushed the idea.

"Frank and Mark didn't seem to be all too concerned with becoming zombies. One time Mom even suggested that they were behind the accident in the first place. I don't think Mom is worried that I'll turn you into a zombie, but I think she is worried that Frank thinks you are a spy."

Me? A government agent? Cool!

"I'm not a secret agent; although, I think that would be pretty rad," I say.

"I know you aren't, otherwise I wouldn't have told you about all of this. The point of sending a spy out here would be to see if we had revealed the secret to anyone. Everyone's greatest fear has been that I'd tell the world, or infect the world," Rachel explains.

"If they want to infect the world, then why would that be a concern for them?" I ask.

"Well, we've been like this for over two years, which is forever in my life, but for scientists that's not very long at all. Frank and Mark think the changes have been great, but the folks at the CDC, at least the group responsible for all of this in the virology department, haven't experienced the changes themselves and are still uncertain. Fact is, no one knows the long term effect. Does the virus have a limited lifespan? Or is it constantly replicating itself, essentially re-staffing the operating team that now controls my body? The thing I don't like to really think about, but have to realize, is that I'm not really myself. I am mostly, because the virus operates my brain, and doesn't seem to have a consciousness of its own, but I don't *feel* the same as I did before. I'm hollow now."

Rachel seems to be making herself small, physically compressing as she contemplates what she is describing as an empty existence. She hunches forward in the seat, hands clasped in her lap. Her hair is hanging down so as to cover her face.

"Wow." That's all I can think to say as *I* contemplate the weight of what she is considering, the loss of some part of herself, and not only the loss, but the awareness that something is missing. Neither of us speaks for a few minutes. We pass a lot of desert as we make our way north on route 33.

Rachel breaks the silence. "Mom is worried that one of these days the Agency - that's how we refer to them at home, I've been calling them the CDC for your benefit, but it really isn't the CDC, it's just one agency, one department of it, that is controlling this. We don't know how far up the chain of command any awareness of the situation goes. Anyway, Mom thinks the Agency will eventually decide we need to be silenced for good. Some leadership change or something at the Agency will lead to them needing to cover us up. Either that or they'll determine that there is too much risk and not enough benefit to this virus and they'll cancel the program.

"Mom expects that we'll either have agents come looking for us or Frank will do something. No matter where the threat comes from, she expects that they are keeping tabs on us and making sure we keep the secret. That's why me spending time alone with you is frightening. There is the risk that I'll tell you about all of this, and as it turns out that fear was justified, but there is also the risk that I could infect you. Granted, that chance is not very high. If it was they never would have let me go to high school," she says.

Given my penchant for conspiracies, I'm eating this up with a spoon, and finding it exhilarating. "Maybe the risk of infection is still high and they let you go to school because even if you do infect everyone they can probably contain it easily enough. You know, just wipe everyone out."

From my periphery I see Rachel's head swing up and she looks at me. I look over and she looks horrified.

"Sorry. I get into conspiracies."

"No, you are probably right. I never thought about it that way. I always figured a small town would be easier to contain information-wise, by keeping the story quiet, not by killing everyone."

Now I did it. She's going to worry more than she was already. I try to be reassuring, "Look, you aren't going to infect me, and I'm not going to tell anyone about this. So as long as we can pacify Frank and your mom then everything's cool."

"Unless the CDC does send someone to eliminate us one day," she says.

"Well, yeah, I guess there's that. But if they haven't done it yet, why would they? Have you felt like you have been deteriorating over the last few years? If they are waiting this out to see if you end up turning into the fictional zombie monsters we see on TV, and you haven't yet, then you should be safe."

"Unless someone with different ethics gets involved at the Agency and they decide this needs to be ended," she says.

"But someone with different ethics might not justify killing five people," I interject.

"Five people who are already dead? It's not the same thing. A perfectly ethical scientist may see us as viruses, potentially dangerous viruses; epidemic level of danger. Pandemic, even. The clear choice would be to kill the virus in the interest of humanity. It would have been done already if we hadn't retained so much of our personalities. And because we retained whatever portion of our personalities that we have is why I haven't tried to kill myself, and I think that's the case for all five of us remaining from the original infection event."

"Is there any evidence to suggest this might be happening in the near future? The extermination, I mean."

"My dad has had a few new men come to work for him. Mom swears they are part of the Agency. When she brought up her concern, Frank dismissed her worries and explained that we are all still in the good graces of the Agency and the work he and Mark are doing is very valuable. That was when Mom started worrying about Frank's agenda and allegiance."

"Have you caught Frank associating with those new guys?" I ask.

"No, I never see anyone do anything around there. Mom says she can spot Agency people anywhere. And she doesn't like the air of superiority that Frank has embraced lately."

"I guess I don't see where the Agency really has to worry about all of you. What would happen if you told someone? They didn't do anything wrong, it'd just be reported that there was an accident with a virus and then for the last two years the situation has been monitored and everything is fine," I say.

Rachel says, "Everything is fine? I know what you are trying to say, but we are zombies, remember?"

"I know, but you aren't killing people and eating their brains!"

We aren't too far from town, but far enough that there aren't any other people around. There's a pull off spot on the road and I park in it.

"Wanna sit outside and talk here?" I ask before cutting the engine.

"Sure."

We get out and I realize that this far from any houses there isn't any irrigation, so the ground is just dirt, rocks and sharp plants. I've never understood why all desert plants are so sharp. What is it about being dry that makes them spear like? Anyway, there's no grass for sitting on. I hop up onto the hood of the car and lie back against the windshield. Rachel follows my lead. I shimmy a little closer to her, and then she reciprocates with a shimmy of her own and we are lying shoulder to shoulder.

For a minute or two we take in the vast nothingness before us and absorb some winter sun. We also absorb some engine heat through the car's hood; it's not altogether unpleasant. She picks up the conversation where we left off.

"None of us ever killed anyone, but it wasn't for lack of desire."

I let that statement sit for a bit. Is she telling me that she wanted to kill someone? Understandably, I guess; I might have wanted to kill someone if they just told me their top secret project resulted in the death and reanimation of my family.

"Are you saying that you wanted to kill someone because they turned you into a zombie?" I ask.

"No. I'm saying that when I was first a zombie the craving for brain matter was slowly building up in me. They didn't realize right away that brains were what we needed to eat, so for the first few days we seemed like we were dying again. No brains makes us weak, remember? So we were all getting weak and sickly, meanwhile each of us had a new desire to eat brains. None of us had ever eaten brain before, and it was several days before Mark had the guts to mention that he had the craving and then we all confessed to having the same hankering."

"Good word choice." I love that word, *hankering.*

"What? Yeah, it's okay." Rachel smiles and rolls her eyes as she shakes her head at me. "Anyway, we all wanted to eat brain. It made sense, though, because brain eating was a behavior observed in the lizards where the virus was originally found."

"That makes sense," I say.

"Those first days, and even weeks, were really confusing for everyone. The Agency started working on a plan for obtaining human brains, ones that didn't die from disease, and weren't slaughtered for our meal, which meant accident victims. It would be possible for them to get the brains in the name of research, but it wasn't as easy as going to McDonalds or something.

"We kept getting weaker and as the craving for brains intensified Mark admitted that he wanted to kill someone and eat their brain. Not only that he wanted to, but he was going to if they didn't provide any other way to feed the craving. That freaked everyone out, and none of the rest of us joined in this confession, but since I'm telling you everything anyway, I did have that same feeling. I wanted to kill someone. Luckily, I was so weak then that I couldn't. When they brought us brains to eat we all started getting better. It wasn't until after we were feeling better that some of us realized we ate the brain of another human being and we labeled ourselves monsters. I made the connection then with movie zombies and threw out their 'reanimate' label. Frank didn't seem to have a problem with eating brain, it was scientific. Mom put on a show of being alright with it, but I don't think she was.

"They started doing tests and what not and determined pretty quickly that animal brains ought to be sufficient. We tried several different species. Not really a whole lot of difference among them. We settled on cow brain for the availability of it. That was the key that linked us to the slaughterhouse here. We've been on cow brain ever since, but the potential to degenerate into the brain-craving monsters has never been so far out of the realm of possibility that we haven't felt the need to be cautious.

"So to answer your question, that's why the Agency doesn't want this getting out. Not until they can figure out how to cure the virus without killing us for good, or until they can figure out how to keep people well-fed and not monster-like. I'm afraid Frank doesn't see it as monster-like and he wants to live freely now, embracing his new nature."

Rachel props herself up on her elbow and faces me.

"But you just said you don't see Frank much, so why do you think he feels this way?" I say.

"Because last night he said 'I am not a monster! This is my new nature, I want to embrace it!' and he waved his fist in the air like this." Rachel waves her fist about like a frustrated old scientist emphasizing his point.

"Well, that will do it," I state the obvious.

"Yeah. After you dropped me off last night I went into the den and found Mom, Dad, Mark and Frank having a discussion. When I walked in they all looked at me, very solemn expressions. I apologized for interrupting and turned to leave, but Frank called me back and asked 'where have you been?' which I thought was odd coming from him instead of my parents," Rachel says.

"Yeah. Did you tell him you were with me?" I ask.

"No, I told him I was out. And then Mom said I was with a new friend from school. To which Frank seemed to get concerned and started asking questions about you, like where you're from and stuff. Apparently they had been talking about the new guys at work with Dad and they had generated the idea that there were spies coming to make sure we haven't let out the secret. Frank assumed they'd send someone to the school to check on me since I'm the one they trust the least. Obviously with you just moving in you fit the profile," she says.

"Makes sense. Do they want to meet me? To try to find out?" I ask.

"Frank said I should invite you over right away, but Mom and Dad were against that. They have been against my having any friends over, ever. They're afraid of infecting anyone, at least as much as they're afraid of me telling anyone the secret. They know they can't stop me from that though, since they can't spend every minute of every day with me. They do trust me with the secret, but are worried about infecting others. I've never understood why they think me going to school is okay but having people over is not.

"Besides, I've already done high school. I was seventeen when I reanimated, so I'll be seventeen forever, essentially. I was almost through senior year. They had me come here as a sophomore to buy some time before dealing with the idea of me going to college or something."

"I hadn't thought about that, you said your cells don't really change, so you don't age. You are nineteen then, in normal years?" I'm dating a college girl, almost, that's rad.

"Yes."

"Well, you don't look a day over seventeen," I say.

Rachel slides off her elbow to rest on her back again.

"Yup. Thanks."

Some clouds pass by overhead and we watch them in silence.

"What's the plan then?" I ask.

"For what?"

"For us. Should I come to your house and meet everyone so they can determine if I'm a threat or not? What's the alternative? Let them worry and try to stop you and I from seeing each other? I've read 'Romeo and Juliet,' I've seen *West Side Story*, that path never ends well. I don't like the wait and see plan."

"Well, I'm already dead, but.... maybe we shouldn't hang out. I have the potential to give you a virus that can kill you and turn you into a monster. I have the potential to kill you and eat your brain if I turn into a monster. I shouldn't have befriended you. I really shouldn't have told you any of this. It was selfish of me."

Rachel sits up and slides off the car. Unsure of what I am hearing from her, I stay put and wait to see where she is going to go, which turns out to be the desert. She's walking away from the car and the road.

"Rachel, where are you going?" I shout.

"Away. I'm just going to go away," she yells without turning around.

I jump off the car and run to catch up with her.

"You can't just walk away from me like that. I know the secret; you aren't alone in this anymore. You aren't going to give me the virus, if it was that dangerous they wouldn't let you go to school. And I'm pretty sure you can't kill me, even if you were craving my sweet brain.

You said you'd be all weak and stuff if it got to that point, anyway."

As I come up next to Rachel, I suddenly find myself lying face down in the dirt with my arms folded behind me and Rachel kneeling on my back.

"You can't take me. I'm not super strong, but my body is strong enough, stronger than I ever was before. And though I may become weak if I'm hungry for brains, the weakness is more of a lethargic thing, not a strength thing. That first week after transitioning it was both, but now it's more a lethargy thing. I'd be slow, but I could still overpower you." Having made her point, Rachel stands up and helps me to my feet. She brushes the dirt from my shirt and apologizes.

"No problem. The example was much more effective than just telling me. I probably wouldn't have really believed you anyway. Now I do," I say.

Only my ego is bruised. Well, that, and possibly my spleen.

"We do pose a threat, and I think maybe the Agency is growing weary of that. I think they have determined that they can't reverse this thing and it's either write us off as a failed experiment or risk an outbreak. I don't think they want the outbreak. Frank, on the other hand, might want the outbreak, or at any rate, he doesn't want to be written off, which in this case means executed," Rachel explains.

"I assumed that's what you meant," I say.

"Yeah."

I ask, "So do you think Frank will try to *write* the rest of you off and get out of town before the Agency shows up? Will it be doctors in lab coats or military assassins?"

"What?"

"When the Agency comes for you," I clarify.

"Who knows. They might try to stage it to look like an accident. Burn the house down or something. Maybe they'll tell us they made a breakthrough and fly us back to Atlanta, and then once they have us in the lab they'll make their move then. That's how my mom thinks it will happen. The Agency has a team for handling things like this, all top secret," Rachel says.

"What does your dad think about all of this? You haven't mentioned him much at all."

"Dad is quiet most of the time. He handles the business stuff that he needs to in order to maintain the cover story, but otherwise he doesn't say much in regards to our 'condition.' He used to work for the...he had an exciting job, and I think he misses it."

"That's too bad," I say.

I notice she stopped herself before saying where her dad used to work. That's curious, but I'll save it for later, I don't think now is the time to pry into things. She's being so forthright with everything I'll let her decide what is best to discuss right now.

I go on, "So what do we do? If the Agency is going to come kill you all, can we stop that? If *Frank* is going to kill you all, can we stop *that*? I'm not excited about either of those possibilities. Especially if in either scenario I end up dead as well."

"See, I never should have brought you into this, now you are at risk. I was just so tired of being alone, and thought that being an outsider to this place you and I would be able to connect easily, and we did, we have, and I'm glad, but now I feel bad about putting you in danger."

"Well, what's done is done." I try to be reassuring, but come across as simply fatalistic.

"I don't know how to get you out of this danger, unless..." Rachel turns back towards the car.

"Unless what?" I ask, my curiosity peaking.

"Unless we make you a zombie, too," she says. My curiosity vanishes.

"Well, from what you've described so far I don't think it's all that unappealing, but just the same, I guess I prefer to stay living. No offense," I explain.

"None taken, it's not like I'm asking you to just change religions or something, I'm asking you to die."

"Well when you put it that way..." I trail off for effect. "How would that help, anyway? I don't see the connection. Would Frank be less insane if more people were zombies? Wouldn't the Agency just want to eliminate me as well in that scenario?"

"I guess so, but then I wouldn't have to be worried about keeping it secret that I told you the secret, because you'd be one of us," Rachel says.

"Yeah, that doesn't make any sense, really, when you really consider things," I say and pat her on the shoulder.

"Careful with the condescending mannerisms, buddy, or I'll turn you into a zombie." Rachel's threat sounds flat and defeated. I take it as a sign that we should change the conversation and the venue. No one wants to dwell on the subject of their murder and transformation into a brain-eating monster.

"How about we head back into town. We can get slushies instead of milkshakes. Maybe on Saturday we can head out of town and find a real milkshake vendor?" I offer.

"Alright. Let's get slushies. I don't think my parents would let me go out of town with you. Not until they figure out whether or not you are with the Agency. Maybe I can talk them into letting you come over for dinner before then. Since we don't eat dinner...in a traditional manner, it might take some work to put on that type of show. And they'll want to do things traditionally so as not to arouse your suspicions."

"If they only knew I have no suspicions."

"If only," she says as she takes my hand in hers. "I'm sorry I brought you into this. I'm sorry I was interested in you. If I just would have ignored you in gym the other day none of this would have happened. But I didn't ignore you, and if I didn't tell you this then you'd think the same things that Trent and the rest think about me. I just didn't want to have that happen all over again. I wish things were different, I really do."

"You wish you were alive, like the other girls?" I ask. Hoping my sarcasm will cheer her up a bit.

"That or I wish you were dead. I could go either way at this point." She takes the bait.

We walk back to the car, hand in hand, trying not to stir up too much of a dust storm in the dry air. I hear a motor and look down the road towards town. There's a car coming, fast. It starts to slow as it gets closer. Rachel gasps and drops my hand when she sees it.

"What is it? Or who is it?" I ask. She looks terrified, but only for a moment.

"It's one of our cars. I think it's Frank," she says as the car pulls up alongside mine.

We are still walking when the car stops and the passenger window goes down. We stop on the passenger side of my car. Looking over the hood and through the open window of the other car I find myself staring into the bifocal covered eyes from earlier today. It is Frank and he isn't smiling.

"Ah, Rachel, and…Eric, is it?" he says.

"Yes, Eric." I confirm. "Hi…Frank?" I pretend like I'm struggling to recall his name, although I of course know his name just as well as he knows mine, but since he pretended I figure I should pretend as well.

"I saw the car stopped and wondered if the driver was in need of assistance, I didn't expect to find the two of you." From the inflection in his voice it sounds like the surprise isn't so much that it is us, but that it is the two of us together.

Rachel says, "Where are you headed, Frank? You don't usually get out of town much." She is on the offensive. Her face looks afraid, but her voice remains steady. Another result of low blood flow, I assume, the fight or flight response doesn't lead to constricted vocal cords. Another side effect that isn't so bad, at least not on the surface.

"Well, I thought I saw a stranded motorist who may have needed my assistance," he says calmly, and slowly drifts his gaze from me to Rachel. I notice he didn't answer the question.

"But how did you know there might have been a stranded motorist out here?" Rachel isn't pulling any punches.

"I was just out for a drive, Rachel, what were the two of you doing out here in the desert? I noticed you two were walking back to the car." Frank is taking on the challenge.

I try to derail the battle that seems to be starting, "I'm having a difficult time adjusting to Cranston, specifically the summer weather during what should be winter. We stopped so I could walk around and Rachel could be my talk-therapist." Maybe I can convince Frank that I'm not a special agent intent on eliminating him. "My family just moved here from Chicago last week. It's quite the culture shock."

"Chicago, eh? You don't say? Yes, I can imagine that's a shift in lifestyle," Frank says.

"Well, we are headed back to town now, so I guess I'll see you later, Frank." Rachel, mostly hidden from

Never Trust a Zombie

Frank's view by my car, nudges me with her elbow. I take the hint.

"Right. Thanks for stopping to check on us, Frank, but we are fine. I hope you have a nice drive." I open Rachel's door for her and wait for her to get into the car before closing it. She doesn't say anything else to Frank.

"Yes, I expect it will be very nice. You two behave yourselves now." Frank gives me a cold hard look and then smiles slightly.

I nod to Frank and walk around the back of the car to the driver side. His car continues to idle in place until I am in the driver's seat. Finally, I look up at him and he looks forward and drives off slowly. I start the car, look over my shoulder, and pull a U-turn to head back to town. Texas is pretty flat, and this road is straight, so it is a good while before Frank's car is barely visible in my rear view mirror. Just as I am about to lose sight of him I think his brake lights come on.

"What do you make of that?" I ask Rachel.

"I don't know. He really hasn't left town in a really long time. I suppose he was trying to find me. To find us. The only question then is whether he took it upon himself to do so or if he is working in conjunction with the Agency. If not for Mom's suspicions of Frank I would have thought she sent him out to spy on us, but I'm pretty sure she is now more suspicious of Frank than she is of me."

"But unless he was there with your mom when you called her, or she told him afterwards, he wouldn't have known you weren't home or weren't coming home right away," I suggest.

"Good point. So Mom is involved somehow. Maybe Frank is making his move, whatever that is going to be, and he's trying to track me down to get us all at the same time. Maybe I should go home now," Rachel says.

"Bring me with you. I'm in this now. Maybe whatever it is Frank wants to do we can divert it by telling everyone that I know about this stuff. That's got to change his plans, even if it's just to add me to his hit list."

Rachel looks at me with an intensity I don't think I've ever experienced before. Thankfully I don't have to experience the fullness of it as I'm trying to keep my eyes on the road.

"You're right, Eric. Let's tell them I told you and see what happens. At least it should bring Frank's agenda out into the open and we can deal with it. Besides, we aren't monsters; we just have a different diet and a deadly virus. Why shouldn't we get to live normal lives?"

"Right," I agree.

"I guess the worst that can happen is that we'll all die. They'll kill you to keep you quiet and they'll kill me for telling, which will mean my parents will likely be killed also, because they wouldn't let anyone kill me for that. But I've already died once, so I'm not really concerned about that; of course it might not be on top of your list of things to do in the near future."

"I live life on the edge, one day at a time, come what may!" What am I saying? I don't want to die tonight!

"You, sir, are either brave or stupid," Rachel says with a smile. "I like it."

I reach over to hold her hand, and she lets me. We drive the next few miles to her house in silence. Maybe we should have come up with a plan for breaking the news, but instead we just enjoyed the silence.

10. Suburban Home

A man I don't recognize is leaning against the front of the house when we pull into the driveway.

"That's my dad," Rachel says.

"He looks like a proper cowboy," I observe. He is wearing boots, jeans, shirt and hat all straight out of a Western; he's a cowboy right down to the way he holds his cigarette.

As though she's reading my mind, Rachel says, "Dad didn't smoke before, but he figured since it doesn't matter now, health-wise, he'd pick it up as part of his image. He grew up watching cowboy movies and stuff."

I'm suddenly blinded by the science of it all. "Does he get the high from the nicotine? If your brain still operates at a normal level is it affected by drugs?" I ask.

"You know, I've never asked him and I don't recall him ever saying anything about that. He just said it went with the image. I've never tried it. One time I tried getting drunk, early on in my life as a zombie. It didn't work. I expect the same would be true for nicotine. I know Tylenol doesn't do anything for me. Not that I really need it, pain isn't the same as it used to be before the virus."

"Interesting." I park the car on the side of the driveway. Rachel's dad doesn't move except to take a drag on the cigarette.

"Are you ready? This is the point of no return. Either we get my parents together and tell them I told you or we don't. We can just play off this visit as me wanting to introduce you to them and then after you leave I can discuss Frank with them. Do you want to play it safe and not tell them I told you?" Rachel seems nervous.

"Let's tell them," I say.

I don't think this is all real to me yet. There is a part of my brain that's saying she's playing a prank on me. I'm pretty sure my subconscious won't fight it anymore if I hear it from her parents. This doesn't seem like the kind of prank most parents would keep up with, or be interested in. I think if we just get it out there then maybe I'll be able to fully accept it.

Maybe then I'll be able to accept that the girl I'm crushing on has a virus that makes her a zombie. That's what I'm hoping for. What a strange thing.

"Okay!" Rachel says as she opens her door.

We both get out of the car. Rachel cheerily greets her dad, who comes to life from his Marlboro man pose and greets her back, just as cheerily. He waits for Rachel to introduce me before he acknowledges my presence.

"Dad, this is my friend, Eric Sterling, the one who just moved in. I wanted to bring him by to meet you. He met Mom yesterday at school," Rachel says.

Rachel's dad diverts his path in walking towards us in order to meet me at the front of the car as I walk around. We shake hands.

He says, "My name is Tom Sutton. Nice to meet you, Eric."

"Good to meet you, Mr. Sutton," I say.

"Dad, is Mom around? I want to talk to you both about something," Rachel says.

Mr. Sutton looks at Rachel, then at me, and then back at Rachel. Looking more like a cowboy than ever, he squints and rubs the back of his neck while speaking. "Yes, she's just inside; do you want me to call her out here?"

"Let's all go inside," Rachel says. Again, Mr. Sutton looks at me and then back to Rachel.

"Alright." Mr. Sutton takes a final drag on his cigarette before dropping it to the loose gravel and packed dirt of the driveway and then grinding it in with the heel of his boot.

"I don't know why you picked up smoking, Dad, it's not a healthy hobby," Rachel says.

"Hmmph." That's all he says about it. I smile covertly. Rachel's dad is cool, for a zombie smoker, I mean.

I follow Rachel and her dad into the house. Dr. Sutton is sitting on the sofa with the television on a news channel. She doesn't look up at us right away, but I assume she must've picked up on our group in her periphery as her eyes snap toward us. Her gaze rests upon me. Initially her face suggests surprise, perhaps alarm, but she quickly forces a smile; however, not fast enough to conceal her initial reaction.

"Hello, Eric, I didn't know you were coming over." At saying this she looks at Rachel with one eyebrow raised in question. Next she looks at Mr. Sutton and both eyebrows rise in what I assume to be an even stronger question.

"Hi Dr. Sutton," I decide to let Rachel take charge here. I'm not going to take the lead on saying anything. I'm just here for the show. I'm hit by the realization that I just entered a house of zombies in the middle of

Nowheresville, TX, without anyone else knowing where I am. Rachel's mom turns off the TV and stands up.

"Well, come on in everyone, no need to stand in the entrance like that," Dr. Sutton says as she waves us all in.

Dutifully Mr. Sutton takes up the recliner as Rachel and I sit on a sofa across from where her mom is. Mr. Sutton kicks the foot rest up on the chair and settles in. If we have time later I'm going to see if he can teach me to mosey. If anyone knows how it's going to be this guy.

Rachel starts the conversation, ending the awkward silence and pained expression of keeping up social politeness on her mother's face. "Mom, I need to tell you and Dad something. You will likely be mad, but please hear me out."

Dr. Sutton immediately looks at me and that initial look of surprise appears again, but this time the alarm I thought I saw at first is gone. I look at the floor.

"I told Eric about us," Rachel says, cutting right to the heart of the matter.

I look up in time to see Dr. Sutton's expression relax. The surprise is gone, and although she isn't smiling, she looks content. Mr. Sutton doesn't stir at all. He remains reclined in the chair, feet up, hat resting on a knee, hands folded on his chest, and his eyes focused on the ceiling, as far as I can tell. Now the doctor smiles and squints briefly, but the smile is insincere.

"What do you mean *about us*,' Rachel?" she asks.

"I mean I told him about Atlanta, the CDC, our virus, why we are living in Texas, our fears about Frank and all that's in between." Rachel maintains a very even composure while saying this. Not surprisingly, I feel my anxiety level increase and with it the brightness of red in my cheeks.

Rachel's parents both look at me, then back at her, and then back at me again. Dr. Sutton asks me, "What did Rachel say about our virus?"

I think the real question she wants to ask is *"do you think we are zombies?"* I follow Rachel's lead and cut right to the thick of it.

"She told me that you have some type of virus that has reanimated your bodies. That you are all dead and the virus is living in your bodies. She said you are zombies," I explain.

Tom Sutton has a laugh like a carnival. Upon hearing the word "zombies" he explodes in a booming laugh, causing his whole body to shake, and consequently the chair he is resting on as well. Arlene Sutton isn't as amused by my response, but she isn't so caught up in the severity of the conversation as to ignore her husband's boisterousness.

With a little smile, Dr. Sutton reaches over and slaps her husband's foot. "Tom, it isn't funny." She says while trying not to laugh as well, though presumably more at her husband than at the shocking revelation she just received of her daughter's failure to keep the family secret.

"Eric," Dr. Sutton begins, with one last sidelong glance at her husband who is attempting to control his laughing fit, "Rachel wasn't supposed to tell you about that. I'm sure she has told you that she wasn't supposed to tell you about it. I've planned for a time like this, in case Rachel did tell someone. I know it isn't easy for her." Now looking to Rachel, she continues, "It isn't about not trusting you, it's just that I figured if I were in your place I wouldn't be able to keep this hidden forever myself. I'm disappointed in the consequences that may follow, but not in you."

She says she is disappointed, but she doesn't sound disappointed at all. Yesterday she seemed pretty relaxed and jovial, but even with that type of personality I would expect a more severe reaction to what is happening right now. Something is off.

"Thanks, Mom. I am sorry for telling him, but I had to," Rachel says.

"I understand." Dr. Sutton returns her attention to me. "As I was saying, I had planned for this situation, and expected that I would flat out lie about it and use some virologist jargon to convince whoever the person was that Rachel was embellishing a story to make it sound *cool*. I know that would likely put me in a bad spot with her, but I always thought it'd be easier to have that discussion with her later than to deal with the reality of someone finding out our secret. But sometimes you just don't know what the right thing to do is until you are in the middle of it, and now that we are in the middle of it, I don't think that plan would be for the best."

Yeah, this is suspicious to me. These people have just had their whole world turned upside down again, by their daughter this time, and they are barely acting anxious about it. Either I'm really a non-threatening person or they don't get worked up about things very easily, or who knows what. I can't help but think that if I were a real life movie monster and my secret identity was revealed I'd be a little more irate. Even if I understood the situation, I think I'd still at least be angry at Rachel for a few minutes. But maybe being a make believe monster in real life gives you a more open mind about accepting life altering information. Perhaps that's another benefit to becoming a zombie.

After a sufficient pause, enough for me to think about everything, Dr. Sutton finishes her explanation, "So, yes, Eric, we are zombies, but not like in the movies, not exactly. Obviously it wasn't something you could tell just from looking at us or talking with us. I hope you understand the importance of keeping this secret."

"Right, I had no idea until Rachel told me, even then I think I was still suspicious of it until now, hearing it from you, too. But I don't understand the need for secrecy. I mean, I guess I can see how you wouldn't want everyone knowing about it and hounding you. This way you get to live normally, mostly. But the fact that you can live mostly normally makes it seem like you should be able to announce this thing to the world and it'd be okay," I say.

The Suttons look at one another. I look at Rachel, who smiles and then takes hold of my hand. Mr. Sutton slides his chair upright and stands up, squaring his hat back on top of his head. He starts for the front door.

Dr. Sutton says, "Eric, you are free to do what you want and tell who you wish about us, but we hope that you will keep our secret safe for us. It makes it difficult for us that Rachel told you, but it is understandable. I'm glad that you appreciate her friendship enough to be so understanding yourself."

Mr. Sutton is now behind me, by the front door. I thought maybe he was going outside to smoke, but instead of a door opening, I hear a strange thud. A split second later I feel the effect of that thud. Unsure of what caused it, I realize that whatever it was it was something solid colliding with the back of my head. For a few seconds more my head reels and I see Dr. Sutton standing up and walking towards me. Someone says something, but I can't distinguish who or what. My final awareness is Rachel's face, her eyes darting from me to her mom and back to me. Her mouth opens, but I don't hear anything. She leans towards me, reaching with outstretched arms, and then darkness.

11. Creep (clean)

I don't know where I am, or who I am, for that matter. There's no telling what the time is. My body hurts. All of it. The room is cool, I think, but my temperature seems to be fluctuating, so I don't really know. It is dark; there's a window in front of me, but no light coming through it. I'm lying on my side on a bed. I manage to roll over and find the bed is flush with a wall. I roll and put the wall to my back again. The wall in front of me has the one window and nothing else. The wall at the head of the bed is blank; opposite that wall is the door to the room, but again, nothing else on that wall either. It is an empty room. It is a dark, cool, empty room, with just this bed and just me on this bed.

It is difficult to focus on the attributes of the room while I'm in such agony, but I'm curious about where I am. My head feels swollen and every muscle in my body is alternating between aches and spasms. I must have a fever, maybe I caught the flu? I don't think I'm at home, though, and this doesn't look like a hospital. I fade out of consciousness several times, each time coming back to the point I left off, wondering where I am and what is wrong with me. I'm unable to capture an image of who I am, but feel like I should be someone and need to find out who.

I just can't do it.

Slowly I begin to notice there is some light in the room. It's very dim, emanating from a small lamp set on the floor next to the head of the bed.

In my confusion I focus on the light. I know what light is, it allows me to see. Seeing is good, and I become aware that I am able to do it. This seems significant, but I don't know why it should. Haven't I always been able to see? I'm not a baby, the realization of this burns into my consciousness; I am not new, I know I've seen before, but the process feels new.

An acrid smell begins to take hold of my awareness. It is repulsive, whatever it is. There is something sickly familiar about it, but still I am unable to place it in my memory. I try to lift myself from the bed, but it hurts and I find myself sapped of strength. I was able to roll earlier, so I try rolling towards the edge of the bed and am able to catch a glimpse of the lamp and the floor beneath me. I think I've found the source of the repugnant odor. Someone, presumably me, has vomited. If it *was* me I'm glad I don't remember it, I hate vomiting. Actually, I do hope it was me, I don't think I could handle lying this close to someone else's vomit.

There's a tingling sensation in my brain, it feels good and is a welcomed relief under the circumstances. I think it was the realization that I don't like vomit that caused the sensation. This is something about who I am, and I've become aware of it. It feels good. I don't like vomit; I don't like doing it, and I really don't like smelling it. I flop onto my back on the bed and look up at the ceiling. It is blank.

I can see and I can smell. Clearly I can feel, as witnessed by the extreme pains pulsing through my body. What is that other one? Taste? Yes, taste. I try to taste and find my mouth extremely dry and difficult to open.

Paul Brodie

Suddenly a grating pain shoots down my throat and my eyes widen. All I can taste is pain.

But pain isn't a flavor. Something's still not right in the taste sensation. I have another moment of self-realization and decide that given the circumstances it is probably best if I ignore the sense of taste for a little while. I can try to figure out hearing.

As though working my way through a preflight checklist, I work through my senses, being driven on this path subconsciously I suppose. It is all I can do to be aware of what is going on inside of my own body. I am inside of my own body, but unaware of it. This is a very frightening realization. I must be dreaming. I know what dreams are; they are thoughts in the brain when you are asleep. Sometimes when I'm sick with a fever I have very strange dreams. I must have a fever, but I don't remember getting sick, or much of anything else, really.

Unable to grasp any specifics on how I got to this point, I return to focusing on hearing. I realize that I've been able to hear ever since I first started regaining consciousness and became aware of the room I'm in. All I've heard is a monotone humming sound, punctuated by rasping.

It's me! I'm making those sounds. I'm groaning in pain and breathing unevenly as a result. An image is recalled and fills the void inside my mind. I see myself sick, in a bed in a different room, surrounded by things, familiar things, watching television. It is from another time when I was sick, and I was moaning and groaning and lying in bed writhing in pain. I remember that time; I had a very high temperature from something that wreaked havoc on my stomach. I must be experiencing the same thing now. The same feelings of restlessness and utter physical exhaustion that I felt then I feel now.

But when did I get sick? And where am I? I'm not in the same room now as I was in that memory. I've moved. That's right, my family moved recently. But I don't think this is my new room. There aren't any things here. This doesn't seem like a hospital, either, so where else would I be if I'm really sick? My family moved. I'm new here. I've met new people. Memories are beginning to flow back as images, captures of moments, but without recognition of details or identities. I need to remember who I am! My frustration swells, coincidently so does my pain, and once again I feel myself slipping into darkness.

***

The room is light, much lighter than what the dim lamp was providing before. My eyes hurt, but I force them open. The tiny muscles in my eyes work to close my pupils as the bright light activates the receptor cells and floods my optic nerve with information. It is too much, too fast, and all I can sense is whiteness. After a few moments of squinting and blinking I begin to notice shapes and shades again. The white, washed out blur diminishes to one brilliant point of light, which I make out to be the window. The lamp is off now.

It must be daytime. As soon as I realize this I also realize the full pain sensation in my body, making it feel too heavy for me to support, even while lying flat on the bed. I test my other senses; the repulsive odor from before is gone, in its place is the pine scented aroma of cleaning liquid. There is no sound other than the bed spring beneath the mattress creaking as I move slightly. My mouth, still parched, tastes like rusty metal. With no recollection of having ever eaten rusty metal, I'm not sure how I come up with that flavor signature, but that's what it is. I still don't know who I am.

"Eric?" a voice whispers. It is a soft, pleasant voice, and I want to hear it again. Not recognizing it, or the meaning of what it said, and not being able to respond or move very much, it isn't long before I get to hear it again.

"Eric? Are you awake? Can you hear me?" This time I can recognize the voice as being female, but it's still difficult to identify specifically.

I try to respond, but a weird groan is all that comes out. I don't even recognize it as my own voice. Not that I know what my voice should sound like, just that I didn't realize the sound I heard was emanating from my throat.

The girl stands up from a chair near the foot of the bed and takes a few steps closer before sitting down at my side and taking my hand in hers. The movement of the bed and the touch of someone else's hands on my own are excruciatingly painful and I almost slip into blackness again, instead I simply scream, or attempt to, but all that comes out is a high pitched squeal.

My visitor laughs at me and then returns my hands to my abdomen and rests one of her own hands gently on my forehead, which also hurts more than it should.

"I see the fever hasn't broken yet. You can't speak either, huh?" she asks.

Whoever this is, she seems to know me, but I can't place her at the moment. Her skin is pale; it stands out against her dark hair and green eyes.

Unable to speak, and not wanting to recreate that little squeal, I do my best to shake my head in answer to her question. But I understood what she asked, so it's a step in the right direction.

"That's fine. I'm sure all you have right now are questions. I'd like to explain things to you, if you feel up to it. Do you want me to talk?"

She seems kind, and I like hearing her voice. If nothing else it does distract me from the pain, and it sounds like she can tell me who I am and why I'm here, wherever it is that I am. I nod.

"Okay," she says.

She stands up and walks towards the window. I relax and stare at the ceiling, hoping the pain will fully subside from a moment ago when she touched me.

"I don't know what you remember right now, Eric, but I guess our history doesn't go so far back that I can't just recount the whole of it right now." She sighs, and a minute or so passes before she continues. Whatever she is about to tell me must be difficult for her.

"I hope you can forgive me someday for all of this. I honestly didn't expect it to turn out the way it has. I know you have issues of your own right now, but things are crazy for me too."

She pauses again, I guess to compose her thoughts. I'm not moving anything except my eyes, following the pacing figure of the girl who seems to have a lot to say, but isn't sure how to say it. Even lying perfectly still is rather painful at the moment.

"I've been waiting for you to wake up. I've wanted to talk to you and explain that I didn't know this was going to happen, and ask you to forgive me. I figure you won't understand yet, but I didn't think I'd be having this much trouble explaining it. Let me just give you the facts and the timeline. Two days ago, after school, you and I went for a drive and then I brought you to my house to meet my parents and tell them that I told you about our virus. Do you remember that?"

She pauses, waiting for my response; honestly, I don't know what she is talking about. I hear the words, but only some of them mean anything to me. It's obvious she and I know each other, but it is still all very foggy about the specifics. When I don't respond she walks over and looks me in the eye. I try to shrug to convey my confusion. She seems to get the message, nods, and walks back towards the window.

"You are still muddled. I guess I'll just keep talking, this can be my practice run, and then we can go over it again later. I don't have anything else to do, and clearly you don't either." She turns back to face me, smiling, but when my expression remains exactly the same, her smile melts into a frown.

She says, "I'm sorry, I don't mean to make light of the situation, just using humor as a coping mechanism. So, three days ago I told you that my family contracted a virus that made us all zombies. After we were infected with the virus the CDC moved us here to live as normal a life as we could…as zombies.

"It was all supposed to be a secret. That was the number one rule I was given, and I broke that rule when I told you about us. Well, after I told you, that night I interrupted a discussion between my parents and the other two scientists who live here, Frank and Mark. Frank was concerned that you were a secret agent from the Agency spying on us. You know, to see if we've told our secret or infected anyone else or something like that. Mom had told them all about you when she got home from school after meeting you. I didn't tell them I told you about us, but became extremely nervous and afraid of what they were saying since I had told you.

"Well, like I told you on Wednesday, Frank wanted to bring you here to find out if you were an agent. My mom didn't think that was necessary, as she had met you and didn't think you were an agent. Frank got angry and left. Later that evening my mom came to my room and explained that she thinks Frank is up to something with the Agency and we might be in danger here. All this time we thought we were safely hidden, but now Mom thinks Frank has been working with someone in the Agency in planning an outbreak of the virus.

"I guess I found my words now, huh? Are you getting any of this?" She looks at me, her face all scrunched up, searching my face for understanding. I'm only catching parts of it, but I don't want her to stop talking, so I nod slightly in hopes of encouraging her to keep it up.

"Okay," she says, mixed with a slight laugh. "You don't look like you are following me, but if you nod so, I'll continue."

I nod again.

"Mom told me that she was concerned that Frank might be about to start spreading the virus in the community, or that someone from the CDC would be coming here, or something. Clearly I don't know what's going on, but Mom was concerned and asked me how I felt. I told her I find the idea of spreading the virus around in public kind of freaky. She told me not to worry too much, that she'd figure something out, but that we might need to leave town soon.

"It was hard not to worry when Frank was at the school Wednesday morning. When I said he never leaves the house, I meant it. That was the first time I saw him out. I kept my worry and suspicion under control all day until, well, you were there after school when we discussed it all. I really thought bringing you here and telling them that you knew about everything would help. I guess I was wrong.

"Mom told me they had to do this to you because we are leaving. They said if I never mentioned it to you then they could have left you alone, but since you knew you couldn't be left behind. If I had waited one more day before telling you..."

She trails off and walks back to the window. She stands looking out for a long while. I lie motionless. I still don't know what she's talking about, but I caught the part where she said "they had to do this to you."

Whatever it is that's wrong with me, they did it to me. But I don't really know who they are yet. I wish I could talk. I have so many questions. Who am I? Who is this girl? What did they do to me? Who are they?

"I guess you aren't ready for conversation yet. I'll come back later; hopefully you'll be further along. We are getting ready to leave. Frank never came back after we saw him the other night. Mom says that's probably bad. I'm really sorry, Eric. I'm sorry this is happening. I really hope you won't hate me and my family. My parents did what they thought they had to. I don't agree with it, but I guess I do understand it. It won't be so bad, after another day or two and the virus takes over fully. Until then it will be awful for you. Just relax as much as you can. You won't be able to sleep, but relax, and I'll be back to see you in a little while."

With that she turns and leaves, closing the door gently behind her. I'm left to try and make sense of what I've just been told. I'll start with what I know: I'm in terrible pain, apparently from something done to me by someone I know; I'm at a friend's house. I guess that's it. Short recap, I don't know much at all. What did she say at the end? A virus? They gave me a virus?

Whoever the girl is, she seems nice enough. Of course, she also admitted to giving me a virus of some kind. A virus that is making me sicker than I've ever been, at least, as far as I can remember, which doesn't seem to be very far. She said I won't be sleeping. How does she know that?

***

Time passes slowly, but it does pass. The girl was right, I'm not sleeping. I just keep picturing her and trying to make sense of what she told me. Her pale face and dark hair are burned into my mind. She isn't gorgeous, but she is attractive. I wonder if she's my girlfriend. I sure hope she isn't my sister. I can't even recall my family at all! But at the thought of family I picture two people and instantly recognize them as mom and dad. That's it, I don't have any siblings. I know it now, and for the moment the pale faced girl is out of my mind. I see Mom and Dad; I see them through my own eyes, in different settings and at different times. First they look young, and then they look older. I suppose I'm flashing through memories. I hear a name again, my parents are saying it over and over. Eric. The pale girl said Eric as well. I wasn't able to comprehend much of what she was saying so I didn't know it was a name, but it's coming together now. My name is Eric.

Upon recognizing my own name it feels as though my consciousness is restored. I remember everything up to the moment I was hit in the head. I was hit in the head! I remember that now, but what I feel is way more than a head injury. The virus, she told me I had a virus. She! Her name is Rachel! Rachel was here, the pale faced girl, she was in this room with me and she told me something, but I didn't understand. I need her to come back now.

"Rachel!"

I try to yell, but it comes out as a hoarse whisper. I need some water. I need some air, I need to move! I try to sit up but the pain comes quickly and reminds me that something is seriously wrong with my body. I fall back on the bed and my head hits the pillow with a thump. I remember there was a loud thump that started all of this, followed by excruciating pain in my head, and subsequently everywhere else. My head throbs and I want to cry. I'm about to break down and sob, but the door to the room opens, distracting me from my emotion.

My eyes fix on the door. As soon as there is enough space cleared, Rachel sticks her head in and looks at me. She gives me a sad, sympathetic smile. The kind I might have really enjoyed seeing if the conditions were different. If I was just down with the flu, in my own bed, in my own house, and she had come to visit me, in that case I would be stoked, but here and now, I'm too confused and in too much pain.

"Hi, Eric, are you able to talk yet?" she asks softly.

Frustration is building inside of me again and I'm not even trying to subdue it. The worst part is that my thoughts are so jumbled I don't even know why it is I'm feeling so frustrated. I try to speak, but an affirming grunt is all I can muster. It's enough, she understands.

"Good. Do you remember anything from what I said before? About giving you the virus?"

The part about hitting me in the head and giving me a virus? Yeah, I remember that part. Of course, I can't speak, so I can't communicate this beyond simply nodding.

Wait! More memory pieces are coming together. They didn't just give me *a* virus, they gave me *their* virus. They made me a zombie!? My frustration takes a turn and focuses on Rachel. Still, I can't communicate this realization.

"Okay. You were deep in the transition before, so I don't think you understood much of what I was saying. Do you remember what happened before we came to my house on Wednesday?" Rachel closes the door and takes up a position sitting cross-legged on the end of the bed, near my feet, but not touching me. This relieves me, but I'm not sure why.

I nod again. I try to ask for some water, but all I get out are some squeaks and grunts before I fall into a coughing fit that leaves me painfully winded and throbbing all over.

"Would you like me to get you some water?" she asks.

I nod as fervently as I can.

"Okay, I'll go for some, but sadly it probably won't help you much. You are in the transition still, and it's just going to run its course. That's why we can't give you any pain killers either. It's brutal, I know, but all we can do is leave you to go through it. If there was anything I could do to make this easier or more comfortable for you... believe me when I say I would." She looks sincere, but the new realization that she and her family just killed me and turned me into a zombie leaves me feeling unfriendly towards her at the moment. "I'll get some water and be right back."

Rachel is off the bed and out the door quickly, leaving it slightly open behind her. I can smell food of some kind now, and hear muffled voices. That's a heavy door if it blocks all of that. I almost lose focus on the moment by being distracted by the physical capability of the door, but I manage to remain on task. The Suttons turned me into a zombie. They gave me a fatal virus. They are murderers. Rachel is a murderer? Why did she do this to me? Weren't we going to tell her family that I knew their secret and that I wasn't going to let it out?

I remember that we did tell them that. I remember thinking they were taking the news of their secret being exposed very well. Now I see that they took it too well. Was it staged? I wish I had understood what Rachel told me earlier. Maybe she was explaining what happened. Did she know this was going to happen to me when we came here to talk to her parents? Was it all an elaborate story to get me into the house where they could turn me into one of them?

If they wanted to eat my brain they would have done it and it'd be over with, but that wouldn't require any kind of back story. It was clear that I was crushing on Rachel; all she would have had to do was say "would you like to come to my house?" and I would have been there.

Man, I guess that's what actually happened, and now I'm a zombie! I need to find out what Rachel's involvement was in this mess.

I try not to let that sink in too much, and work over what I remember of what Rachel said. Wednesday. She said Wednesday as though it happened in the past, not today. That means I've been here for more than a day? Did she say how many days it has been? I can't remember. How long have I been in this agony? I look down and realize for the first time in all of this that I'm wearing hospital scrubs. I know I didn't come here wearing these. So many questions.

What about my parents? Did the Suttons call them and give them some story about where I am? Did they invite my parents over and kill them, too? Did my mom even know I was with Rachel? She might not have had any idea where I was, and if she eventually figured out I might have been with Rachel and somehow figured out how to contact the Suttons would it have been late enough for them to have cooked up a plausible alibi for Rachel and just dismissed my disappearance as a mystery to them?

Rachel is back with the water, and I am none too pleased with her. I try to start in with some of my questions, but am met once again with the dry coughing that leaves me pulsing with pain. Rachel smiles sadly and hands me the water when I stop shaking. I prop myself up on one elbow and gulp down the water, only to find that it doesn't help to relieve the pain and, in fact, burns a little as it passes through my esophagus. It does seem to restore some life to my mouth, however, keeping my tongue and cheeks from sticking to my teeth, if only momentarily.

"Does it help at all?" Rachel asks hopefully.

I croak out, "A little." My first intelligible uttered words in who knows how long.

"You can talk!" she says. At first I take offense at this, but then I realize that she doesn't seem to be operating under the same perspective as me right now. Rather than throw an angry glance at her I shrug and bobble my head about.

Rachel says, "And you can move! You are supporting your weight on that elbow pretty well. You seem to be progressing faster than Mom expected, although you probably have another day or two before you are up to strength according to her guess. But progress is progress."

Rachel's mom, I remember her, the kindly scientist who can't keep a straight face when trying to tease her daughter's friends. She has plotted a schedule for my monster morph. I think I'd like to talk with her soon.

"So do you remember coming here to the house and talking with my parents?" Rachel asks.

I nod again. I could probably say yes, but I'm not going to push it.

"Okay. I'll recap again. We told my parents that I told you about the virus. Unknown to me at the time, my parents were planning on us getting out of town because Frank is off his rocker, literally, the chair has been empty in the den since we saw him Wednesday night." She pauses and tries to fight a smile from breaking out on her face. "No good? Alright, I'll stick with the story and hold off on the jokes for a bit. You look pretty miserable and I don't know what I can do to alleviate your suffering. I hoped humor would do it. Anyway, my dad hit you with a board. He hit you hard, not enough to kill you, but enough to knock you out."

Yeah, wouldn't want to kill me before you can infect me with your killing virus. At least I can respond to her in my head. Even if she can't hear it, it will help me. But my face must have revealed my thought, even through my grimacing in response to the pain I'm still experiencing.

"Honestly, he wasn't trying to kill you with the board!" Rachel exclaims. "At least, that's what they told me."

I guess she misread my face. I don't care about his intent with the board, it doesn't matter if that was just to knock me out or not, the end result is that I'm dead. But I remain silent, this time only partly due to the pain; I'm primarily interested in the rest of her narrative.

Rachel exhales and pulls the chair from beyond the foot of the bed up closer to my head, and then sits down.

"So Dad hit you with the board, you went woozy and then passed out. Left a pretty good bruise, which might not really ever go away, come to think of it, but don't worry about that, it's hidden by your hair, mostly." Rachel pauses, and then continues. "I guess you don't need those kinds of details right now. Back to the story. You see, with Frank's actions raising some concerns for my mom they decided we need to leave this place.

"That's when you and I come in and say you know about us. Dad realized we couldn't just leave you behind knowing about us, so he hit you. Believe me, I gave them both a stern yelling at in response to it. Not that that helps any now. But it was a while before they got me to calm down and were able to explain things to me. Dad said he needed to buy time to figure out what to do with you. I don't know why he thought hitting you was the best thing, it's not like you were about to run out to the newspaper or something…"

Rachel stops her report. Her lips purse and her forehead scrunches up. She must be thinking. I'd like to ask her what about. She looks at me and I look back at her. Shaking her head, Rachel stands up, puts her hands into her pockets, and wanders over to the window, but then comes right back over and sits down again.

"I just took their explanation at face value, but now, in retrospect it doesn't make so much sense," Rachel says, and just leaves the thought hanging. I've been building up anger towards her, grouping her with her parents in the attack on me, but maybe she wasn't part of it after all. She continues her story, but more pensively.

"When I was asking Dad why he hit you, he said he needed time to figure out what to do with you in relation to our getting out of town. Mom suggested that we pass off your head injury as some kind of accident and then flat out deny any stories you might tell afterwards attributing them to concussion induced confusion. Dad didn't think that was going to work, so he suggested we give you the virus and take you with us. I protested, but Mom agreed with Dad and said that Frank was likely going to cause trouble for you if we didn't take you with us. It seemed like the best thing to do at the time. Now I'm not so sure."

Her family murdered me, but she didn't. I wish I knew what was going on. I wish I could talk more.

Rachel stands up and walks to the door. She stands for a moment, silent. Then grabs the door knob and pulls, but before she leaves the room she looks back at me.

"Things didn't go as planned, did they?"

I shake my head and try to smile, but the pain is too much and I black out again.

12. Say Anything (Else)

Hours have passed since my visit with Rachel. I don't know how many, but the light outside is dimming. I really don't know anything right now. I think Rachel said it is Friday, and we went to speak to her parents on Wednesday. Rachel and I only met on Monday. I've only been in Cranston for eight days! Time flies when you are transforming into a living monster.

Surprisingly the pain has subsided significantly. It happened gradually while I was lying here ruminating over my visit with Rachel. I didn't have the strength to get up or I would likely have pounded on the door or checked the window for a viable escape route. Without sufficient strength I was left to ponder my situation. Initially it was anger that fueled my thoughts and produced nothing but a list of pointy questions I was hoping to injure Dr. Sutton with. But those faded out of awareness as the pain subsided and new feelings emerged. I didn't even realize that the pain was going away until I had a sudden feeling of comfort. It was a warm feeling, similar to a high fever, but void of the associated pain and aches. I replayed the scenario Rachel had painted for me. I still didn't see the logic in turning me into a zombie, but I tried to make the best of it with a pros and cons list about my new life. This was fine for a few minutes until I remembered my parents and realized I have no idea what they are thinking or what they know about my disappearance for the past few days. My anger towards the Suttons returned, and if it hadn't been for another hour or so of time alone in this room, along with a new sensation in my brain, I might have lit into Dr. Sutton when she appeared with some food for me.

I am sitting on the bed when I hear the lock on the door click, followed by a quick knock, and then the door opens. Startled I swing my legs up and fall back onto the bed.

"Hi Eric, how are you feeling?" Dr. Sutton asks as though she is making the rounds in a hospital.

Though my anger has subsided significantly, I feel a surge of it return, and my sarcasm is in full supply. "Fine Doc, I've never felt so dead in all my life!"

Dr. Sutton smiles, but from amusement or disgust, I can't tell. "Are you hungry, Eric?"

The anger quickly subsides, unusually quickly, and I decide to cooperate. What do I have to gain from being stubborn in this situation?

"I don't feel very hungry, not like I would expect to after not eating anything for a few days, but I guess it's kind of like after having the flu and vomiting everything up for several days. You think you should eat, but your body remembers the pain of getting rid of the last things you ate and it hesitates." I answer.

"Well, I don't think I've ever read anything like that in a text book during medical school, but I understand what you are saying. And your body certainly did work to get rid of everything in it over the last few days. Mark has been wonderful in taking care of cleaning you up. Your clothes are downstairs. We had an idea of what to expect so we've been dressing you in scrubs since the beginning.

"Tell me this, rather than feeling hungry, do you feel a craving for something that you can't quite identify?" the doctor asks.

Who is Mark again? I need a program for this show. For the time being, I'll answer her question.

"Yeah, I have that. It's sort of like I'm anticipating something, but I don't know what. Like I'm waiting for Christmas, but I don't know if that's what I'm waiting for," I say.

"That's the effect of the virus telling your body you need to eat brain now. Interestingly it isn't so obvious at first that you know you need brain, but having experienced this all before I can tell you that's what it is. Of course, as Rachel has told you, we don't eat human brains. She mentioned you didn't agree that we should be calling ourselves vegetarian zombies, what did you recommend? Carnibulls?"

"Yes, or cownivores."

Dr. Sutton laughs. I wish I could've been this normal with Rachel earlier; her mother is the one I should be angry with but I'm carrying on like normal with her. Maybe it was just the pain. Maybe I really don't mind being a zombie. Or perhaps my solid gold good nature just can't be kept down for long.

"Well, however you want to define it, we don't eat human brains because we aren't monsters. We may technically define ourselves in a way that could be compared to the fantasy monster that is the zombie, but we aren't monsters and really aren't zombies in the Hollywood fashion at all. I could bore you with the technical details of why the virus needs the body to eat brain, but you won't understand it. Suffice it to say that cow brains are an adequate substitute. It is much more palatable; not to mention culturally acceptable in many countries, even in some areas of the U.S. The only downside is that cow brains don't satiate the craving as well as human brains, but as far as sustenance, there is hardly any noticeable difference. Before you start forming questions you may or may not be afraid to ask, I *am* speaking from personal experience."

Dr. Sutton's voice implies that this topic of conversation is now over with. I won't push it. Besides, I'm more concerned about my murder and my parents than I am about diet.

"So you brought me some cow brains then?" I ask.

"Yes." Dr. Sutton hands me the covered bowl she brought into the room with her. I sit up in the bed and remove the lid. The smell isn't altogether unappealing, though it is different from anything I'm familiar with. She produces a knife and fork from a pocket on her white lab coat and hands them to me. Next she produces a cloth napkin and hands it over.

"Well, you are moving quite well. Rachel reported you were moving and attempting to speak. I was surprised, you are transitioning very quickly."

I'm momentarily filled with that same rage from a few moments ago. "You sound pleased at that, I would have expected you to express some remorse over the spur of the moment murder of your daughter's friend." Hey! That was a good one! Let's see how Dr. Sutton handles it.

"Dig in, it is better when it is warm." That's all she says. I guess she learned how to keep a straight face. Being accused of murder probably has that effect on most people. She turns to leave, but I stop her with a question, going for broke on my offensive.

"What do my parents know about all of this?"

"Eat first, and then we'll discuss everything else. Don't get up right away after eating; give your body a few minutes. Then come downstairs and we'll all talk." She delivers this instruction matter-of-factly and leaves the room, but this time the door remains open.

The craving in my brain is louder now, presumably because the brain, or rather, my dinner, is right in front of me. I stick the fork into the bowl. My serving of brain looks like pan fried chunks of a mixture between fish and chicken. I'm not sure what they prepared it with, but honestly it doesn't taste that bad, but that might just be the virus speaking.

13. Comedown

It doesn't take me long to finish the brain. I'm surprised I'm not nauseated simply by the thought of it. Maybe an iron stomach is another benefit of being a zombie. Regardless, I eat it all and almost enjoy it. Following Dr. Sutton's orders, I lie on the bed for a few minutes after setting the empty bowl on the chair. I feel fine, but I'm not going to take the chance at standing up too soon. Of course, if I'm a zombie now, what does a little light-headedness matter? Will I get dizzy and fall over? I wonder what would happen if I break a bone. I need to get a notebook to write down all of these questions I have. Or, I should be enraged that someone just killed me and turned me into a living (sort of) monster. I really need to get a handle on my emotional response to this scenario. Anger or acceptance: which will it be?

I think it has been long enough of a wait now, it's not like I'm going swimming, I just need to walk down some steps. Still, I stand up slowly, with my hands out to my sides, ready to brace for impact should I topple. I stand without trouble. I feel fine. I decide to bring the brain bowl down with me. Just because I'm a monster doesn't mean I can forget my manners, even with the rage I feel over having been murdered.

Standing up is fine; however, walking proves to be a little bit of a challenge. I wobble a bit and my legs feel sore and jelly-like, just like after running the mile during gym class. It is dark out in the hallway so I pause for a moment at the door. The pause serves two purposes, it lets my eyes adjust a bit and rests my weak frame. To my surprise, my eyes adjust quickly. The only light seems to be what is spilling out of the room I'm leaving, but I can see just fine almost immediately, even beyond the stretch of the light. Are my eyes better now? Another question for the list. I'm not going to remember any of these.

I make my way to the stairs and find that they go down a bit and then turn around a corner. The stairs are steep and narrow; luckily there is a hand rail. I grab hold and descend into the darkness. The walls in the stairwell are like the walls in the room I occupied, just vertical wooden plank. It helps to remind me I'm on a ranch. At the bottom of the first set of stairs I turn the corner and find a similar stair case that looks like it leads down to a hallway. There is a door at the end of the stairs, and it is open providing more light. It is now like I'm in a different house, the floor is carpeted, the walls are painted a cool blue color and there is one picture hanging on every stretch of wall between doors. There are three doors on the right, only one on the left, and then a railing that leads to more stairs. I hadn't realized this was a three story house. Of course, I have died and reanimated since I last saw it from the outside.

The pictures are old, two look like they could be of the ranch pastures, or they could really be any open field. There are three photos of people, again, maybe they are Sutton ancestors, or maybe they are just old pictures that came with the house. I don't need to add these questions to my list, they aren't important, which means these are probably the only questions I'll remember to ask. As I reach the top of the next set of stairs I hear voices from below, but not clearly enough to decipher the words; I think there is a television on as well. The steps aren't carpeted, so my footsteps rattle loud enough to announce my approach. The voices hush.

From the bottom of the stairs I see down the hall the television that had been on a few days ago when I first entered this house. I get a strange déjà vu feeling, only not really déjà vu, more like the feeling I got when walking into Wrigley field in Chicago. I had only ever seen the stadium on television, but then there I was, walking through the entry way, coming out into the seats and seeing the field in person. It was something I knew but had never seen in person until that moment. That's how I feel now. Not that I'm entering a situation I've experienced before, but that I'm seeing something I've never seen in person before. Except I have seen it in person, that's the only way I've seen this room before. I saw it in person two days ago, and now I'm seeing it through reanimated eyes, no longer in person. Will I experience this feeling everywhere I go? I didn't feel it when I saw Rachel or her mom. Maybe I'm just feeling strange because I know that's the room where I was betrayed, lied to, and assaulted. That's certainly a possibility.

As I stand in contemplation, an old man turns into the hallway and jumps slightly at seeing me.

"Oh, you startled me, Eric. We haven't met properly yet," the man says as he offers me an outstretched hand. I shake his hand and he continues, "I'm Mark, I suppose you've heard my name by now. It is a pleasure to meet you."

"Hi, Mark. You've been changing my clothes and keeping me clean, I hear."

He chuckles a bit and avoids making eye contact.

"Ah, yes. That has been my responsibility," he says with a smile.

He doesn't say anything else, or move away. If he is waiting for an expression of gratitude, I don't think he's going to get it. I'll carry my used dishes down, but I'm not ready to thank anyone for turning me into a zombie. Not just yet.

Mark meets my eyes again and says, "Well, it is a tough transition. You seem to have made it well enough. Everyone is in the dining room, right through that door there."

The smile leaves Mark's round, drooping white-whiskered face as he points back towards the door he had come through. He reminds me of Mickey Rooney, my mom's favorite actor, at least when he was smiling he did. Mark makes his way past me and up the stairs. I enter the dining room.

Dr. Sutton smiles and stands up upon my arrival.

"Rachel, will you take Eric's dishes into the kitchen, please." Rachel complies with her mother's request. She doesn't make eye contact with me; her eyes stay fixed low through the dish handoff. Part of me seems to remember the crush I had on this pale girl, only a few days ago, but that part isn't as loud as the part of me that recognizes I'm in the same room as my murderers.

"Eric, how do you feel?" Dr. Sutton asks.

"Well, better than I would ever have expected for being dead and having just eaten cow brain," I reply.

"You know, cow brain is eaten by a lot of people, even in America, as a regular meal option, so it isn't that out of the ordinary," Frank says.

I remember Frank, but in the story I've been told Frank is the enemy! Now he's one of the family again? Rachel said he hadn't returned yet when she was last in my room with me. How long ago was that?

"Well, I'm 17 and have lived in America all my life and even died in America, and this is the first time I've ever eaten any kind of brain, let alone even had it offered to me. At least knowingly, I've eaten a lot of hot dogs, so maybe I can't say that for sure, but knowingly this is the first time for me. So ordinary or not *in general*, it's odd for me." I'll be playing this conversation from the frustration angle I see. Seeing Frank here like this, I don't know how else to play it.

"Good point," Mr. Sutton says. "Sorry about the blow to the head, Eric."

The cowboy is sitting at the far end of the large, oval wooden table. No cowboy hat to be seen. His hands are folded in front of him, resting on the table. He is intently studying them with his eyes.

"I don't actually feel any pain from it anymore, so I forgive you. It's not like it killed me." Tom Sutton looks up at me when I say this. I see anger in his eyes.

"Well…"

The word hangs out as though it is waiting to be followed, but I don't think he ever had any plan to say more than that.

Rachel returns from the kitchen and takes up the seat next to her father, her eyes on the table top, her face sullen. I look to Dr. Sutton and find her staring intently at me, and then to Frank to find the same posture. Tom is passively hostile. Rachel looks scared. Mickey Rooney seemed jovial out in the hallway. What a crew.

When I last saw Rachel she seemed to be questioning the story she had been told, I'm questioning it right now as well.

"Eric, I'm sure that in time you will understand our reasoning for doing what we did. Not only understand, but hopefully you will appreciate it. You are a pioneer!" Dr. Sutton suddenly becomes very animated and enthusiastic, like the car salesman that time my dad told him what price range he was looking to buy from.

"A pioneer? I think pioneers are usually volunteers," I say.

Rachel stands up quickly, nearly knocking her chair over in the process.

"May I be excused?" she asks. I look over and she is looking at her mom.

Dr. Sutton looks at her daughter for a moment and then says, "Yes."

Rachel leaves without saying anything else or looking in my direction. Is it just me or was that strange?

Dr. Sutton looks at her husband, who has been watching his wife since Rachel asked to be excused. He just shrugs at the doctor now.

"Eric," Dr. Sutton starts in, with a sickly smile, reminiscent of nearly every handle-bar-mustachioed villain I've ever seen in a cartoon, "You'll have to excuse Rachel. She just learned some things that will take her some time to process. I guess the two of you have that in common."

This is getting interesting. Rather, this continues to increase in its level of interest.

"What's going on?" I think that sums up all of my questions.

"Eric, what Rachel has told you isn't all true. She didn't know until just a few minutes ago; we didn't want to worry her with the truth. Ever since we left Atlanta we have been living a lie. The Agency was going to exterminate us, all of us. Mark, Frank, my family; we were marked to be cast away as a failed experiment! But we were not failed, we were alive! We are alive now, almost 3 years later, but only because we are smart. You seem smart to me, Eric, tell me what you would have done if you had been in our position. What would you have done if you and your family and team mates were to be thrown away like dead rodents?"

Caught off guard by this new narrative I don't answer straight away. Besides, it sounds like a rhetorical question, but after a short, however awkward, silence, I do give an answer, "I would probably try to protect my family and friends."

I'm not sure where this story is headed and if I want to find out I should probably present myself as being cooperative.

"Of course you would, and that's all that we have done," Dr. Sutton stops. Well, I hoped the story would go further than that.

No one is saying anything. Dr. Sutton and Frank are looking at each other approvingly; Tom Sutton seems to be sitting this one out. The silence is broken by Mark's return to the dining room. Yes, he looks like Mickey Rooney alright. He has a binder, which he delivers to Dr. Sutton. She takes the binder and sets it on the table in front of her.

"Eric, this is our work. These pages contain our research, theories, hypotheses, plans for further experimentation and everything that we know about our virus. It was started a long time ago before our team ever even had the virus on hand to work with. We have kept up our research all these years and logged everything in this binder. This is our life's work."

I suddenly recall the stereotypical movie scene when the villain reveals their master plan to the hero, thinking they have the hero incapacitated, but only too soon will the hero be free and, having full knowledge of the plan, be able to stop it in time to save the world. Why is she telling me about the importance of this binder?

"Why are you telling me about the importance of this binder?" I ask.

"We want to impress upon you the significance of the work we are doing here, and though you were initially brought here by deception, we want to embrace you into our family as our first live trial for our personalized strain of the virus."

Dr. Sutton is a villain. An evil, maniacal villain; and old Frank is her henchman. Both of them look pleased to death right now at the thought of their experiment progressing so well.

"I'm not a scientist, but I took a psychology class last year and I seem to recall something about informed consent being really important in research experiments and live trials for drug testing." I get them to stop smiling with that quip.

"Again, in time I expect you will understand, Eric. If you are looking for an apology from me, you won't find any." Dr. Sutton becomes all business.

"Don't worry, I won't ask for one, not right now. I'm too confused. Maybe you can clear some things up for me real quick?" I ask.

"Sure, what's on your mind?" Dr. Sutton sits back down in her chair and waves a hand, inviting me to take a seat as well. I take her up on the offer and sit across the table from her.

"Rachel told me the CDC, or the Agency, whatever you are calling it, sent you here, is that true?" I ask.

"No, they did not send us here. We came here on our own," Dr. Sutton says.

"So you left Atlanta and have been living here ever since and Rachel didn't know anything about that?"

"We told Rachel the CDC was sending us here because we didn't want her to worry and feel like a fugitive, but it was still important that she keep our secret safe, so we told her that they keep tabs on us. They wanted to kill us, fearing an outbreak, but our team knew enough about the virus to know that the likelihood of such an event was minimal."

When she says she's been lying to her own daughter for several years, on top of what she has done to me now, I have a hard time trusting her.

I ask my next question, "What is this about me being a pioneer?"

"This is the exciting part, Eric! We've been studying the virus in ourselves for three years now. We've been doing experiments with strains of the virus. We've done animal trials with what looks to be our optimal strain, but haven't introduced it to a human yet, not until you walked in the other night. You are the first human trial for the new virus. Obviously the virus is sustainable, as we are living proof, but there were a few things we wanted to improve to make it stronger. We believe we have achieved that. And look at you! You've transitioned quickly!" Dr. Sutton says this with all the pride of a young parent watching her toddler throw and catch a ball for the first time.

"Did I mention that pioneers are usually volunteers, or at least, forced by necessity, to enter into their pioneering?"

No response from the monster gallery.

I go on, "Tell me this, did Rachel know you were going to make me your first test case? Did she bring me here to do this to me?"

Dr. Sutton says, "I told you she didn't know the full story, but that doesn't mean she didn't bring you here with the hope of making you a zombie. You are the first friend she has ever brought home. And she told you about us before she brought you here, is that correct? Maybe she wanted you to join our family before we decided that ourselves."

This gives me reason to pause and think. Rachel indicated that her dad's attack on me was spontaneous, but it sounds like I was marked as a trial case already. If Frank is here now, then he wasn't a threat then, which means the Suttons were never planning to leave town, and that makes the story Rachel gave me full of holes. I think someone is lying to me, but I don't know who.

"What about Frank?" I look over at him and he looks up at me with a bit of surprise on his face. I look back to Dr. Sutton. "You told Rachel that Frank was going to do something to cause an outbreak and you were against that. I guess that was all a lie, as she said Frank left town and hadn't been back since, but here he is now, and you don't seem to be at odds with each other."

"Rachel was mistaken. Frank and I are working together on this project," Dr. Sutton says.

"I did just get back in town, however, so maybe Rachel's imagination ran away with her," Frank adds.

"I see." I'm forgetting my plan to be cooperative in the interest of finding out more information about what's really going on. "So you chose me to test the new virus on and then conveniently Rachel brought me here?"

"I suppose you can call it convenience. It doesn't matter now, you are a part of our family and now we will get to see the effects of the virus in you. This is exciting, Eric!" Dr. Sutton is back to her car salesman tone.

I need to talk to Rachel again. Did she bring me here with a purpose I wasn't aware of? Did she honestly misunderstand what was going on here, or is her mom lying to me now? More importantly, I remember my parents.

"Okay, I guess I understand what you are telling me, but I have a more pressing question for you. If I've been here for two days, have you contacted my parents? Do they know anything about where I am or what's going on? If not they must be worried to death."

Frank responds to my query, "They are here, Eric."

"Who is where?" I ask to clarify.

He says, "Your parents are here, in this house, Eric."

My head spins a little, like I've been disconnected from reality, but I still see everything around me. "What do you mean?"

Frank rolls his eyes, and then continues, cooly, too cooly for the topic, he *is* a henchman, "Wednesday, after we gave you the injection we called your folks to let them know that you had come here with Rachel, but had suddenly taken ill. Your mother was most concerned; your father wasn't at home yet. Dr. Sutton was able to convince your mother that, being a doctor, she was the best attendant you would be able to find within thirty miles. Assuring your mother that you were likely experiencing mild food poisoning or a standard stomach virus, she agreed that you could be put up in an empty bedroom here for the night so as not to move you and risk any unnecessary spreading of the virus to your family, if a virus it was." He smiles in a way that makes my zombified skin crawl. "Your mother was hesitant, obviously concerned and wanting to be with you, but she consigned to the doctor's recommendation and asked if she could come over briefly when your father returned from work.

"Your parents came by that night. You were feverish and unconscious. They said they'd come back Thursday after your dad got out of work. Luckily, they didn't see you in the thralls of agony associated with the transformation, happily you won't be able to recall the severity of the pain. We don't recall it from our experiences, but we have since witnessed it in our animal test subjects and now in a few human cases."

"A few?! Dr. Sutton just told me I'm the first…Wait, you didn't do this to my parents?!" I shout.

"Absolutely we did!" Frank is one cold dude. "They are in another room, experiencing the same agony you experienced. You see, when they returned Thursday evening we couldn't let them see you as that would have caused them to sound the general alarm. Instead we gave them a treatment similar to what you received and they are transitioning now. We have given you your family, Eric. You will now all be together, with us," Frank finishes and relaxes into his chair.

I'm speechless. What do you say, or do, when you are in a room full of movie monsters who just murdered your family, and yet you are still able to stand before them and seem to be alive? Surely this is unprecedented. It is for me, at any rate. This is where I would probably need to sit down and take a minute to compose myself, probably exercise some deep breathing, but I'm a zombie. I want to be outraged and experience powerful emotion, just as I've wanted to do since I found out that they transformed me, but I can't. I think these feelings, and I feel them, but only in a brilliant flash of energy before the emotion dissipates and I'm left neutral again. Everything is hollow.

Rachel told me that the virus reanimates the body's cells, including the brain. She said that means that personality and memory and anything stored in the brain still exists as a zombie, because it's all just a mass of neural connections that are triggered by electricity and chemicals. Well, she didn't say it like that, I'm putting her words into the appropriate context based on what I learned in psych last year and a little extra curricular reading I did because I found neuroscience so interesting. The point is that I continue to exist as a shell of myself. Whatever makes me *me* is gone, but the shadow of it all remains like computer files in my brain. The virus loads up certain files and I operate, but it's not me. I can't hold onto the emotion.

"Frank, I think you are a monster. You are all…correction, *we* are all monsters. Zombies are not humans, they are virus controlled corpses. We might all look normal; no rotting flesh or anything like that, but we aren't human! You just told me that you murdered my parents and I'm outraged, but a few seconds later it doesn't even matter. I feel like I should be horrified and angry, but I have trouble holding onto it. I don't think I like it, and it confuses me a great deal. If you don't have emotion, what motivates you to do what you are doing?" I slam my fist on the table as I finish, and then sit down.

Frank chuckles to himself, but doesn't say anything. Dr. Sutton just looks at me, expressionless.

Mark speaks, "You are right, Eric, we aren't human anymore. You can call us monsters, I suppose we fit the definition, but we aren't evil. Society has taught you that monsters are bad and evil. Television has taught you that the so-called 'living dead' are evil and murderous. You have charged us with murder, but are you dead? Are you really dead?"

Is he serious? They aren't evil?

"Are you serious? Of course I'm really dead! My heart's barely even beating; I have a virus inhabiting my body! Just because the virus is sending organized signals through my brain, which by the way makes no sense as to how that is even possible, doesn't mean that I'm alive. Television has taught me that the living dead are murderous, yes, and you have proven TV right."

I think these people have been too long in the world of zombies, they don't seem to have the ability to reason.

Dr. Sutton takes over. "Eric, you are proving a theory we have considered for some time. We know that the virus cannot completely mimic life, that is, a fully functioning brain, but it comes awfully close, and as you said, it is astounding that it can do anything even remotely close to what it does. Your perspective right now is closer to human than any of ours are. You are closer to emotion than we are. Over time we expect you will lose those feelings as much as we have. You will have the feelings, but as you said, they won't last. The signals will be there in the brain, biologically, but the spirit of them, the memory of them, will fade quickly and not remain constant.

"We each still enjoy books, movies and music that we previously found enjoyable. Things you enjoyed while living will be things you will enjoy as a reanimate, only the feelings won't last as long. If you get hurt the pain signal will trigger, but it won't be sustained. When you experience joy you will feel it, but it will fade. But emotional ties to people seem to fade to non-existance. Mr. Sutton and I know we were once married and loved each other deeply, but those feelings no longer exist for us. There is seemingly no need to love or to be loved in the virus, and that is manifest through our brains into our conduct."

"So what you are telling me is that I am angry that you killed me and my parents now, but it is only a reaction, not a real feeling? That in the moment I recognize what happened I react to it, but after the initial reaction the thought has no lasting presence or effect on me?" I ask.

"That's a very astute way of saying it, yes," Dr. Sutton says.

"Well that's dumb," I say.

Tom laughs at my comment and then stands up, stretches, and leaves the room, saying he is going for a cigarette as he passes through the doorway.

"This is why I told you that in time you will understand, because you won't be tied to all of these emotions anymore. You will then be able to appreciate what we have done for you and your parents." Dr. Sutton puts on her sweet voice as though she is talking to a hurt child. I guess she has taught herself to use this voice for manipulative purposes, because she just admitted that she doesn't care about me or anyone else.

"Oh, and Eric, will you please stop saying that we 'killed' you? It isn't very nice to hear and it really isn't completely true," she adds.

"No, Doctor, I won't stop. You did kill me, and according to Frank you also killed my parents. We are dead; if I can't hold onto an emotional feeling by my own control then I am dead. If what you are saying about all of this brain stuff is true, then in time I suppose I will forget the heat I feel right now, and maybe then we can all sit back and have a laugh over a steaming hot cup of brain juice about how crazy I was upon *transitioning*, but until then, until the virus runs every part of who I am out the window, I'm not giving this part up on my own. You killed me." Upon finishing my speech I have the urge to stand and applaud myself. But I don't.

"I'm sorry you feel that way, Eric," Dr. Sutton says and stands up from the table.

"I'd like to see my parents," I say.

Frank starts, "I can take you…" But he is interrupted by Dr. Sutton.

"It might be easier if you stop thinking of them as *your* parents, Eric. The meaning associated with that link will soon be dormant in your mind, you might want to start getting used to it." Her tone is harsh and cold. How anyone can sound like that without emotion is beyond me. This zombie thing is confusing.

"A moment ago you were welcoming me into your family, now family doesn't matter?" I say.

Caught in her manipulation, she doesn't respond verbally, but her eyes try to cut through me. She's not going to respond.

"May I still see them?" I ask the doctor.

"Frank, take him to their room if you don't mind." She leaves the room and kicks the stop holding the door to the kitchen so that it swings slowly closed behind her.

I look to Frank and nod. He stands up and smiles, then waves a hand indicating for me to follow him. Mark announces he'll come with us.

***

We don't have to go far to find the room my parents are being held in. There is a door recessed a bit, alongside the stairs. It seems like a good location for a closet, but the door opens up into a rather spacious room. I suppose this would be considered a den, if it hadn't been transformed into a makeshift laboratory for studying deadly viruses. Carpeting remains along the edges of the walls, but it has been torn out of the middle of the room, exposing the concrete slab of the house's foundation.

Several metal tables are lined up with all the standard glassware and small electronic devices and machines one would expect to see in a chemistry lab. There are plastic boxes stacked all around. Some furniture is gathered in one corner of the room; likely it hasn't been touched since it was piled there years ago when this room was converted to a lab. Some old pictures like the ones upstairs still hang on the walls. Along one wall are a few animal cages, but they appear to be uninhabited at the moment.

As I survey the lab, Frank makes his way to a door in the right wall. He opens the door, but doesn't enter the room. It is dark in there; must not have any windows.

"Your parents are in here," Frank says.

I walk over and look inside, but still can't see anything. "Have any lights in there?"

"The switch is inside on the left," Frank says with a smile.

I step inside and reach for where I'd expect a switch to be, but before I can find it I'm pushed forward and I fall on my face. The light flooding in from the lab disappears as the door is pulled shut behind me. Realizing there isn't much I can do at the moment, I stay lying face down to think for a moment. The first thing that comes to mind is that my parents aren't actually in this room. If that was a lie, then maybe they aren't even in this house at all. Maybe there never was any contact between my parents and the Suttons. If the Suttons didn't call my mom it is unlikely that she would have known I was here. She might have expected it after I brought Rachel home the day before, but she wouldn't have been able to prove anything, and it would have been easy enough for Dr. Sutton to convince my mom that they had no idea what happened to me or where I was.

This brings a fleeting sense of relief to consider that my parents may be alright; extremely worried, yes, but alive. So if my parents aren't involved here, then why tell me they were? And why lock me in a dark room, alone? The good doctor said I was a human trial for her new virus strain. Maybe this is my observation cage. The pretense of accepting me into their zombie family was just to gauge what state my mind is in and determine what level of control they'd need to exercise over me. My defiance must have earned me these beautiful living quarters. If that is what this is.

I push up from the floor. It is carpeted, likely the same cream color as the remnants in the main room this is attached to. I rest on my knees and feel out in front of me, considering for a moment that maybe this is a closet, which would explain why there aren't any windows. I don't feel walls anywhere around me from where I kneel, so I stand up slowly. I turn around and put my hands out in front of me, feeling for the door I just came through. I find the door knob and attempt to give it a turn, but it's locked. I reach for the light switch, again, but my hands just glide across the papered walls without finding anything. With my hands on the wall, I use my right leg as a low feeler and start shuffling to the right, intending to search the perimeter of the room. Maybe there is a lamp on a table.

Only a few feet from my starting position there is a dresser or a wooden chest or desk or something. I reach down with my right hand and find that it isn't very tall, whatever it is. The top is smooth and rounded on the edges a bit. I slide along the side of it, but there is nothing attached to it on the top or sides, and no light, which is my primary target. The end of the object is snug in the corner. I guess this wall from the door is about ten feet. I start feeling along the side wall and my foot makes another contact after a few side-steps. Again, I reach down, and find this object to be as low as the previous one. I reach across it and find the back wall. Suddenly I recognize what these objects are.

Coffins. If my heart were operating at normal human standards I'm sure I'd have that sensation of it skipping a beat and jamming up into my throat, but I'm a zombie. I have a flood of anxious fear soak through my brain, but then it stops. For a few seconds I appreciate this new inability to feel. I try not to form the thought again, but how can I avoid it? Frank said he would take me to my parents, he brought me to this room, and there are two coffins in it. What other conclusion can I draw right now? I use my zombie power of apathy to put those thoughts off for the moment and continue my circuit around the room. Beyond the casket the wall extends a few feet past where I figure the door should be on the opposite wall. I find the other side wall without coming into contact with anything on the wall or the floor. Nothing on the side wall either. As I round out my search and find the door jamb on the original wall, I also find a light switch. It's at the right height, but why would it be on the side of the door with the hinges, especially when the door opens inward? As I contemplate the awful architectural design, I flip the switch.

The room is instantly filled with yellow light, and instantly I regret having done it. As I turn around to face the room I realize I can't block the idea that my parents are lying dead just a few feet from me when I can see the coffins plain as day. I don't want to open them up, and I can't right off, as the return of the anxious fear has paralyzed me momentarily. But it fades, and I have to know. I take a step towards the first coffin and the pain of fear floods my mind again. I close my eyes and a few seconds later it dissipates.

"Man, this is annoying!" I say aloud to myself. These thoughts trigger an emotional reaction which releases the chemicals which feel like anguish and then it's gone, as quickly as it comes on. It's not comfortable. Before my transition I would just sit down and cry it out, then move on, I suppose. But now I have to keep reliving the intensity of the pain fresh each time I react to the thought. Dr. Sutton said this would fade. I hope it does, although I fear that means losing more of my *me*.

For now, I need to open a casket and see if it holds my mom or dad. I struggle through another bout of feeling and kneel alongside one casket. I don't know how I'm going to react to whatever I find once this lid is open. I slide the heavy box away from the wall to make room for the hinges on the lid to open, and then fix my fingers under the edge of the lid and lift.

14. Seeing Red

Nothing. No bodies, no vampire collectibles, not even a sick note saying "Gotcha!" The flood of relief is welcomed, but it quickly fades. I push back and fall into a sitting position on the floor. Since I'm here, and have nothing else to do, I'll check the other casket. I spin myself around on the carpet and scooch closer to the casket. Perching on my knees once again for leverage, I pop the top on the second coffin. Empty again.

"Well, that was anti-climatic. But that's good in this case," I say out loud to myself.

I close the lid on the second box and sit on top of it, slouching backward against the wall. In this posture I notice the camera fixed in the opposite corner from me, way up near the ceiling. I wave to it and then fix my eyes on the ceiling above me and sit motionless.

So they are watching me. This has been an experiment, but what was the question they were hoping to answer? Were they just trying to see how I would respond to the fear that my parents were dead and in these caskets? Maybe they were curious to see if I would even care enough to open the boxes to find out. Maybe it's all coincidence, the caskets were here and this is the only room they have without windows where they can imprison me. Didn't Trent tell me this house used to be a funeral parlor before the Suttons moved in? I'll have to wait and see. I'm not going to think about any of it until they give me more information. There's no point in speculating about the welfare of my parents, or my status as a prisoner.

I make it through singing only a few of my favorite songs to myself before there's a knock on the door, followed by the click of a key in the lock, and then the door opening. Dr. Sutton appears with her white lab coat on, and a clipboard in hand.

"Hello, Doctor," I say, trying to sound as disturbed as possible. "What's going on?"

"As I mentioned before, you are our first human trial with the new strain of virus. We need to observe you and see how you take to the transition. I'll tell you flat out, we haven't had very good viability with our previous tests using rats, rabbits, and a cow. They weren't reanimating. It took us a while, but we think we figured it out, and felt confident enough to try it on a human."

"I don't understand you at all. I don't understand this virus business. I don't understand why you are doing this to me and I certainly don't understand why I want to be angry but keep returning to a relaxed state of calm! It aggravates me, now and then," I say.

Dr. Sutton replies, "Eric, your experience so far has been very interesting to us. We don't remember the full details of our transitioning due to the passage of time. Like good scientists we recorded as much data as we could, but our notes still miss some vital details, or at least we realize they do now after observing you. Aside from the quick fading of emotional responses you keep mentioning, you don't seem to be experiencing any difficulty with memory recall, or even spatial or social recognition. Quite phenomenal when compared with the process each of us went through.

"This room, and the story about your parents, was designed to test your personal relationship retention. We needed to see if you still had loyalty. It appears that you do. The quick fade of emotions is interfering with it, perhaps, but you still opened both caskets. Why did you do it?" Dr. Sutton's tone is very formal and scientific.

I don't want to answer her because I don't like being an observed experiment, but once again I realize that it doesn't really matter. The situation being what it is compliance on my part seems to be the best path, at least until I figure out what really has happened with my parents.

"When Frank threw me in here with the lights off, I was caught off guard, and slightly offended, but I thought my parents were in here. I figured the lights were off and that they were each in a bed, similar to how I found myself upon waking, upstairs. I was disturbed that I was locked in, but decided to find the light switch and see what was going on anyway; thinking that perhaps I had been lied to again and my parents weren't actually here, and this room would be my new prison cell. Well, the light switch is in a stupid location so I didn't find it for a while. By that point I had already come up with the idea that my parents might be in these coffins and I had to know for sure.

"The feeling of suddenly imagining my parents both dead just a few feet from me was crippling, but since it kept fading I was able to open both boxes and find out. The worst was when I found the first one empty and the thought that both were shoved in the other box as a way of torturing me came to mind. I also thought you might have put a note in one of them indicating this as a joke, but there was just a whole lot of nothing. Then when I sat down I noticed the camera in the corner and realized you are running tests on me." I rattle this all off without ever looking at Dr. Sutton.

"Wow. Excellent response, very thorough. Your science teachers must have enjoyed your lab reports. But also wow for your thought processes through all of this. Do you feel like your thinking is any different now than it was before your transition?" Dr. Sutton is obviously excited about something.

"Do you mean do I think differently now than I did when I was alive? Before you killed me?" I know she doesn't like me using this language, but all this zombie stuff aside, I'm still a 17 year-old boy.

"Eric, we did you a favor," she reminds me.

"Making me a zombie is doing me a favor?" I ask.

"Okay, first of all, look up the definition of zombie next time you see a dictionary, you don't meet the terms of the definition, none of us do. We use the term loosely, mostly for fun, but also because Rachel seemed to take to it more than 'reanimate.' We keep it up for her sake, mostly. It's not a big deal, but in the interest of pure science, we aren't zombies. And when you answer my question I think you'll find that even you don't really think that we killed you at all. Do dead people have conversations like this?"

She has a point. I haven't even checked myself for a pulse yet. All I know is I've been very sick and I've been told a lot of stories. I reach up and press a few fingers alongside my neck.

"What are you doing?" Dr. Sutton asks, surprised.

"Checking for a pulse...I haven't done this yet. All I know is that I've been really sick, but maybe I'm not actually dead like you." It's no good, just like with Rachel the other day; I can't discern a pulse by touch.

"You won't be able to feel a pulse; your blood pressure is way too low. But you can take my word for it, your body expired and has been reanimated. By way of explanation, the virus replicates to all of your cells and, for lack of better terminology, operates them. So your heart is being operated, it is beating, but remarkably slower and less powerful than before, therefore a much lower blood pressure. It does beat, but without the virus there is no way it would be considered life sustaining."

"So then without the virus I'm dead! See! I was right!" I jump off the coffin and point an index finger at the doctor.

Without skipping a beat or revealing any surprise by my action, Dr. Sutton says, "I know you have never been dead before, yourself, but surely you have seen someone at a wake or funeral that was dead? Do you feel anything right now like you observed in that situation?"

I don't think she's going to let me get away with not answering this question.

"Alright, no, right now for all intents and purposes I don't appear to be dead. But to answer your first question, yes there is a difference between my thinking today when compared to my thinking from a few days ago, before my *transition*. Aside from the messed up way I'm experiencing emotional reactions, I feel slightly detached and at times I've felt a strange déjà vu or 'outside looking in' effect. I did have the memory problems you mentioned at first, and had trouble recognizing Rachel and remembering you and Frank, but that went away after a while. I guess I can tell a difference, but really if you would have just told me that I was really sick for a few days I might not even realize I've been reanimated, hence my self pulse check a moment ago. Reanimate. Zombie. I think I'm with Rachel on that one; I'm going to keep using it, whether Webster approves or not." I sit back down on the edge of the casket.

"Fascinating. You have no regard for using words according to proper definition." She says as she makes a mark on her clipboard.

I chortle at Dr. Sutton's attempt at humor and then roll my eyes dramatically to the right, like a couple of fighter jets in an air show fly by.

"You still have a sense of humor, I see," Dr. Sutton says. So that was a test comment.

"Apparently."

"Well, Eric, it is fascinating, the experience you are having, when compared to the rest of us. Your state of fugue lasted hours; we each experienced it to varying degrees, but over the course of days. There did seem to be a correlation with age, Rachel having the quickest recovery after transition and Frank having the slowest. Your recovery is significantly quicker than Rachel's was, and you are older than she was, though not by much more than a year. Tom and I are the same age, and we were only hours different really, so age seems to be the primary factor without gender influence." Dr. Sutton looks at me and seems to sense my disinterest, or at least assumes I'm not interested in the details, so she just continues.

"We all experienced the emotional reaction with quick dissipation, but it was coupled with a deep apathy. We felt things, but didn't care so much. You seem to care a great deal. By your repeated use of the word 'kill' you clearly show you care. In your concern for your parents you clearly show you care. If I read your expression correctly, you have care in regards to Rachel, though I'm not sure what the details are in that regard." She pauses. If she thinks I'm going to volunteer some information about my feelings toward Rachel this will be a long awkward silence for her.

With no response from me, she continues. "We've been working on the virus, primarily trying to make it more environmentally viable. We've been strengthening it against UV light and antiviral drugs. It's not easy to replicate it outside of a host, so the virus struggles in that regard, but we have built a strong virus. Of course, the best part of all, as you said it yourself, if you didn't know what had happened to you, you wouldn't realize you had transitioned." Dr. Sutton *is* a mad scientist.

If I were James Bond I suppose I would need to tell her she'll never get away with this, but I'm still not clear on what her goal is. I'm starting to think she wants to spread the virus to the public, but I'm not one hundred percent on that, yet.

I recall Rachel telling me that this was Frank's agenda. She said her mom told her Frank wanted to cause an outbreak. Was Rachel lying to me, or was Dr. Sutton lying to Rachel?

"Come with me, Eric, let's have a seat in the living room. I've been on my feet most of the day," Dr. Sutton says.

"Fine. But can you tell me what is going on with my parents? For real this time."

"Your parents are here, and they are transitioning, just like we told you. There is another room upstairs, across the hall from the one you were in. That's where they are. We called them Wednesday night to tell them you had come down with something and that I was going to take you under my care until you were better. Your mother was very concerned. When your father returned home from work they both came over to see you. I didn't argue against it because I didn't want to raise any unnecessary suspicion. When they got here we brought them to you. It was so soon after exposure that you appeared as though you were simply under the effect of a high fever, eyes closed, writhing a bit, moaning in pain. It was unsettling for your parents, particularly your mother, but they trusted my recommendation.

"We had a nice visit with them downstairs, they stayed nearly an hour, we had coffee. After we chatted for a while they came back up to see you, and supposing you were finally resting comfortably they didn't attempt to rouse you, but left the room quietly. Had they gone in for closer inspection they may have found you were no longer breathing. We were prepared if that happened. Fortunately they returned home for the night. The next day your mother came over early and wanted to see you. She sat by your bed for a few minutes, but it was difficult for her to see you in that much pain. It took some effort on my part, but I was able to convince her that everything was alright. She said she would come back with your father later that night.

"When they returned we led them upstairs and into the room across the hall from where you were. They followed right in. Obviously you weren't in there, so when your dad started to ask, well, no need for the details, Tom subdued your parents and we injected them with the same strain as we gave you. As I mentioned, age slows the recovery from the transition, so it will be a little bit longer for them than for you, but I don't expect very much longer after observing the great results of your trial," Dr. Sutton concludes.

She smiles, I guess at her supposed success, which makes me angry. But only for a second. And then again a few seconds later, but this time also only briefly. Stupid reanimated brain.

I suppose she'll interpret my compliance as defeat, but I'm hardly defeated, my resolve is strong, fleeting from moment to moment, but overall strong. I need to find out the whole story. I need to know what Rachel knew about all of this. Is she as guilty as her mom, or was she manipulated in order to get me here? Did she know about my parents when she came up to talk with me? I don't recall her saying anything about them. They must have been across the hall by then, but I don't have a clear concept of the timeline.

I tell the doctor, "I'll go sit in the living room with you now. But I want to know everything. I want to know why you are doing all of this. Why aren't you working to find a cure for this virus? Why are you making it stronger? What do you expect to do with it?"

We leave the coffin room, head through the lab, down the hall and enter the last place I saw through living eyes.

***

I sit in the spot Dr. Sutton was in the other day, this way no one can sneak up on me from behind. It also means I'm cornered with no escape, but that kind of thing doesn't matter so much when you are already dead. I guess, to be fair, it also wouldn't matter if someone snuck up on me from behind. It might hurt to get planked in the head again, but only for a few seconds, like all of these other feelings. I certainly don't seem to have lost my scattered imagination through the *transition*. It feels good to be sarcastic, even if I'm the only one aware of it.

"Would you like anything to drink, Eric?" Dr. Sutton asks as though I've just arrived at her house for a book club meeting.

"Sure, formaldehyde, on the rocks, if you don't mind." That's another good one, I think. It just came to me.

"Are you sure? We have that..." She trails off as she enters the kitchen, returning moments later with a couple of cans of soda. "You can eat or drink whatever you want, really. Your body will process it, but it doesn't really have need of the same nutrients as before. Now, whatever the virus requires will be provided by brain. It is still important to keep hydrated, but not quite as important as it used to be for you. If you like soda, drink soda. That's what I do, and I don't have to worry about diet anymore. So that's a plus."

Initially I'm put off by Dr. Sutton's sudden casual demeanor, but I adjust to it quickly. I accept the cola and take a drink. I've noticed some differences in my perception of smell and sound, also touch and sight, but until now I haven't tasted anything previously familiar to me. The brain tasted fine, but it wasn't something I could compare to in the past, so I didn't yet know if my perception of taste was also different. Reason suggested it would be, and reason has been proven correct. I recognize the cola flavor, and the sugar sensation, but it is different; still favorable, but noticeably different. Life, or whatever this can be called, will never be the same.

Dr. Sutton sits opposite from me, taking up my previous seat in this room. I wonder if the balance of power in this discussion will change with the new seating arrangement, or I'll just have to handle that on my own.

I go on the offensive. "So, you've successfully turned me and my parents into zom-, I mean, reanimates. You've proven your new virus in human test cases. What's next for your virus and for my family?"

Dr. Sutton takes a long sip of soda and then looks at me. I wait for her response.

Finally she says, "Naturally we'd like to continue observing your family for a few weeks. Two days hardly makes for conclusive evidence in such a study. It'll be a few days yet before your parents are even conscious. You will all stay here with us for a while. Don't worry about the school or your father's work. It has all been taken care of."

"How?" I interrupt.

"Well, with a cover story. One that fits what you have been so often repeating: that your family is dead. You were killed in an automobile accident, all of you, Thursday night, when your parents were driving you to the hospital. Your dad was driving way too fast, but understandably so, you were very sick. Tom has provided sufficient evidence for this to be convincing…"

I interrupt again, " 'Sufficient evidence'? What does that mean?"

"Well, it required a little deception on the part of some people in roles of authority, but there are no ties to us. We aren't in hiding from everyone, Eric. We aren't alone in our project."

That's news to me, and very interesting. Scary, but interesting. Rachel either lied to me about everything, or she was deep in the dark on all of this. I'd sure like to know which it is.

Dr. Sutton continues, "All of your property will be handled however the local officials handle such things. You, Eric Sutton, no longer exist in your old identity. If you need anything, in the way of clothes or objects, we will get it for you. Until our observation phase is complete you will not be allowed to leave the house, use the phone, or access the Internet. You are on lockdown, but please don't take offense and feel like a prisoner, this is in the interest of science."

"Didn't Hitler and the Nazis use a similar line about the Holocaust?" This time my question brings a serious reaction from the doctor. I guess no one likes being compared to a Nazi, not even a zombie mad scientist.

"I'm going to ignore that observation. You are restricted, yes, but it is for your own good. Once we've determined that the virus is settled and you are fully functional we will develop a new identity for you and help you relocate to wherever you would like to go. Of course, by that time, if you are interested, we'd be happy to have you stay with us and help in our work."

"Do you mean help on the ranch and in the slaughterhouse?" I ask.

"No, with the lab work and our next goal." Dr. Sutton seems to want to tell me, but she wants me to ask. This is so cliché for mad scientists. Just like the parking lot full of pickup trucks, all stereotypes, even ones reserved for mostly fictional characters, are based on facts. Mad scientists are just looking for attention.

"Well, I guess we'll have to see how it goes over the next few weeks. And maybe you can give me a rundown of your next goal. But not now. I'd really like to go see my parents, and maybe take some time to think about things for a while. I assume I have free run of the house and can claim the room I transitioned in as my own?" I ask.

Dr. Sutton answers, "Of course. The room is yours, feel free to visit your parents. You are free to roam the house, unless of course a door is locked, but that's just good manners to respect that. Generally, the lab is the only door we lock. If you want to eat, the kitchen is kept stocked with standard human fare; you may or may not want to eat in order to satiate inclinations towards it in your mind. There is another kitchen in the basement, which is accessible through the kitchen up here, where the brain is stored and prepared. Feel free to ask one of us for assistance if you get the craving. Learning the new cuisine is best through observation rather than listening to someone talk."

"Okay, thank you," I say.

I stand up and finish off the last of the can of soda. "You recycle?" The irony strikes me and I decide to laugh about it later.

"Only people." Dr. Sutton apparently catches on to the humor as well. "Just kidding, there is a bucket under the counter next to the dishwasher in the kitchen."

"Got it." I drop off the can and on my way back through I stop to ask another question.

"Dr. Sutton?"

"Yes?"

"When I was transitioning and mostly out of it, Rachel came to talk to me, I don't remember a lot of what she said, but one thing stuck and I wanted to ask about it, she said something about sleeping. Do I not need to sleep anymore, or was she referring to during the transition?" I ask.

"You can sleep, but you don't need to. We haven't found any amount of hours awake that will induce drowsiness. The only thing close to being tired is if we go too long without eating brain, then the virus weakens and with it we do as well. It is an awful feeling and we avoid it as best we can, but occasionally with scheduling at the slaughterhouse and through our beef trade we do end up without brain to eat for long enough to have an effect. It isn't often.

"So if you go up to the bed and lie down it is possible you will sleep, but for how long or if you'll feel well rested after you wake up, there's no rhyme or reason to it that we've found, yet."

"Alright, well, I'll see you around." And with that I'm on my way up the stairs.

15. Monsters

I guess it is Saturday morning now. The sun is just lighting up the sky out the window. I hear cow noises, whatever the technical term is for that, but I don't see the responsible parties. It's still relatively dark. I'm standing at the window in my new bedroom. After my last conversation with Dr. Sutton I found my parents lying in separate beds in the room across the hall. Neither one seemed living, but they weren't dead either. I stood in the room through several waves of pain before getting sick of the emotional…not roller coaster…what's the carnival ride that lifts you up real high in a chair and then just drops you? An emotional one of those. There's nothing I can do for them except wait for them to regain consciousness and then coach them through the confusion.

How am I going to do that?

I thought about going to see Rachel right after leaving my parents, but decided to take some time alone to contemplate things. I must have fallen asleep after lying down to think, I don't really know, my concept of time is all out of whack. I think I should go find Rachel and talk to her about everything. Maybe she can give me a head's up on her mom's plans, if she knows any more about them than I do. If she does know more it might be because she knew all along, in which case I don't want to talk to her.

Someone is knocking at the door.

The door opens before I can respond to the knock. It's Rachel.

"Hey, I was just thinking about going to find you. I'd like to talk, if that's okay with you?" I say.

"Yes, that's why I came up here. But let's go for a walk outside, okay?" she says.

Rachel seems different, but I don't know if that's because everything seems different to me or if she's changed as well. She isn't expressing any obvious emotion right now. She's dressed simply, as usual, with her hair up.

"I don't know if I'm supposed to leave the house, according to your mom's rules of my observation phase," I say.

"Alone. You aren't allowed to leave alone, but really that just means don't be seen in public by anyone who knows you and believes you were killed in a car crash a few days ago. The public might not respond well to seeing you alive when you are supposed to be dead. You can walk around the ranch with me, no one will see us."

This is the kind of statement that should scare a person, when it is a zombie saying it to them, but that's not how I responded when presented with similar invitations before, and now I'm a zombie myself. More importantly, Rachel mentioned the car crash story, so she knows about that part, but did she know about it before we last spoke? That's what I need to find out.

"Alright, let's go," I say.

Neither one of us speaks as we descend the two flights of stairs and make our way out the front door, not until we are outside and beyond hearing range from the house. Even then we walk in silence for a short while.

I try to get the conversation going with a little humor, that's how Rachel and I used to talk – used to, all of three days ago.

"Rachel, when you came up to the room to get me I told you I had been planning to find you so we could talk. You said that's why you were there. Did you mean you were there to talk or you were there because you knew I was planning to find you?"

"What?" Rachel asks with confusion apparent in her voice.

"I mean, we don't have some kind of *zombie mind link* or something, do we? You weren't reading my mind because we are both zombies? You just meant that you wanted to talk to me, not that you knew what I was thinking?"

I'm trying to be humorous, obviously we wouldn't have a mind link, but it sounds like something Hollywood might try; however, I'm not entirely sure something like that might not be possible. After all, *I am a zombie.* I really can't stress that enough. Talk about paradigm shifts!

"Oh, yeah, we don't have any kind of *mind link*. Your thoughts are safe from me or anyone else. We are just reanimated corpses, not telepathic zombies."

Rachel laughs a little, which is really all that I was going for. Of course, it's good to know she can't read my mind. Not that I'm so concerned about her, but until I figure out Dr. Sutton better I don't want her to know I'm not actually as accepting as I'm pretending to be right now.

"Good. I think that would be difficult to deal with," I say, feigning significant relief by wiping my forearm across my forehead.

"Why, you have a lot of thoughts that you don't want anyone to know about?" Her eyes are squinty and suspicious. This is more like how we used to talk – used to, three days ago, yes.

"Nothing specific, it's just a matter of individual liberty, that's all. My life was taken from me; I'd like to at least keep my mind for myself."

Honest, but perhaps not the most sensitive thing to say to someone before attempting to fish incriminating information from her.

Rachel stops walking and turns away from me. I shouldn't have said that. I hope I don't lose her over it. I decide to wait for her this time, let her take whatever time she needs to craft her words.

"Eric, I'm sorry my mom and dad did this to you. I didn't know, honestly. Maybe I suspected it, but I really didn't think it would happen. And then your parents, too. I don't like it."

I guess she didn't need much time to mount a response after all, and it sounds like my lament wasn't as out of line as I thought. She agrees with me. Or she's pretending to. I'll remain cautious.

She turns to look at me and continues, "I wanted you to come out here to talk with me because I need your help. I'm afraid of what Mom is going to do next. She's been lying to me, Eric. For nearly three years. Everything I told you the other day, what she had been telling me for all this time, was just a cover. All that stuff about Frank, it was all a lie. Mom explained it after I found your parents.

"I didn't know they came here Wednesday night because I was hiding in my room trying to make sense of what my parents had done to you. I was out for a walk when they came by on Thursday. It wasn't until after I spoke with you yesterday morning, when you were really awake, that I knew they were here. I met Frank in the hallway; I hadn't seen him since I was with you out on the highway. I still thought he was up to something and we were going to be leaving, just as soon as you transitioned. But it was all lies, I can't believe I was so stupid to believe it all." Rachel looks like she might cry, but she doesn't.

I really want to believe what she is telling me. It absolves her of any guilt in my murder, but I just don't know yet.

"It's not stupid to believe your parents. Especially in such a strange situation as you've had. I don't think anyone would blame you for believing your mom. That doesn't excuse her, but you probably shouldn't beat yourself up over it." I try to be encouraging and comforting.

Rachel's demeanor doesn't change. She says, "Yeah, I guess. It's just so crazy. I thought Frank was off declaring war on humanity, but he was just out, I don't know where, while right under my nose my mom was the one waging that war. When I saw Frank I called for my dad. We were on the second floor and he was just in his room, so he was there quickly. When he didn't freak at the sight of Frank, I got really scared. I had just left you with a feeling of suspicion about my parents reasoning for doing this to you. I asked what was going on and Frank said 'I guess the jig is up, Tom.' He actually said that the jig was up. It'd be funny if it wasn't so serious."

I interrupt, "No, it's still pretty funny picturing Frank saying that. Did he look serious when he said it?"

"Yeah, kind of, I mean, I think he was being sincere." Rachel and I both laugh for real, but only briefly. It's still good to laugh with her, however short.

She returns to her story, "Upon hearing the jig was up, Dad said 'I think we should talk with your mother.' So they took me downstairs and we found Mom. She explained everything to me, about her secret work these last few years, about your parents, about Frank. She apologized for lying, but said it was necessary to keep me safe. She told me about you. She said from the moment she met you she considered you as the perfect trial. She liked that you were new to town first, but then she thought that our friendship was a nice touch, you and me, I mean. She said she just generally liked you. That's when she came up with the story about Frank, in hopes of motivating me to bring you into my confidence and, well, doing exactly what I did."

"Talk about making a good first impression," I say.

Rachel laughs again, but this time it's the kind of laugh usually reserved for police and morticians. She shakes her head and starts walking again, further out toward the pastures. I don't start moving until she has a ten yard lead, or thereabouts. I start out after her and catch up after she stops at the fence around the pasture area. She's leaning on the upper rail of the wooden fence, so I lean, too.

Rachel starts talking again. "It's been a few months, apparently, since Mom and Frank and Mark figured out whatever it was they figured out to make the virus strain they used on you. Mom became very excitable when talking about it. They kept it all secret. I didn't even know Mom was working on anything scientific. I never saw her in the lab. I thought it was just Frank and Mark tinkering and keeping themselves occupied." Rachel stops and turns towards me. With a straight face she says, "They want to release the virus. They think this is the next step in human evolution."

"The next step in human evolution is to kill all humans?" I ask, turning my body to face her.

"I don't understand it either. But that's what they are planning. As scientists they need to do their trials and make sure the virus is going to do what they hope it will do in humans. So now they have their test cases. You, and your parents. Oh, it's terrible what they've done! I don't know how they think they pulled off their cover story. Won't the police be suspicious that there aren't any bodies? Not to be morbid, but…" Rachel lets me finish the thought on my own.

"Your mom told me they had a little help from some friends with some form of authority. I supposed they were more in allegiance with the Agency than you had told me," I say.

She thinks about this for a moment. "That sounds plausible. I didn't tell you before, but my dad used to work for the Agency. When I told you he used to have an exciting job and that he seemed depressed living out this life here on the ranch, the exciting job was working for the Agency. I thought he lost that job when we came here, but maybe he never really left it. He doesn't leave home for extended periods of time like he did before we transitioned, but that doesn't mean he's not working with them somehow. Look what my mom has been able to do without me knowing about it. My parents are murderous liars."

We are still standing face to face, so I nod, consolingly. What can I say, it's true. I'm not going to dispute it, but all the same, I feel for her. Once again, my timing may be poor, but it's time to challenge her story and find out if she's being sincere with me. If her story is true, she and I are on the same team and we are victims in her mother's war on humanity. If her story is not true, then she's doing her mother's work in trying to force me to be a team player.

I want to believe Rachel is being honest with me, because, let's face it, up until a few days ago I thought I'd be asking her out on a proper date. Some of that mindset is still in my head, being processed intermittently by the virus. Like it or not for the virus, this body is crushing on Rachel still, but not if she is a knowing accomplice to my murder or the murder of my parents.

"Rachel, I appreciate you filling in all of these details for me. I hope you can forgive me for what I say next, but I have to say it either way. I've been assaulted, murdered, lied to and orphaned in only three days time, by your parents and their 'family.' You invited me to your house on Wednesday, and here we are on Saturday, zombies on a cattle ranch in the middle of nowhere. My parents have also been killed. An elaborate hoax has been enacted to make it seem like we were killed in a car accident. Now you are telling me that human kind is in danger of extinction through the introduction of a virus that a few mad scientist zombies think is the next stage in human evolution."

This time Rachel interrupts me, "What's your point?"

"My point? I have a point, I'm just building up momentum."

"Okay, sorry for interrupting."

"No problem. So all of that stuff has happened and is happening, and I need to know one thing. Are you telling me the truth? I would honestly love nothing more than to believe what you are telling me, and to take confidence in our friendship, but, hopefully you can appreciate it, I'm having a tough time with this. How can I know you aren't lying to me now, as another aspect of your mom's devious plans?"

Rachel looks hurt, I'm inclined to take this as my answer, but I want to hear what she has to say.

"You can't know. I guess that's all there is to it. You either trust me or you don't. What made you believe me Tuesday night, and not write me off as a loon? What made you talk to me Wednesday morning, and then agree to spend time with me alone after I confessed to being a zombie? Why did you believe me then, but not now?" she asks.

That's not exactly what I was expecting her to say. I thought she'd defend herself a little more. But she raises some valid questions. I suppose I need to be completely open with her if I want the same in return.

"I believed you then because I didn't fully believe you. Or, I didn't fully appreciate what you were saying, that it was possible. I don't know why I didn't dismiss you as a loon. Possibly it was because I had a major crush developing. I don't know how to explain how or why that happens, but I know it can make a person dismiss reality in some ways. Maybe that's what it was for me. But when you told me you were a zombie, it felt like you were telling the truth. I can't recall with enough clarity how it felt when we were talking on Tuesday and Wednesday. Obviously now I know you were telling the truth about the zombie thing, and I really want to believe that you didn't know what was going to happen and that you've only found this all out yesterday. However, your mom has said a few things that make me suspicious, that perhaps you have been on her side all along.

"Seeing your reaction to my words makes me pretty sure you are sincere, but there's that old saying, you know, turn me into a zombie once, shame on me, enlist me in your evil plans to destroy human kind, shame on you. Something like that."

Rachel doesn't laugh at my joke. I guess I didn't expect her to. It's wrapped in some pretty sharp barbs and dripping with jellyfish toxins. That's a painful thought.

"Well, Eric, it sounds like you've already made up your mind about me and for some reason you are leaning more towards what you inferred from what my mom said than towards what I'm telling you straight. My mom, the one who did this to you, is the one you are trusting, against our history, however short it has been, and your instinct when you see my reaction to your words. I don't know what I can do for you to prove my honesty. This isn't television so I'm not going to just kiss you, if that's what you are looking for."

I smile and shake my head.

"This conversation can go both ways, you know," she continues. "You've spent more time with my mom in the last day than you have with me. I don't know what has changed in you through the transition. I don't know if you aren't the one being used to manipulate me, as you seem to believe is true of me. So I could demand a sign of trust from you just like you are demanding of me."

Checkmate.

"I guess kissing you won't do the trick?" I say, suddenly feeling the weight of my suspicion and accusation come crashing down on me like an avalanche. I think I've been unfair. I wanted to believe Rachel. She makes a good point, why then did I give so much credibility to what her mom said? Because I want to know what her mom plans to do. I don't want to get played again, but I don't have anyone else to trust. If I choose to trust Rachel and she does rat me out, what difference does it really make? My parents and I are dead. I could run away and try to get to the CDC, but what about my parents? And then what about me? Will the CDC just lock me up the same way Dr. Sutton has? Will they cure my virus by killing me? What's left of me, that is.

I've been looking at my feet, contemplating, so I look up at Rachel, she isn't looking at me, but soon meets my gaze. We don't speak, just look. I was so intent on getting her to prove her trustworthiness that I accused her of dishonesty and damaged what credibility she saw in me.

Rachel takes control of the moment. "I know you don't have any real reason to trust me. I understand your perspective on what has happened. Remember, we didn't ask for this to happen to us, either. My mom and the others are trying to make the best of the situation. After three years, I think it's getting to them. I think Dad is starting to enjoy it. He seems more alive in the last few days now that he has some secret agent stuff to do again. I'm really worried about all of them. I think they are going to release the virus soon. As soon as they are confident it won't turn Cranston into a city of rotting corpses. They prefer living corpses. But not me, I don't like any of it. If my parents hadn't kept promising me a normal life all this time I might have tried to end it myself. For myself, I mean. But I remained trusting and hopeful that I would be able to live as though I weren't a zombie. I realize now that it isn't possible.

"All the needed secrecy at school made me an outsider. When I met you, I felt something. Something good. I wanted to see what would happen without the secrecy. I realized that I couldn't have healthy, normal relationships without the other person knowing about my virus. You took it well. I really didn't think you'd be so understanding and accepting. I don't have any reason now to be suspicious of you, but your accusation of me being accomplice to what has happened to you and your parents makes me defensive. And if you can think I'm working for my mom, then why can't I think you are doing the same thing? You really should have been frightened when I told you about the virus. But you weren't, so that's odd. I don't know, it's been a rough week," she says, exasperated, and sits down on the dry grass with her back against the rails of the fence.

I laugh a little and sit down next to her. We sit for a few minutes and say nothing. I don't know what she's thinking about, but I'm trying to figure out what I can say to restore our relationship and figure out what our next move should be. After a few minutes more I think I've got it.

"You are absolutely right."

"About it being a rough week?" she asks.

"About everything. Rachel, listen, I'm really sorry I was suspicious of you, and for accusing you of being part of Dr. Sutton's crimes against humanity, literally. From what I can recall of our time together, I can see you've been sincere with me. I'm sure if I could recall everything a little more clearly I'd realize that even more. I hope I haven't damaged your opinion of me so much that you can't trust me now. I don't want to use it as an excuse, but I was turned into a zombie this week, that should cut me some slack, right?"

"Mhhm."

"Okay, I'm going to trust you, Rachel. I trusted you before and I will trust you again. My primary concern now is to get my parents and go on our way. I don't know what that means really, or how we'll fare as zombies. We'll probably end up in a hospital quarantine or something and we'll die as they observe and study us and do whatever they can to cure the virus. I think that's what I want at this point. I don't want to be a zombie. But then there's you," I say.

Rachel seems a little shocked, but I'm not sure at what.

"But you don't have to die…again…you can live like this, don't you feel mostly the same as you did before?" she asks.

"I do, but not completely the same. There is enough difference for me to wonder about what will happen in the future. Will something change in me after a few years so that I'm the one looking to advance human evolution by introducing a fatal virus that reanimates dead bodies and makes them walk around like a puppet oblivious to the fact that they should be buried in a cemetery? I mean, eventually whatever remnant of me that is left in the wiring of my brain is going to fade or something and I won't be me anymore; I probably won't even realize it is happening. I don't want that."

"But what about your parents?" Rachel asks.

"I'm going to explain this to them and see what they think."

She follows up with, "Then what about me? You said you want to get your parents and leave, perhaps let yourselves all die again, but then there's me. So what about me, Eric?"

"That is the question," I say and look off into the distance.

16. This is the End

I look into Rachel's green eyes. "Were your eyes green before you became a zombie?" I ask.

"What? My eye color? Of course it was the same. Did you think it would have changed?" she returns.

"I don't know, I just wondered."

I'm still working out how to respond to her question. After my eye color question Rachel looks at me funny and turns her head in the opposite direction.

I finally respond to her question, but a little standoffishly, "You just said you've wanted this to be over with if you can't have a normal life. After this week do you see that normalcy isn't a likely outcome?"

Rachel doesn't respond or even look back at me immediately. Instead she pulls a tuft of tall grass from the parched ground and shakes the dry dirt loose from the roots. She tosses the grass off into the air and turns to face me.

"I do see that, but I also see that in my attempt at developing a normal friendship I ended up with you. This isn't what I was hoping for, I promise, but it seems convenient enough now. You and I are dead, right? Our parents are dead, right? We can't go back to school now, at least, you can't and I simply don't want to. Let's leave. You and me. I can get money for us, and we can just go.

This is what I brought you out here to talk about. I want to leave and I want you to come with me. What do you think about that? And you still didn't answer my question; remember how I'm attentive to your tendency to do that?" Rachel says.

"Hmm. I'll need a minute to consider your new question, but I guess I can answer your original one," I say, and reposition myself on the ground, stretching my legs out straight. I'm still wearing the scrubs they dressed me in while I was transitioning. Rachel offered me a pair of sandals from a shoe mat by the front door on our way out. The sun is rising and warming the ground. It doesn't feel bad at all. All around us are wide open pastures. Plenty of cows, but no other people, living or reliving.

"You want to run away from all of this?" I ask stretching my arms out to measure the grandeur of the scene.

"That doesn't sound like an answer to my question, Eric." Rachel is serious. She really wants to know what I think about her, and probably not just in regards to my plan for getting my parents and getting out of here.

I better give it to her straight. "I'm considering you in my plans. I'd like whatever happens next for me to involve you. However, I'm not over my parents and I can't leave them. I don't need to think about any of the rest of it, that's enough for right now; I'm not leaving my parents. I'd like to keep getting to know you and, as you pointed out, we have a lot in common, certain aspects of which no one else in the world shares, but I don't think I can go with you right now. If you want to go, I wish you well, but I've got to stay until I can figure something else out.

"And if you are going, before you go I want you to know I don't hate you for all of this, I don't think you are behind it, and I don't want you to feel bad about it. I don't hate you, but your mom, well, I think I probably do hate her."

Something changes as I say this. I think sometimes you just need to say what you think, or write it down, and then hear or read it in order to really understand it. It's not enough to form a thought in your mind; you have to follow through the action of speaking it or writing it to know how you feel about it. A moment ago I was only thinking about me, my parents, and Rachel. But Rachel is right, my parents are dead. They will be reanimated soon, but like I'm realizing, that's not the same thing as living. I also realize now that there are a lot more people in danger than the four people I'm concerned with.

Rachel doesn't respond to my monologue. She just sits with her eyes cast downward.

I speak again. "I've never been very socially conscious before, I try to be polite and all that, but I've never seen myself as a superhero. However, if your mom is looking to infect this town with a zombie virus, I feel inclined to stop her. It's too late for me and my parents, but there are still a lot of people out there who are in danger. Well, it's Cranston, so not a lot of people, really, in the grand scheme of it all, but quite a few innocent lives are in peril. I suddenly feel responsible to help them. If there is anything you can tell me about your mom or the operation she's got going on here that might help me, I'd appreciate if you'd let me know before you leave. If you still plan on leaving. You could help me help Cranston."

Rachel looks up at me, reaches over, and takes hold of my hand. "She'll just kill you. Mom will kill you if you try to stop her. I don't know any details about Mom's plan. Until yesterday morning I had no idea she was involved with research on the virus at all. I didn't know she and Frank and Mark were looking to introduce the virus into the public. At this point you probably know as much about all of that as I do."

"I guess I need to find out then. Once my parents are mobile, I'll figure something out to get them out of here, and then I'll get into the lab and find their stores of the virus and destroy it. I'll just destroy the whole lab. If they are thinking of waging biological warfare on people then this is war. And regarding your mom trying to kill me, she's already done it once, I'm not afraid of her." If I was holding sun glasses, now would be the time to put them on.

"Why don't you just burn the house down then? Get your parents out and torch it," Rachel suggests.

"I don't want to kill your family, I just want to destroy the virus, I can then report all of this to the CDC, if I can get a phone number for them, and if they believe me," I say. "We really don't know what the relationship is between your mom and the CDC and the Agency at this point."

With our hands still joined, Rachel says, "That's not my family any more. I wish it was, sometimes I think it is, but in reality it isn't. I'd burn the house down myself, but I'm too afraid. You wouldn't have any problem notifying the CDC. Just tell them you know where Dr. Arlene Carter is and they'll come running. Carter is our real last name."

"Carter? I'm confused," I say.

"Remember the story I told you? We were sent to live here peacefully and quietly, hidden in plain view from the public? Well, I was told changing our last name was just part of that. It never meant anything to me so I've never thought about it since. But in light of my mom telling me yesterday that we ran away from the Agency and weren't actually sent here, I guess it does mean something," Rachel explains.

"Well. Just when I thought all the surprises were on the table. So you don't actually have ties to the Sutton ranch then. That fits with something Trent said about the suspicion about your family, actually."

"I don't know what Trent was talking about, but the ranch was in our family, only it was my mom's maternal grandfather who started it. His name was Sutton, so it's twice removed through marriage by the time we got here. Actually I'm surprised the Agency hasn't tracked us down yet, we are under an assumed name, but it's not that far off, and this ranch along with the slaughterhouse has been here for a long time now." Rachel trails off, her mind seemingly switching tracks and considering something important for the first time.

I give her a minute and then ask, "What are you thinking about?"

"Why hasn't the Agency ever caught up to us? If we actually escaped from them like Mom said yesterday, why haven't they ever found us? It's not like this is some local police investigation team, this is a high-level secret operations group. For example, what would *you* do if you were launching a top secret manhunt for a group of escaped zombie scientists?" Rachel asks, her energy level swelling.

"Me? Well, I…" I start, but she quickly interrupts me.

"Wouldn't you try to contact any of their living relatives? My great-grandmother Sutton is still alive. She lives in New Mexico with my great uncle's family. My mom's parents are still alive, too. Wouldn't they find my mom's parents and start asking questions? Then my grandmother would easily give up the name of her brother and mother in New Mexico and they'd have Sutton. Right?"

"What do I look like, Ancestry.com? You lost me." I'm trying to do the family math, but after the part about twice removed through marriage I think I forgot to carry the great-uncle.

"I'll draw you a family tree sometime, but don't they have profilers and stuff? Granted, zombie profiling might not be as advanced a science as profiling bank robbers or serial killers, but after three years, couldn't they figure it out? We'd need brains; Sutton's used to have a slaughterhouse. I guess hindsight is 50/50…"

"I think you mean 20/20."

"What? 20/20? What did I say?" she asks.

"50/50," I answer.

"Oh, not that. 20/20. Which means this all makes sense to me now, but I probably wouldn't have figured it out before. Obviously I never did," Rachel concludes.

"But you aren't a special operative trained for this kind of thing. It does beg the question of why they haven't found you yet," I say.

Rachel is sitting with her knees pulled up to her chest, arms wrapped tightly around her knees. With her excitement she looks like she'll implode from the force she is squeezing herself with, but it fades and she drops her forehead down to rest on her knees.

"My parents lied to me for three years, shouldn't surprise me that yesterday's reveal still held some details back. What did you say about my mom saying they had some help from some friends in authority?"

"That's exactly what she said. They got some help from some friends with authority," I say.

Rachel speculates, "Maybe they didn't run away from the Agency. Maybe the first story I was told was the truth, but only partially. What if they ran away from the CDC, but not the Agency? Maybe some faction of the Agency has sanctioned this research and my mom is still working for them. Maybe the Agency is the group of 'friends in authority.' Maybe that's why they never tracked us down, because they knew we were here and in fact were the ones who sent us here."

"Your dad worked for the Agency," I say, not as a question, but rather looking for confirmation.

"Right. He did. When they told me yesterday that we were fugitives it was the fact that Dad used to work for the Agency that made me think it was plausible that we'd been able to successfully hide all this time. But maybe it's actually his affiliation that brought us here and has allowed my mom and Frank to get to this point in their work. Maybe we should try to find out more information?"

I concur with Rachel. "I think that's a good idea."

For the moment, the discussion of *us* fades away. We are distracted by the mystery of the whole situation. We are no longer crushing teenagers trying to figure out how to develop a relationship when life is pulling us in different directions. We are now zombie teenagers wondering whether or not a nefarious scheme is afoot that hopes to end with the viral infection of the human race. To quote one of the greats, "This is heavy."

I say to Rachel, "We do need to find out more, but I don't know how. For now I think it is best if you and I stay together. We don't know what is going on, which means we don't know who, if anyone, we can trust."

Rachel looks at me. She doesn't say anything. I wish we did have that zombie mind link I was joking about before. At least between the two of us, that would have made this whole conversation easier. But less exciting, perhaps. We sit and stare for a moment.

Looking at this girl, sitting pensively in a cattle pasture on a bright, mid-winter morning in Texas, you'd never expect she was a zombie. I guess the same could be said for me, except changing the details to boy instead of girl, but the point is that we don't look like zombies. Dr.

Sutton said we weren't technically zombies, but even using the term reanimate, I don't think anyone would suspect us of being that. Of course, I don't think anyone would know what to expect by that term. I'm getting lost in the semantics. There are more important things to think about now. And Rachel seems to have thought of them.

"Super soldiers. Isn't that what combat units are always after? They want to remove the biological weaknesses of man and replace them with strength," she says.

"You mean the Agency? Do you think that's what your mom is working towards? Super soldier formulas for the Agency?"

"Why not?" she asks.

"Good point. It's all speculation at this point. So, have you ever heard any discussion about what would happen if a reanimate were shot?" I ask.

"Depends on where and how many times. Remember, kill the virus, kill the body. I suppose we could be shot and still function more than the average human. Plus, we don't need to eat or drink as much or as often. We don't need sleep…"

Rachel stops her brainstorming when I roll over onto my stomach and begin doing pushups.

"I can't usually do more than twenty five of these at a time."

"Only twenty five?"

"Okay, twenty, I didn't want to sound like a wimp."

Rachel laughs. I keep pushing and don't feel the need to stop when I hit twenty, or even twenty five. I stop at thirty five, not feeling weak or tired, having answered the question in my mind.

"We don't tire like an average human. It may not be that we are that much stronger, but our muscles don't tire like a living person's would. We sound like pretty valuable creatures for combat. We are already dead, we can take more physical damage before going down, we don't need much food or water, we don't need sleep, we have better stamina, and we are functionally stronger than the average person," I say.

"Sounds plausible to me," Rachel says.

"Who do you think is behind this?" I ask.

"I don't think it matters. Apparently my mom and dad, Frank, and Mark are all in on it and they have someone either in the Agency or CDC, or perhaps the U.S. Military, backing them. Frank used to be an agent, I usually refer to the initial research team as my mom's team, but Frank was lead scientist on the project attempting to use the virus for Alzheimer's therapy. You know, maybe this super soldier bit is the reason they were working on the virus in the first place. Maybe the accident wasn't as accidental as has been claimed. Maybe it wasn't supposed to spread to the families, but maybe it was. More data, better research," Rachel says. I nod in agreement.

"I think it all sounds plausible. If it's accurate, then maybe the target isn't to initiate a public outbreak in Cranston. Maybe this is just the secret laboratory. Which makes me the first super soldier...I'm Captain America!"

Rachel raises her eyebrows and smiles slightly at my burst of enthusiasm. I settle back down and continue.

"But why me? I'm not exactly the super solider type. Wouldn't Trent have made a better candidate?" I ask.

"Don't look at me, I didn't know what was going on."

"Okay, so I'm the first live trial, now they want to test me to see how I behave, but also to see if all of their tweaks to the virus are doing what they want them to do. If my trial goes well then it might be down to mass production and release to whoever it is that wants this stuff. Maybe just the Agency, but maybe they are on a military contract, like you suggested. Maybe not even for our own military. Who knows where this will end up if we don't stop it?" I say.

"Well that means calling the CDC is out. If we call them, it'll go to the Agency to follow up on, and if they are in on it, then they'll be after *us*. If we tell the local police they'll either end up dead, transitioned and imprisoned, or they'll call for Federal help which will likely lead back to the CDC and the Agency. As soon as anyone comes near this place Mom will call quarantine and they'll call the CDC," Rachel adds.

"So we are on our own? You and me against the world? Is that what you are thinking?" I ask with a hint of sarcasm.

"Yeah, just like the movies, huh?"

"Just like it."

We sit in silence for a while more as the sun warms us to the point of discomfort and then agree to head back to the house. On the walk back we laugh at how we've cooked up a story that features the two of us as the only thing standing between the world and something bad. World domination by a despot in control of an army of zombies, maybe? Or maybe the plan actually is what Rachel initially suspected, a simple outbreak of a fatal virus. Either way, we stand between life and death for a lot of people. Us, a couple of zombie kids. Who only moments ago were about to part ways.

"This is a lot of responsibility for a couple of 17 year olds," I say.

Rachel corrects me. "I was 16 when we transitioned. Counting from birth I'm actually 19 now."

"Right. And yet you are still hanging around with high school boys. Classy," I tease.

"I think it is safe to say my emotional development halted when I turned into a zombie," she says.

"Good point. All the more reason to prevent this virus from spreading. Think of all the children that would be stuck, never having any opportunity to advance in life. That isn't fair. Sure, sometimes it happens naturally, or even by accident, but for one person to bring about such outcomes for another person is unnatural and seems very unjust," I say, adopting the role of crusader rather easily.

"I agree."

"Then let's just burn the house down now," I say.

We stop walking and face each other.

"What do you mean?" Rachel asks.

"I'm saying that if we are pretty confident that no good will come from the existence of this virus, and there isn't anyone we can contact for help, then why not destroy it right now? I'm thinking about this as if it really were a movie. You know, when the hero has the villain against the wall and the action that will end any and all threat is simple enough to perform right then, but the hero hesitates or takes a moment to crack a joke allowing the villain to escape, and the story stretches on for another hour? It all could have been prevented if the hero just took action in the first moment when a solution presented itself. It happens all the time in action stories and when I'm watching them I always say 'just pull the trigger already!' or 'handcuff him and *then* call for backup!' Or whatever the case may be. It happens all the time, the hero doesn't act when a simple solution presents itself and has to struggle on for a while longer until a more difficult solution is realized.

"In books and movies it makes sense, good for the story and all that, but in real life, why not just do the easy thing and prevent further trouble? We go get some gasoline, douse the outside of the lab and throw a match.

Your parents and Frank and Mark will likely get out before the house goes up, but hopefully the lab will be destroyed, and with it all remnants of the virus they have stored." I'm growing confident in my new plan.

"I think you make a strong argument, but we can't destroy the virus unless we kill everyone who has transitioned and then make sure no one comes in contact with the bodies until the virus is dead. So even if we destroy the lab and the house, the virus will exist," Rachel says.

"Right, the plan isn't perfect, but without the lab and the extra virus, and hopefully without any documents or research notes, your mom's team will be set back enough to prevent any short term epidemic," I respond.

"What about your parents? Once the house is in flames we won't be able to get them out, and it's highly unlikely that anyone inside will make an effort to get them out. That's a big sacrifice for you to make." Rachel reaches for my hand again. I let her take it.

This is why I'll never be a Hollywood-successful hero.

I say, "My parents are already dead. Your mom or Frank or whoever pushed the plunger on the syringe already killed them. The corpses of my parents lie on a couple of beds in a third story bedroom over there, being infected by a dangerous virus, but those aren't, and never will be, my parents. If I get hung up on the possibility of reestablishing some form of family with zombie parents then I'll doom humanity. I'm 17 and highly self-focused, but I'm not stupid."

"Should we get you a cape to wear before we pour the gasoline?" Rachel asks.

"I don't see how it could hurt. Unless the cape drags through the spilled gasoline and I go up in flames with the house, in which case it would certainly hurt." This makes us both laugh, and the laughter seems to lighten the weight of what we are planning to do.

"Should we wait until night? They don't all sleep, but they might be less likely to catch us."

"What do you think would be more suspicious to them? Us playing outside during the day or during the night? Also, do we have access to gasoline without arousing suspicion?" I ask.

"There are several cans of gas in the shed for the mower. It'd be easier to get that out unnoticed in the darkness, but you are probably right that they'll be less suspicious of us being out here during the day than during the night. Unless we catch them while they are eating! If they are all in the basement together we could start this thing up and we might even trap them all." Rachel says.

"Well, let me ask you then, are you prepared to do this to your family?" I ask.

Rachel gives me a look of sincerity, "It's like you said, my parents are dead. They actually died a long time ago. I've come to realize that any attachment or feelings I've had for them are just remnants of memory, and not current emotions. Besides, if it's them or the world, I think the right thing to do is to stop them."

"Alright. Then it's settled. Will they call you for breakfast? Do they eat breakfast? What are your normal meal times?" There is so much I don't know about being a zombie.

"It's more of a daily meal time, and it'll be around 6pm. No reason behind that, it's just what we've become accustomed to," Rachel explains.

"That's still a long time away. I'm hesitant to wait that long, but it does sound good to trap them all in the house and get it over with. Especially in the event that your dad gets out of the house, he'd probably rip my head right off, wouldn't he?"

"Most likely. If we do the fire now we need to be prepared to face them or run. If we run we won't know what happens here, but we might be able to get away. If we face them, well, without some weapons I don't think we stand a chance."

"But waiting borders on that Hollywood scenario when the hero waits for whatever reason and ends up making things worse. We can get the virus now, at increased risk to ourselves, or we can try to play it safer for ourselves and take it all out later. So much for declaring it settled already." I guess I should reserve final judgment until all plans are actually in place and reviewed a second time.

"Whether or not we are alive in the end, we should probably consider what will happen if they all make it out of the fire," Rachel suggests.

I recap. "Good point. If they get out, the virus still exists, and it is feasible that they could go into town and start infecting people. If that's the plan to begin with, we haven't stopped it, just forced their hand and perhaps made it a slower, sloppier process. But, if they are working towards giving a virus serum to a military leader with a screw loose, we may have set them back a good while. Of course they still have the virus. The only sure way to settle it is to get the house and the zombies. This, in all honesty, includes you and me." Uncle Ben was right, and I don't mean the rice guy.

"So let's call the police," Rachel says.

"And tell them what, exactly? Do we make something up, or what? We've already considered the local force and how they probably aren't prepared for what is going on here," I say.

"We can tell them there is a meth lab being run from the house. They'll bring more than just the local deputy to investigate that, hopefully, but by the time they arrive the house will already be burned, suggesting there was a meth lab that may have exploded. But that's too uncertain with timing. We need the police here, and in good numbers, before we light the fire."

She's right. "I agree, but how do we get them here? And how do we get them here and then light a match without obviously being the ones lighting the match? Or without their arrival pulling everyone out of the house?"

"That I don't know," Rachel answers.

"I know, neither do I, but those are the questions we need to answer before we go any further." Suddenly the idea hits me. "I'll be on the inside when you light the match."

I can tell from the squint in Rachel's eyes that she isn't immediately picking up on what I'm saying.

"I'll go inside and gather everyone somewhere, either into the lab if I can think of a reason, or maybe into the kitchen, the one in the basement. If I have them all engaged in conversation with me in one location it should secure enough time for you to get the fuel, douse the house and scratch the match," I say.

"You couldn't rhyme fuel?"

I just laugh.

She continues, "You really should have a cape if you are going to sacrifice yourself like that. But you are already dead, right? So it doesn't really matter." Rachel seems hurt by my willingness to take one for the team.

That team being the human race in this case, which I'm not technically part of anymore. I always wondered how Superman felt, I guess now I know. It's almost the same thing.

"I'll wear a cape if it will make you happy. And yes, I am dead. These bodies, they aren't us, they are just reanimated masses of flesh and bones. We are gone, I don't know where we are, or how it works, but we aren't here. You and I never actually met. Public threat or not, it's ridiculous for us to do anything different than stop this all, here and now. I'm sorry if that's a little harsh, but I guess I just haven't had the same experience as you have. We both caught the virus without consent, but your situation was accidental. Mine wasn't. Mine was part of an evil plan, either to enslave the masses or who knows what. I don't want this."

"What about me, then? Should I light the match and then run inside to join you? Or am I supposed to go make a new life on my own somehow?" She isn't angry, but her tone is flirting with frustration.

"I don't know, Rachel. I'm just not thinking about you right now. There are bigger issues to consider. I'm sorry."

"Fine," she says.

I think I've lost her, again, but maybe this time for real. Whatever connection we had is gone. If not for my new found spirit of being a super hero I think I'd be trying to fix that. As it stands I just hope she carries out this plan with me.

"So do you want me to get the fire going now, or are we going to wait until later?" She looks at her feet while speaking, and then raises her eyes to mine.

"This is the best way to handle the situation," I say.

"I said 'fine.' When do we do it?"

Yeah, I guess 'us' is over. And the question of what I think about her is answered. I can see that's how she is interpreting it. I can stand around wishing circumstances were different, that she and I met when we were *both* living humans and never knew anything about zombie viruses, but that's not the way it happened.

"Right now. No point in putting it off. I'll go inside and gather everyone as best I can. My primary goal will be to reel in your parents; hopefully I can get them all. Be prepared in case something doesn't go right and someone gets out. Keep your eyes open after you start the blaze."

I add, "Do you want to call the police? If we call them right now they might get here just in time to see the fire really take hold. It should be too late for them to stop that, but they might be able to offer some protection to you. You could call and tell them Frank's gone mad or something, that way they expect trouble, and if he gets out of the house when the fire starts he'll be the target for the cops. What do you think?"

"Yeah. That sounds like a good idea. You go find everyone, I'll get the gasoline. Dad's got lighters all over the place; I'll grab one from the car on my way over. I'll call the Sheriff on my way." She sounds detached and sleepy.

"This is for the best, Rachel. Too bad you and I didn't meet for real."

"I'm almost three years older than you," she says.

"Right."

I turn towards the house and stop.

"Hey!" I face her again. "I got one for 'fuel!' Ready? You mule the fuel, douse the house, and scratch the match!" I'm very pleased with my accomplishment. Rachel isn't as enthusiastic.

"Nice work, but it's just not the same after the moment has passed."

Well, that's a letdown.

"Bye, Rachel," I say.

"Goodbye, Eric."

17. Nightmare

Inside the house I don't find anyone in the living room, upstairs kitchen or dining room. I decide to check the basement next, and then work my way up. The door to the basement is heavy, with an old fashioned door knob, quite possibly original to the house. It opens noiselessly on well oiled hinges. The basement has obviously been renovated recently, despite the old door. The stairwell is enclosed with metal hand rails. I flip the light switch and realize that the chance of anyone being down there is slim, since the lights had been off. Out of curiosity I follow the steps down to where they turn to the right. The basement isn't very large; it opens up into one room. It must not run the whole length of the house.

Directly ahead of me is the kitchenette setup. Three refrigerators or large freezers are lined up on the wall to my left, then a sink just past them in the corner. Around the corner, bordering the sink is an oven. A few cabinets and an island counter round out the set. The rest of the basement is a nicely furnished room with a living room feel. There aren't any windows, but there is a door on the wall to my right. I'd like to check if it leads outside or to another room, but remembering my mission, I realize I've taken too much time on this diversion already. It's a nice basement, but I've got monsters to corral.

I head back up the steps and through the familiar downstairs rooms. I decide to knock on the lab door, in case they are in there. That would end my search sooner, as well as prevent the need for knocking on bedroom doors. That seems a little too nosey for me, even under the current circumstances.

The lab door, in contrast to the basement door, is very modern, and made of metal. It's painted white, perhaps to make its composition less noticeable from a distance. But my knuckles can tell, and the muffled sound my knocking makes is a dead giveaway. I knock and wait. I can't hear anyone or anything inside, so I knock again and count to fifteen.

"Hello?" A voice comes from upstairs. I think it's Mark. I realize now that I haven't yet come up with a story for why I need to gather everyone. Better think quickly.

"Hi, Mark?" I ask.

"Yes," Mark replies.

"It's Eric."

Duh.

"Where is everyone?" I ask.

Mark is down to the bend in the stairs now and I look up at him.

"Arlene and Frank are in with your parents, making observations. Tom is around somewhere, I believe, I don't think he has left for the slaughterhouse yet, doesn't usually go this early on Saturdays. I'm just doing some reading. I thought I heard knocking so I came out into the hallway."

"Yeah, I was just looking for Dr. Sutton and figured I'd check down low before going up the stairs. I thought maybe she was in the lab."

"Nope, no one is in there at the moment."

"Thanks, Mark. I guess I'll just head up to see Dr. Sutton then."

"Okay, that'll be fine." Mark says and begins climbing the stairs. I jump up the steps, two at a time, and catch up with him.

"Actually, I've got something I'd like to talk to everyone about. Do you think you could find Tom and bring him up?" I ask, trying not to betray my flash flood of anxiety, and hoping that Mark doesn't ask for details, or ask if I'd like to involve Rachel in my discussion as well.

He doesn't seem suspicious.

"Sure, I'll see if he's in his bedroom and bring him up. Got some more questions about your new life, eh?"

"Yes, still trying to figure this all out. Thanks."

"Sure, sure." Mark says as we walk side by side down the hall towards the next stair case. Mark stops at the last door and knocks. I continue on up the stairs, concerned that Tom might be able to read my expression and become suspicious of my request for a grand council.

Tom answers the door and I hear Mark explaining my request as I set foot onto the third level floor. The door to the room my parents are in is open slightly. I approach quietly, but don't hear anything from inside. I knock lightly on the door frame and step inside.

"Hello, Eric," says Dr. Sutton.

Frank looks up at me from his rocking chair and then back down to the clipboard and papers in his hands. Clearly I'm not very interesting to him at the moment. If he only knew what I was about to do. Actually, it's definitely better that he doesn't know. This phrase isn't really useful in a situation like this. I wonder when it would be useful.

"What's up, Doc?" If I'm going to die for good in a few minutes, I don't want it to be without ever having said that to an official doctor.

"Quite," Dr. Sutton says. Is she suddenly British?

"Do you need something, or were you just coming up to visit your parents?" she adds.

"I was hoping I could have a chat with everyone. I saw Mark downstairs; he's going to see if he can bring Mr. Sutton up. I have some 'life as a zom-... reanimate' questions and I wanted to get everyone's perspectives on it," I say.

Frank looks up again and eyes me studiously for a moment before going back to his papers.

"Very well. We can have a little session with you," the doctor says.

Mark and Tom Sutton enter the room. Mark makes for the only other open chair in the room, a simple straight backed wooden chair, probably part of a dining room set at some point. Tom leans against the wall right inside the door. He speaks first.

"Good morning, Eric. You have some questions?"

"Yes I do. Probably not very scientific, but some things I thought up over night. Does anyone mind answering my questions?"

I try to play it off as casual and be extra polite. All I need to do is buy some time. I hope Rachel has everything under control outside. If this doesn't go according to plan, not that we really have much of a plan, things could get pretty dicey.

Tom shrugs in response to my question. Mark says he doesn't mind. Frank says nothing.

"What's on your mind?" Dr. Sutton asks.

"Well, first just a few stupid, but curious, questions." I still don't have any questions, time to adlib. "Will my hair continue growing? Will I need to shave and get haircuts?"

Tom says "Hmmph," while blowing air out his nose. "That's an interesting question. I don't think I wondered about that myself until a few months after the transition and I realized I hadn't had a hair cut since."

Good. He seems to be taking the question seriously and isn't raising suspicion.

"Hair still grows, but significantly slower than it did before for you. A good haircut will last a lot longer now. It's a good benefit," Dr. Sutton says.

"Of course, a bad haircut..." Tom lets silence finish his remark, which has the intended effect: we laugh.

"Okay, how about, bathroom stuff. You said I can eat whatever I want and my body will process it. Is digestion the same as before, just doesn't absorb nutrients the same?" I ask.

I do wonder about these things, but it doesn't matter if I find out the answers now as I expect we'll all be dead in short order. I hope we will be.

"What have you eaten in the last few days?" Dr. Sutton asks.

"I guess since Wednesday lunch, I haven't eaten anything except for the dish of brains you brought me, when was that, yesterday? I had a little water at some point."

"Right, so in four days you haven't eaten much or had anything to drink, but do you feel hungry? Have you felt the urge to visit the restroom?" Dr. Sutton asks.

"No, I feel fine. So I won't go to the bathroom anymore?" I say.

"Not as often. But you will. We have delved into the science of it a little, if you'd like to get deeper into it at some point we can do that, but I assume right now you just have some entry level curiosity."

"Right. I'm just curious. Maybe someday we can get into the science behind it all. But that's good enough for now," I say.

"I have a question for *you*," says Frank.

Taken by surprise, I say "Okay, shoot."

"Why are you wasting our time with these questions?"

No one says anything. Either they are all thinking this, or zombies don't have patience for eager learners. I don't mind. It opens the door to ask the one question I'm actually interested in knowing the answer to.

"Well, I have one big question I want to ask, but didn't know how to go about getting everyone together in order to ask it. I was trying to work up to it, but I don't want to waste anyone's time, so I'll just ask it."

I pause a moment, as much to kill time as to phrase the question in my mind.

"What do you all intend to do with this virus? Why have you spent these last three years researching it in secret and why are you now doing human trials with it?" I ask.

Tom chuckles and stands upright from his leaning position on the wall. He walks towards the one window in the room, which has been blocked by curtains thus far. I begin to sweat, though not physically, I don't know if that's possible, but in my mind I'm sweating. I sure hope Rachel isn't in view of this window, wherever that might be. Or if she's already started the fire I hope the smoke and flames aren't visible here. Tom stops short of the window and turns back to face me. That's convenient.

"You must have a theory yourself, Eric, otherwise you wouldn't ask this question," the cowboy says coolly.

I look at Dr. Sutton who is waiting for my response. Frank and Mark are also "eyes on" me.

"I don't have a theory, I'm just curious. You made me a zombie; you made my parents zombies, what's next? There must be a reason. I'm trying to figure it out. I guess if I have a theory it's that you want to give this virus to everyone, but I don't understand why. That's what I'd like to know. Why?"

Tom nods slowly but doesn't say anything.

Dr. Sutton takes over. "The virus doesn't make people into zombies, it reanimates their bodies. In the process it eliminates a lot of what makes people weak. It doesn't make them immortal, but it does *reduce* their mortality. You will live longer like this than you could ever have hoped for without the virus. Many things that would have killed you before won't kill you now. They won't even hurt you. This is the next stage in human evolution. We are going to make the world stronger. You are the first. You are proof that this is possible and over the next few weeks and months we'll determine to what extent the benefits reach. This is historic!"

I say, "But what about individual will and consent? You did this to me, I never asked for it. You didn't even offer me a brochure and have me consider the transition as an option. You just did it. What if I don't want to have *reduced* mortality? And what about the children, or the really old? Do you want to give them the virus as well and trap them in extended states of childhood or old age?" I feel my temper rising toward anger, but then it stops. And then it starts again.

Dr. Sutton seems pleased to have these questions to contend with. Frank has put his papers down on the floor next to his chair and folded his hands in his lap. He is finally taking interest in my little meeting. Mark is also sitting attentively in his chair against the wall. My parents are both lying motionless in their beds. Dead, reanimated, I have no idea. Tom Sutton is standing a few steps from the window, arms folded, smiling at me.

"To answer your last question first, the virus will kill the weak, the sick, the very young and the very old. We aren't sure what the age brackets are, but we know that Rachel transitioned at 16 and Frank at 68. I suppose in all honesty we don't *know* that the virus will kill those groups, but we definitely expect it to. That is a hard process to recreate with rats as their development is very different in matters of time than it is for humans. One of our associates during the accident that resulted in our transitioning did have young children, and they weren't looking good during the transition. Our teammate didn't like the whole process and ended things for himself and his family, so we never got to see what would have happened with the children. It is too bad."

As Dr. Sutton laments her mad scientist memory, I challenge her again. "Then you are prepared to release a viral agent into the public that may instantly kill, and not reanimate, a huge portion of the population, just like that?"

"Yes. Yes, Eric, we are willing to kill a large portion of the population in order to improve things for an even larger portion of the population. That's our plan." Dr. Sutton seems frustrated with me, but she has admitted her evil intent yet again.

"Who died and left you in charge of the future of the human race? Can your virus-operated corpse bodies procreate?" I match her frustration wit for wit.

"We don't need procreation. We will continue to exist, unbound and unfettered by the animal demands of life, almost completely. We will be able to focus on progression. Free from needs to earn money and work ourselves to death just to survive. Education and enlightenment will take top priority and focus in the lives of the survivors. You are young Eric, what do you know about the struggles that exist in the world?" Dr. Sutton is in her full mad scientist element now.

"What do I know of the struggles of the world? What do you mean? Poverty, war, famine?" I seek to clarify.

"Yes, those things. What causes them? I'll tell you. Mortal weakness. The animal passions of the human race. If we eliminate those passions, we eliminate the problems that follow. We are providing peace and security," she explains.

I still don't know if they are operating alone or on a larger scale, but it sounds like the super soldier theory is out. I suppose I'm not Captain America after all, I'm just a modern version of Frankenstein's monster. Unless I pull this mission off, in which case I'll reinstate my Captain America status, but not for the super soldier bit, just for the heroics. I wonder how Rachel's fire is going out there.

"Maybe you are providing peace and security, but at what cost?" I ask.

"What cost? The loss of sickness, weakness and death," Frank answers.

I turn to face him, "Minus the initial death count, right?"

"You have to break some eggs…" he says.

"And all of you are in on this? Mark, Mr. Sutton?" I ask.

"Yes," Mark says.

Tom simply nods.

"Well, I wish I never got mixed up with you people. I'm not happy about how things have turned out, but I'm glad that Rachel brought me so that I can stop you. I guess if it wasn't me here now I'd eventually have faced the virus anyway. I'm glad then that it *is* this way so that I can stop it."

Tom laughs, another big laugh like when I first met him a few days ago. "You can't stop this, boy!" and he continues laughing.

I smell smoke. Rachel has done it.

"Maybe I can't, not alone, not right now, but the stopping is already in motion." That doesn't make sense. 'The stopping is already in motion'? Oh well, it's said, can't take it back now.

Tom's face goes blank, and then fills with suspicious hostility. "Where is Rachel?"

Dr. Sutton's eyes open so wide I half expect her eyeballs to fall out. She shrugs in answer to Tom's question.

Tom scowls at me and then comes charging in my direction. He grabs my collar with one hand and the other clenches around my left bicep. I'm slammed against the wall next to the door. With his face only an inch or so away from mine, he says, "You can't stop us."

I am thrown to the side and I crumple into a heap when I hit the ground. Tom is out of the room and I can hear his steps pounding on the stairs before I can even lift myself back up. Frank is right out the door behind him, followed by Dr. Sutton. Mark is standing over me.

"What have you done, my boy?" he asks.

"This isn't right. You can't expose people to a fatal virus like this. It's evil," I say.

"Evil is in the eye of the beholder," Mark says, right before kicking me square in the nose.

***

I don't lose consciousness, but it is a minute or two before I can stand up. The smell of smoke is stronger now. The air in the room is becoming hazy. It's just me and my parents left in the room. They both lie as though dead. That's how I think of them otherwise I might not be able to leave them. I struggle to stand. Without looking at the beds, I say goodbye and exit the room. There is much more smoke in the hallway, it's coming from the stairwell. I see no flames yet, and can't sense any increase in temperature. I don't know where the fire was started, but it seems to be going. I hope it destroys the lab. It is likely that everyone has gotten out. I hope Rachel gets away from them.

The smell of the smoke stings in my brain, but I don't feel it in my throat or lungs as I should, if I was alive. I'm still reeling a bit from the head kick, which, by the way, was totally unexpected. It wouldn't have surprised me as much from Frank, but quiet Mickey Rooney? That caught me way off guard. The stairs are now covered with black smoke. I feel my way down to the next landing and drop to the floor in an effort to see beneath the smoke. Visibility is low. I'm realizing that fire might not really have been as much of a captivating method as I originally thought. I wasn't figuring for how little physical effect the smoke has on me. I suppose the others have simply run right out the front door.

Visibility is much better from the floor, I stay down and crawl towards the next stair case. I start to feel the heat, a lot, the closer I get to the stairs. This end of the house is where the lab is. I guess Rachel started the fire here. Good. Hopefully that means the lab is destroyed; even if we don't get the walking virus samples, we'll get the stuff in the lab. The heat is stifling. Maybe fire wasn't such a bad plan after all, I just lost my audience too soon. I'll have to rehearse better next time.

Next time. There is no next time. This is it for me. I'm not going to attempt to make it down these stairs. I'll melt or burst into flames in the process. Zombie Eric might be able to withstand greater physical pain, but he isn't invincible. Do I just give up then? Just lie here on the floor until the flames consume me? If I'm not affected by smoke inhalation it's likely to be a very painful process of succumbing to flames. I'm getting second thoughts about this plan. I think I'd rather take my chances getting out and having Tom rip my head off. Yes, that sounds more appealing than burning to death. I'm next to one of the bedroom doors, so I push through and find that the smoke hasn't filled this room extensively yet. I close the door behind me to maintain the clearer atmosphere.

I spare no time in making my way to the window. I rip the curtains open and the rod pulls down with the violent tug. The window slides up and I kick out the screen. Sticking my head out I feel the heat from the flames engulfing the house to my left. Flames are also climbing up the right side of the structure. She either started fire on both ends or it has already wrapped around the front of the house. Lucky for me there isn't any fire directly below this window. Neither is there any ground for a good 15 feet or so. I wonder if my bones are stronger as a zombie. This certainly isn't a fatal fall height, but that doesn't mean it isn't a bone shattering height.

I take a moment to look around the room, maybe there's some mountain climbing equipment. No such luck, but it was worth the look. I tear off the bed sheets and try to wrap them into ropes. I tie the two together and somehow end up with a "rope" that seems shorter than one of the sheets alone. This isn't as easy as they make it look on television. I abandon this project as I realize I'll get only a foot or two of rope after tying it off to something inside the room. Those two feet might make a difference, but only if I'm going to break my legs on the straight fall. If I survive it won't matter. Yeah, that's good rationalizing.

I climb feet first out the window and maintain a solid grip on the bottom sill. Sliding my feet down the siding I hang flat against the wall. I can't look down, but it suddenly feels like I'm even higher than when I was looking down from inside the room. I can give myself another few inches by sliding my hands to the outer edge of the window. First with one hand, I slide it out and take the best grip I can with just my fingers on the outer edge of the window. There is a bit of a recess where the window pane seats into the frame, this provides something for me to hold onto. Next I move the other hand out and successfully move myself six or so inches closer to the ground. That's it, I can't go any further. Unless when super heated my zombie body will stretch like rubber. Probably not, and I don't really want to wait to find out. The heat is pretty gnarly as it is.

It's now or in another fifteen seconds when my fingers give out. I think I want to be prepared for the fall so I count to three and push off.

Falling is a basic activity. It doesn't take much effort. Impacting the ground is another story. I land on my feet, but with a strong backward force that pulls me down into a seated position. On the way down my face meets with my knees, but only for a second before I roll onto my back and over my head. The end result is me lying face down in the grass with acute pain in my feet, ankles, knees, nose, tailbone and neck. But it doesn't last. By the time I'm able to recover my wits the pain is gone, or rather, not gone, but simply a shadow of the initial pulse of it.

Pushing myself up to rest on my knees, I look left and right, but no one is around. The flames on the house have reached the roof and are working their way towards the middle. The smoke is billowing into the sky, white in some spots, black in others; spiraling together like a mixed chocolate and vanilla soft serve cone for a bit, and then mixing into an indiscriminate grey fog. I look up to the window I jumped from, okay, fell from, and it does look high. I critique my form and suppose I might have been better off turning to face out, away from the house, after pushing off from the wall. That way I could have hit the ground and transitioned into a forward somersault. I've seen the guys do it on TV. I could have pulled it off. Maybe.

I stand all the way up, and surprisingly, I feel alright. Looking left again I see a gas can. That must be where Rachel ended the soak. I take an oblique path towards that end of the house, increasing the distance between the house and myself, as the heat increases in intensity the closer I get to the end. I clear the corner of the house before I see anyone. It's a body, but I'm not sure who it used to belong to. My arc has to increase to get me further from the flames, but I continue towards the front corner of the house where the body is lying, uncomfortably close to the fire from my judgment.

It's a short, stout body, which means it must be Frank or Mark. The car is gone from the driveway. I wonder if Rachel got away or if it was someone else. I pull my shirt up over my head and run to the body. The heat is unbearable, I get close enough only to confirm that it is Frank, but it's not close enough to determine what killed him. I assume he's dead; he wouldn't be able to stand the heat if he wasn't. But did he drop there because of the flames or by some other means? I run from the body, straight towards the road. My eyes dart around in every direction, looking for any sign of Rachel, or anyone else. But I see no one. Did the others get out and leave in the car? Are they running away from the house? Did they get trapped inside?

Tom and Frank left the room upstairs first; if Frank is outside it begs that Tom made it as well. Unless he stopped inside to get something, that's very possible.

Maybe he didn't make it out. If Frank only made it that far before succumbing to the heat, perhaps Tom, Dr. Sutton and Mark didn't even make it out of the house. That's only if Tom didn't get out the door first.

My attention is pulled from wondering about the others by an exploding window on the second floor. The fire is definitely doing its job destroying the house. I wonder if my parent's remains will ever be found and if they are, if they'll determine who they are. How will that reconcile with the story Dr. Sutton and her friends made up?

"Hey! Are you alright?" Again my attention is jerked away from what I'm thinking about, this time the sound comes from behind me and is a voice. I spin round to find a man with a concerned expression leaning over from the driver seat of an old pickup truck, yelling to me through the windowless passenger door. "Son, are you okay?" He repeats.

"Yes! I'm okay, a little in shock, mentally, I guess, but I think I'm fine physically," I yell back.

"Get in, nothing you can do here. Let's get a safe distance away. I already called this in when I saw it from my field a few minutes ago. I drove over to see if I could do anything."

I hop the drainage trench alongside the road and climb up into the truck. A momentary shock of pain extends up my leg and then dissipates as the signal fades out in my brain. Maybe my fall did significant damage after all.

The man drives down the road a stretch, well past the house and then pulls off the road and into the pasture through a shallow part of the ditch.

"That house is lost. Fire is a real danger out here. Might seem like an obvious statement, but the age of these houses, the dry climate, the distance from significant emergency services. There ain't much hope of putting a fire like this out. Were you inside when it started?" the man asks me, eyeing my disheveled appearance. I'm still wearing scrubs, but I lost the sandals somewhere along the way. So much for my clothes and wallet.

"Inside? Yeah, I was inside, we smelled smoke and ran for it. I jumped out a window."

"We? Were the Suttons all home? Did they get out? I didn't see anyone else outside when I drove up," he asks, the sound of fear picking up in his voice.

"I don't know. I meant I smelled smoke. The Suttons were home, but I don't know where anyone is now. The car is gone, so someone may have left. I looked around after I got out but didn't see anyone." That's not true, I did see someone. I'm not going to correct it. It won't matter in the long run.

"Maybe someone was injured and they left for the hospital. You are lucky to have gotten out when you did. I'm going to head over and make a sweep around the house, see if I can find anyone else. Are you okay to stay here alone?"

"I'm fine, I'll come with you," I say. "My name is Eric, by the way."

"Eric, my name is Jack. Sorry to meet you under these circumstances." Jack hops out his side of the truck and makes his way around.

"Me too."

I jump out and trot to catch up to Jack. He walks briskly, and then breaks into a jog. I keep up with him. When we get close enough to the house to feel the heat we hear the first sirens of emergency responders. I wonder if Rachel called it in or if this is from Jack's call.

We circle the entire house and Jack sees Frank's body. He curses under his breath and grabs my sleeve to pull me towards the road. We run out and cross the road to get away from the heat. The Sheriff pulls up next to us. Shortly after the Sheriff come the first of the volunteer fire fighters.

Jack and I return to his truck in order to get out of the way. Jack drops the tailgate on his truck and offers me a seat. I hop up and crawl into the bed of the truck, taking up a position sitting on the left tire-well hump so I can watch the fire fight. Due to the time it took for everyone to show up, efforts are directed toward preventing the flames from spreading to the pastures, the shed and the barn. The house is a total loss. Everyone could tell when they showed up.

"What a shame," Jack says. He is standing on the passenger side of the vehicle, leaning against the wall of the bed.

I don't say anything, but I disagree with Jack. It's no shame from my point of view. The fatal virus that was no more than a few months away from an epidemic outbreak has been destroyed. Those responsible are hopefully destroyed along with it. The only shame is that I don't know, and might not ever know if they were. More than just a shame is that my family had to be destroyed.

What will I do now? Pretty soon the authorities here will start asking me questions. They'll want to know who I am, what I was doing here, who else was here, if I have any idea how the fire started. What do I tell them? I could give them the truth, but they won't believe it. Not until they take me to the hospital and try to run some vitals and lab work on me. Then I'll go back under observation, just like Dr. Sutton had planned for me. I don't think I like that idea. But what other options do I have?

The Sheriff's car is moving. The cruiser pulls gingerly off the road and into the field, coming to a stop alongside Jack's pickup.

I have two options. Lie and possibly get some semblance of a normal life back, or tell the truth and live in a cage. The self-preservation instinct is powerful. I think I heard that recently. I fully understand it right now.

18. My Friends

Today is June 14th. Flag Day. It's also graduation day for Cranston High. I'm graduating high school. This is the day I've been waiting years for. The day when I can start to make my own plans and decide where I will live and for how long. No more moving whenever Dad changes jobs. No more being the new guy. At least, not like being the new guy in public school. I'll go to college and be new, but so will everyone else in my classes, mostly. I'll be just like them. Except for the fact that I'm a zombie orphan now, which is why this day isn't so important anymore. I've been able to go wherever and do whatever I've wanted to for several months now. But knowing it is important to finish what I start, I stuck around Cranston to see high school through.

Almost five months have passed since the fire; since I lost my parents, and my own life, too. I'm doing remarkably well for someone who lost his life. Obviously, I lied about what happened at the Suttons' house. So far none of the Suttons have shown up. No bodies were recovered from the fire, except for Frank. They declared everyone dead in the fire, everyone being Tom, Arlene and Rachel. There was some surprise over my being there, when they had only two days earlier declared me dead with my parents in a vehicle accident. I'm not sure how this worked with the story the Sutton's cooked up about the accident, but they couldn't argue with the fact that I was standing there in front of them. It's not like I could have come back from the dead, right? That's what I asked them. They took my word for it.

I gave them the story that I had been over to the Sutton's house for dinner that Wednesday night, after which I took ill. Dr. Sutton decided to keep me there to care for me. I was barely conscious for two days with the illness, and when I was just getting back to normal the house was on fire. This allowed me to be vague on who was at the house and any other important details. Happily, they didn't push for anything more. Partly, I assume, because they realized that if I had been unconsciously ill for a few days, I didn't know that my parents were dead. The Sheriff took it upon himself to break the bad news to me. I responded honestly, and truly did grieve the death of my parents. Inwardly I knew they were murdered, but to keep up appearances, I went along with the car accident story.

My aunt had come into town to handle all the legal and property issues for my parents. She arrived Saturday morning in Cranston and went to the house. The Sheriff brought me there after a brief interview out at the Sutton's. My aunt nearly passed out when she saw me, being under the belief that I was dead, too. It was traumatic for her, but after a bit she calmed down. We spent the next week with the funeral, going through everything in the house, conversations with lawyers (graciously provided by the company Dad had been working for), and establishing me as a legal adult. It worked out so that I could keep the house, at least through the end of high school. I don't know how it worked out, but it did, and two weeks after my first day of school at Cranston High, I completed my fourth day of school there.

The return to school was very strange, to say the least, but I adjusted. It got around that I had been at the Sutton's house for a few days before the fire. Then the fact that they never recovered any bodies from the scene and the Suttons haven't been seen or heard from since. So with me being the only survivor, having just come out of some sort of coma – let's just say there was suspicion and talking. There still is.

Trent and his crew warmed up to me after a few weeks, but it wasn't quite the same as when I first got into town. They already thought the Suttons were strange, before the house fire and disappearance. They said it wasn't too out of the ordinary not to recover the bodies after such a fire, but I had told Jack the neighbor that one of the cars was missing, and that made its way into the police report, and then into the gossip stream. Since no Suttons ever showed up at any of the area hospitals, or have been seen in Cranston since, it's all very suspicious.

I didn't play baseball. Trent didn't push the issue with me. Maybe I should have played, I might actually have been able to keep up with my zombie endurance. Of course, the pre-sports physical would likely have weeded me out. I still can't believe they didn't force me to see an EMT at the fire. That would have raised a few eyebrows.

What I believe happened was Tom and Arlene and possibly Mark went after some important information, either in the lab or somewhere else, and then were trapped inside. Or they just never made it down the stairs. Rachel must have lit the fire and then lit out in the car, never looking back. Who knows where she ended up. She didn't seem thrilled about taking off on her own, but I guess she managed. Sometimes I miss her, but then I remember that she's a zombie and I think about everything her family did to me, and I don't miss her anymore. Even a seventeen year old boy can see past a pretty face in this situation. A seventeen year old zombie boy, that is.

The graduation ceremony is being held on the football field at the school. I need to be there in forty minutes for our last rehearsal. The actual ceremony will be later this afternoon. I get to sit on the stage as I wound up being the Valedictorian. Having no family and not needing sleep proved to be helpful for improving my study habits. It didn't hurt that for the most part all the other kids avoid me. I've heard the rumors, and they aren't friendly towards me, but I don't care. In a few more weeks Cranston will be nothing but a bad memory. A really bad memory.

Someone is knocking at the door. I peek out my bedroom window; I can't see the front door from here, but I can see most of the driveway and the road in front of the house. No cars, no people. Another knock. I cinch up the tie I'm tying and head for the front door. I open it and no one is there, but an envelope is lying on the step outside. I look all around before picking up the envelope, no one in sight. Alright, I've seen this on TV; no one is so fast that they can simply disappear during the time it took me to get from the bedroom to the front door. Barefoot, I sprint for the left side of the house, past the garage. No one. Next I break for the other side of the house. Still no one.

Shoving the envelope into my pants pocket, I run for the backyard. No one here either. I walk along the back of the house, checking windows and the door for any signs of tampering. I even look underneath the overturned trash barrel in case someone is hiding under it like a cartoon character. Nothing. There aren't any fences or large plants where someone could be hiding back here. I finish my circuit of the house and go back inside, locking the door behind me. Whoever dropped off the letter must have run and hid behind another house. Rather odd behavior, I'd say.

I jump over the back of the couch that sits perpendicular to the door and lie flat to read the paper I pulled from the envelope.

> *Eric,*
>
> *You have performed miraculously these last few months. We are so proud of you. You truly have come to appreciate your new life. We knew you would. We look forward to reuniting with you after graduation. It is regrettable how things turned out at our separation, but all's well that ends well, and this is going to end well. Don't worry about finding us, we'll find you and fill you in on all the details. See you soon!*
>
> *Arlene, Tom and Rachel*
> *P.S. Congratulations on being Valedictorian!*

If I wasn't a zombie, I'd likely do one of those shudder things and be entirely creeped out. But I am a zombie, so I'm not especially affected by this letter, and the mysterious delivery no longer bothers me either. I've developed a sort of apathy towards danger these five months since the event. It is a bit of a letdown to know the Suttons are still alive and well. I was content with the thought of Rachel being out there somewhere, but not the mad scientist and her secret agent husband.

I hoped Rachel would be fine, but I don't define 'fine' as being with her parents. This is slightly confusing and very interesting. I'll worry about it all later, though, for now I have a valedictory speech to deliver.

***

Today was hot. The ceremony was miserable for the heat. Luckily, it's such a small class that the whole process wasn't much more than an hour long. Without any meaningful friendships, I didn't have to stick around for hugs and photographs. I shook a few hands on my way to the parking lot and then returned home. I'm now waiting in the living room with the front door wide open. If they wanted to hurt me they wouldn't have left the letter, so I see no point in hiding.

Back to back superhero movies on cable pass before the Suttons show up. I don't hear a car, or anything else, until a voice from someone in the room with me.

"Eric, you look well." It's Dr. Sutton. She is standing in the doorway.

"Thanks, come on in. Where's the rest of the family?" I ask.

"We're here," says Tom, as he enters, with Rachel a few steps behind.

"Great. It's been a few months, I wasn't sure if you made it out of the house or not," I say.

"We did, thank you for your concern," says Dr. Sutton, full of false sincerity.

We both know I wanted her to die in that fire. If I wasn't so curious about what they've been up to since then I might have tried catching them in a trap tonight to finish the job. Maybe it's the loss of humanity, or maybe it's the sheer isolation, socially speaking, but I don't care as much about the threat the Suttons pose as I used to, and will sacrifice public safety a little in order to indulge my curiosity. Plus, I've got to find out about Rachel.

"Well come in, everyone, have a seat. Can I get anything for anyone?" I say and stand up.

All three come in and sit down together on the sofa. I pull in a chair from the kitchen and sit directly in front of them, a comfortable distance away. Once seated, I look at Rachel, and she looks back at me with hollow eyes. No one says a word.

"So what's up?" I say to get things going.

"We just came to see how things were going for you and to congratulate you on finishing high school," Dr. Sutton says.

"Thanks. Where did you go?" I ask.

"Well, after you so thoroughly destroyed our operation here we had to set up new quarters elsewhere. Initially we spent some time with another group doing the same thing we were doing here. Preparing."

"Preparing for what?" I ask the doctor. "Another group?!"

"For the release, of course. The release of human kind from the bondage of mortality," she answers.

"What? Oh, right, death," I say.

Tom rolls his eyes, Dr. Sutton gives an exasperated huff, and Rachel almost looks like she is going to smile. Seeing her with them I immediately think she's on their side, but maybe not.

"Cranston hasn't been our only project, Eric. We have family members in several other locations. The operation is bigger than you have probably imagined. This isn't just an errant group of scientists, as you have likely conceptualized it. We were one sanctioned group. We were the first, of course, because the initial exposure was accidental, and well ahead of schedule. But the results were hopeful so we entered phase two," Dr. Sutton says.

"Phase two? Who is behind this project? Who are the other groups?" I ask.

Tom joins in the discussion. "Eric, you aren't stupid, but you are trusting, and in this case the two are mostly the same."

"We lied, Eric, you weren't the first human trial we did with our improved virus. You have turned out to be the most disagreeable, but you weren't the first. Well, not the first over all, you were the first for us," Dr. Sutton says. "After we made it through a few months successfully, the Agency set up similar installations across the country and staffed them with scientists, living covertly in the same way we were. Those scientists received the first strain we created. You received version two."

"The Agency. What is 'The Agency'? Can you explain that to me? I never asked before, but this is some crazy stuff. How can something like this exist in the U.S.?" I ask.

"Maybe you are stupid, Eric," Tom says.

"I can see you are still a little defiant, Eric. We came to invite you to participate in our mission, and help us build a supply of the virus. But perhaps you aren't ready for that yet," Dr. Sutton says.

I don't respond right away. This is worse than I had ever suspected, and I am powerless to stop it.

"You want me to help you grow the virus? I'm not a biologist, or chemist, or evil mad scientist of any kind. I don't think I would be able to help, even if I wanted to," I say.

"And I don't," I add, just to make sure they realize it.

"We gathered that," Tom says.

"We don't grow the virus, Eric, we are the virus. Our blood is all we need to transmit the virus to another person. We would provide you with a freezer and phlebotomy equipment. All you would need to do is draw a few milliliters of blood twice a month and freeze it. Our blood doesn't replace very quickly, but it does, given enough time. Essentially a few tablespoons a month is all we can spare, but it is sufficient. And even though it seems slow, it is still more efficient than trying to replicate the virus in the lab.

"We didn't expect you'd be sticking around Cranston now that high school is over, but if you let us know your destination we would make sure you were comfortable. We take care of our family members. You wouldn't want for anything. But if you aren't interested in participating…" Dr. Sutton explains.

"Why?" I ask.

"You keep asking that one," Tom says. "This is the future! We have made you as close to immortal as any human has ever been! We are the future of the human race, just like we talked about a few months ago, except, once again, we didn't give you the full story. I'm still with the Agency. Arlene is still with the CDC. Everything we are doing *is* sanctioned and supported by the government. You proved to be a good test case for us because you actually fought back. You were the first to do that, and it kind of shook up our whole operation. But now we know a little more of what to expect when we go all out."

Dr. Sutton takes over, "Of course, we still aren't ready to go 'all out' just yet. We need more virus and more locations. We want the transition to be as expansive as possible in order to prevent any kind of organized rebellion. We don't want anything like what you tried to mount against us in January but on a larger scale."

Did she single me out as the instigator because she doesn't know Rachel was involved or because they have decided to just pin it on me alone and forgive Rachel's involvement? I look at Rachel, whose eyes haven't left me since we sat down, but she reveals nothing to me.

Tom thinks I'm stupid and too trusting. We'll see who the stupid one is. "I see. I'm asking these questions because I want to know the real story. I figured what you told me back then wasn't the full truth. And as I've had time to think about this for a few months now, I have come to the conclusion that living this way isn't that much different than how it was before. I'm no longer Eric Sterling, but I'm a close shadow copy of him. And that's not too bad, right? I still don't know if I support the universal transition you are working towards, but what's the harm in saving some of my blood for you each month? Especially if you are paying me."

"It isn't that we'll be paying you, but there will be some factors we take care of in your behalf," says Dr. Sutton. She looks at me cautiously, but I think she believes my sudden flip-flop on the issue. She *is* a bureaucrat. Tom on the other hand doesn't seem to be buying it; I can tell by the way he looks at his wife when she corrects my statement so matter-of-factly.

"Cash, rent, brain money, whatever, it's all the same in the end. I'll do it. I'm headed back to Illinois for college, so let's figure out where you will be putting me up. That reanimate apathy you alluded to is setting in. I don't want to pull the trigger myself, but I'm less concerned about handing you the gun," I say.

"Nice analogy," says Tom, clearly suspicious of me.

"Here's the catch, Eric. You can go wherever you want, but you can't go to college just yet. We can't have you associating with the general public; it's too risky for our timeline. We don't want an accidental outbreak," Dr. Sutton says.

"But, Dr. Sutton, what about these last few months? You've left me here, hasn't this been a risk?" I ask.

"It could have been, but that's why we chose Cranston. It is small and controllable in the event of an accident. You never realized it, but Mark has been living in town, keeping his eyes and ears open for any information that would indicate our project had been compromised here."

"Mark made it out of the house, too," I say.

"Eric, what do you think happened at the fire?" Tom asks.

"I'll tell you what I experienced. You all went running out of the room, Mark kicked me in the head. I made my way down to the second floor and realized I was trapped, so I jumped out a bedroom window. I think I fractured my leg a bit, but after a few weeks it was alright. I circled the house and only found Frank's body. The car was gone so I assumed Ra-, I assumed the rest of you had gotten away or were trapped in the house. They reported no bodies found in the charred remains of the house, not even my parents."

I don't want to betray Rachel, not until I know if she has betrayed me.

"No report of Frank then, either?" Tom asks.

"No," I say.

He follows up with, "You didn't find that suspicious?"

"I guess I wasn't paying much attention to it at the time. I've still never even been down the road that far since. But now that we are discussing it, one of your neighbors arrived first, he and I walked around the house and we saw Frank's body. He must have reported it. I never thought about why that was never mentioned." I'm surprised I missed that one. I'm usually very observant.

"Frank's finger prints registered and the CDC was contacted. Of course we had already phoned in about the fire. Federal investigators came out and told a story about Frank being a high clearance level consultant that was visiting with Dr. Sutton from the CDC. It was sensitive information and they asked that it be left out of the local news, in the name of public safety. Sometimes it is too easy to cover our tracks," Tom says.

I don't like the way Tom said that, or the way he is looking at me now, as though I'm a track about to be easily covered. He must not be buying my sudden agreement to their proposition. I can't blame him; it was a pretty weak performance on my part. I'll keep up this line of conversation for now. Until I figure something else out.

"So Mark has been watching me to make sure I don't infect anyone ahead of schedule. Is he going to follow me to my next town? And if I can't go to school, what will you have me do?" I ask.

"Mark won't be following you. You'll be in a secure facility. We'll provide plenty for your comfort and entertainment, but you will not be able to interact socially. From what we heard about you recently, that shouldn't be a problem," Dr. Sutton says.

"Will the three of you be with me at the secure facility?" I ask.

"No, we are moving on to the next town. Our overall goal is to have a launching point in twenty five states. Some of the smaller states combined count as one, and the larger as two, to be accurate it's more like twenty five geographical zones. If we hadn't lost the house here, you would represent this zone, but things as they are, we'll have to find another representative. Luckily Illinois isn't taken yet, so we can set you up there," Dr. Sutton says, apparently still unaware of my deception.

"If you have that many more locations to secure, and you are doing them one in two years, this project is going to take quite a while to roll out, huh?" I guess when you are semi-immortal time isn't as important anymore.

"That would be the case if we were the only team in operation, but remember, we have others established already. And by recruiting from our organization, which is easier than recruiting civilians, we have made great progress in two years. In total there are seventeen locations. We figure approximately four more years until we roll out the big finale!" Dr. Sutton explains with flourish.

"Eric, you've believed nearly everything you've heard, from Rachel's initial confession to everything else we've told you, even though it was completely outlandish. I have a piece of advice for you. You might find an honest vampire from time to time, maybe even a werewolf, but never trust a zombie," Tom Sutton says with a laugh.

He and his wife stand up. Rachel remains seated.

They start walking around the couch towards the door.

"Just keep on with your regular plans and get ready to move. We'll be in touch shortly," Tom says, no longer looking the part of the cowboy, but rather every bit the conniving secret operative with the trust-no-one approach to life and business.

I don't respond. I think if I don't do something to help myself, and soon, I won't live very long. He'll be back sooner rather than later to 'cover his tracks.' He sees right through me and my flimsy deception.

Rachel finally stands up.

"I have to agree with my dad, Eric, you should never trust a zombie."

She pulls her hand from the purse she has slung over her shoulder and in it is a handgun. Two well-aimed shots drop her zombie parents to the floor. They never had a chance to react.

19. Moment in the Sun

My shock at the first shot knocks me backward in my chair. Still lying flat on my back I lift myself up on my elbows and look to Rachel.

"Are you going to shoot me?" I ask.

"Why would I do that? It took five months to get back here. I'll explain in the car, grab what you need and make it fast, we've gotta get moving," Rachel says, rather calmly for someone who just killed her parents, even if they were zombies.

I scramble to my feet and start off towards my room, but stop. "Don't we need to do something to the bodies? Is a single bullet enough?"

Rachel says, "I'll check them while you get your stuff. If I severed the spinal cord then it's sufficient, if not, well, either way they won't recover from this. The virus won't be dead, but the body won't be able to respond enough to keep it alive. The virus will starve to death. At any rate the locals are all going to freak out when they find them. So we ought to get moving now or we'll be found with them, and that won't be as much fun...for us."

I grab my backpack and dump the remaining notebooks onto the bed. What do you grab when you are making a hasty, late evening, zombie homicide getaway? I stuff the bag with some clothes and my toothbrush. I grab a folder I keep my legal documents in, but figure I probably won't need it. If I'm not here when the cops show up, I'll likely become the prime suspect. My identity is as good as garbage. And that seems fitting. My life was ended, and now finally my identity is catching up. It's like I told Dr. Sutton, I'm no longer Eric Sterling, just a shadow of him. I suppose it's time for who I really am to take center stage. I put the folder back on the shelf.

When I return to the living room, Rachel has closed the front door and shut off the lights. She grabs my arm and leads me to the back door.

"Mark is waiting with a car around the corner," she explains while peaking out the window on the door. She looks like she's in a movie.

We leave through the back door in full sprint, straight through the backyard neighbor's yard and out to the street. No one is outside, but I notice a few faces peeking out behind curtains. The sirens have started and are coming this way from town.

When we reach the car Rachel tells me to take shotgun. She goes to the driver's door and opens it.

The gun is in her hand again. "Out," she orders.

"Rachel, what's going on? What are you doing?" Mark asks, fear or anger causing his voice to shake.

"Change of plans. Get out or I'll shoot you," she says. Fixed and calm.

Rachel steps back, allowing room for Mark to get out of the car without putting herself within range of a counterattack from the old man.

Mark stands up from the car and turns to face Rachel. She pulls the trigger again and the old man falls in a heap.

"I guess I meant *and* instead of *or*," she says. What has she become since I last saw her?

She puts the gun in her bag, throws the bag over the driver's seat into the back and gets in the car. I do the same.

Starting the car and shifting to drive in nearly one motion, Rachel sets us on our way out of Cranston, leaving the local authorities to wonder and puzzle.

"Congrats on being Valedictorian! I'm pretty jealous I didn't get to graduate, too. I still haven't been able to graduate high school yet and I've spent nearly six years in it." Rachel speaks as though we are friends just out for a drive.

"Thanks," I say. A little shaken, but due to the quick dissipation of feeling, not as out of sorts as a regular person would be at this point. "So that was a lot of killing back there, where'd you learn to shoot like that?"

"That was nothing. My dad trained me extensively these last few months," she explains.

"Never trust a zombie," I repeat from earlier.

"Exactly, it should be my family's motto," Rachel says.

"You could get it on a T-shirt."

"Maybe I will."

We sit in silence for a few minutes. Rachel has gone through the neighborhoods and back onto Highway 33 North. We are out of Cranston and hitting the uninhabited part of the desert. There won't be any houses or likely any traffic for several miles. There aren't any cars following us, so even if the calls went in describing the car at the scene of the second shooting we should be safe now. We'll be long gone before they start sweeping the area.

"There's a CD in my bag. Will you grab it?" Rachel asks.

Dutifully I reach into the back seat and pull the bag up to my lap. I reach in and feel the barrel of the gun, still warm to the touch. It startles me and I flinch. Then I find the case and remove the CD.

"It's a collection of songs I made for this drive. I'm glad you're with me for it. The first song is by one of the bands you told me about," Rachel says.

I put the CD in and recognize the song immediately. "Moment in the Sun" by the Living End. I'm pretty good at Name that Tune.

"Good choice," I say.

As I listen to the lyrics I realize it's very fitting for this moment.

I add, "Great choice."

"I figured you'd like it," Rachel says and smiles. After all that's happened she looks like the pale girl I saw on my first day in a new school five months ago.

"So where are we headed?" I ask.

"North. Don't worry about that now. I want to explain what happened after the fire."

"Shoot. I mean, go for it! Don't shoot!" Stupid colloquialisms.

"Funny. Well, after you went inside I got the lighter and the gas cans. I started at the lab side of the house, wrapped around the front, and then to the other side. I doused it good. I was worried over not getting the gas all the way around the house as it left the back door untouched. But it was what it was, so I lit it up and the flames took off. It was pretty crazy. I ran around to the car and realized I didn't have the key. So it actually was fortuitous that the back door wasn't engulfed in flames yet. I ran back around, opened the door grabbed the keys from the hook and returned to the car. By the time I had the car started I saw Frank coming through the front door. Suddenly he was thrown to the side and my dad was standing there.

"He looked right at me and I waved frantically for him to come to the car, Mom was right behind him. They ran to the car and got in. I told them I was out for a walk and saw the house on fire and went running back. I shouted for them but didn't hear a response and I got scared, so I was going to drive for help. Either they believed me or they didn't care; Dad said to drive and get away from Cranston, so I did. My allegiance was never questioned, whether it was to them or to you. We spent the last few months touring the other locations. I tried to gauge the other situations, to see if any of the non-volunteers they transitioned had the rebellious spirit you did. I don't think any of them do. Mom didn't give you the full details. There are over one hundred zombies out there. Of course, most of them volunteered. But even the few who were treated like you don't seem to be fighting it.

"As for you, I'm glad you made it out. Apparently Mark had gotten out of the house, long enough after my parents so that we didn't see him, but not so long that he didn't see the car driving away. He set out on foot towards the slaughterhouse and took one of the trucks from there. He eventually called in to the supervisor in Atlanta who was then able to link him back up with us. It was decided that since you were the only person in Cranston who knew who Mark was that he could be placed back in town and lay low, providing good intelligence about your situation. He proved to be helpful in that role."

Rachel finishes this part of the story and we sit quietly again. Rachel is a much better secret agent than I have given her credit for. It's true, you can't trust a zombie. Which leaves me wondering about my current situation; how do I trust someone who has repeatedly said they can't be trusted?

Rachel says, "Now we come to tonight. My parents decided it was time to check in on you and explain the next portion of the plan. They thought by now you'd have calmed down and would be supportive of their objective. I was pretty sure you wouldn't be, but I almost gave up hope during the conversation. It seemed like you were really going to just give in and go along with them. I almost shot all three of you."

So my deception worked on the Sutton women, but not Mr. Sutton, presumably.

"Why didn't you?" I ask.

"Because when you looked up at me from the floor, after you'd fallen backwards, you were smiling."

"I was?" That's news to me.

"Yes. I knew then that you were still opposed to turning this virus loose on the public. I knew that you were still ready to wear the cape. And that's what I need you to do now, Eric, wear the cape. I know all of the secure facilities, as my mom liked to call them, where the virus is being harvested. We're going to shut them down. We have a couple of years, in theory, but if we get away with tonight's actions then the schedule might change. Once they find out we eliminated one of their teams they'll certainly come after us. Do you feel up to the task?" Rachel asks.

Do I feel up to the task?

"Are you asking me if I'm prepared to become a superhero?"

"In a way, yes," she says.

"You said never to trust a zombie. How can I know you aren't taking me to the CDC now to turn me in as the one who killed your parents?"

"I guess you don't know. You can't know. You won't know until we take down the first house and you see the freezer full of vials of blood. Even then you won't know the full story, but you'll see part of it. I'd like for you to trust me, but I don't expect you to. I held true to our arrangement with the fire, at least the first part, but then self-preservation took over. That's why you can't trust a zombie. At least, not the first wave of us. You are different. You can be trusted. Somehow you didn't lose your regard for other people. That's why I need you to wear the cape. So will you do it?"

She doesn't let me respond.

"But really, after all that has happened, if you play this '*I don't know if I can trust you*' bit again, we're going to have trouble." She adds.

She makes a strong argument. Now that I've seen what she is capable of, I think it's best to drop my suspicions once and for all. She did just shoot her parents in front of me. What more do I need to see? And if we have a legitimate chance at stopping the virus then there's no other option for me. College can wait. Besides, I never did get to ask her out on a proper date.

She waits through the silence as I contemplate things, and then asks, "Are you in?"

"I'm in," I say, "but first, can we stop for milkshakes?"

About the Author

Paul Brodie's first interests in writing appeared during elementary school in the form of writing short stories. Over the years his interest in writing came and went. After high school it was channeled into writing songs for the rock band he fronted. Years later, work provided opportunity for Paul to do a little technical writing for training material. When he began university studies at the age of twenty-six Paul found an appreciation for academic writing. During his undergrad he began writing a blog. Paul's writing ability continued to improve through graduate studies. Finally, at the age of thirty-one, Paul returned to his creative writing roots and began writing fiction. *Never Trust a Zombie* marks Paul's first serious attempt at writing a novel. He describes the experience as a great challenge in problem solving. Each piece of the story needs to connect to the pieces before it and after it. He looks forward to more writing.

Paul lives in Vermont, but originally hails from New Jersey. He and his wife, Kathy, have one daughter, Megan, and are anxiously awaiting the birth of their second child.

Please visit this book at Amazon.com and leave a review.

Comments or questions for the author?

e-mail: Paul.Brodie.Writing@gmail.com